GRIN AND BARE IT

The Rigan came clumping back into the room carrying an armload of paraphernalia, which he dumped on the floor in front of Anderson. His collection was pretty complete: wearing apparel, traditional sash, a few items of jewelry, a small green mnemeplast card, and, of course, the inevitable weapon carried by all mature Turgorn males.

"Where's the owner?" Anderson asked, pushing through the Rigan's booty with one foot.

The Rigan's perpetual smile deepened somewhat, but he said nothing. He didn't have to. A few shreds of pale meat still hung wedged between his fangs.

By Leslie Gadallah
Published by Ballantine Books:

CAT'S PAWN

THE LOREMASTERS

CAT'S GAMBIT

CAT'S PAWN

Leslie Gadallah

A Del Rey Book

BALLANTINE BOOKS • NEW YORK

A Del Rey Book
Published by Ballantine Books

Copyright © 1987 by Leslie Gadallah

Library of Congress Catalog Card Number: 86-91586

ISBN 0-345-33742-5

Printed in Canada

First Edition: March 1987
Second Printing: March 1990

Cover Art by Barclay Shaw

for the three of you
who discussed the Kazi threat with me
over the dinner table and far into the night

Prologue: The Ambassador

Melissa Larkin had been told that the ambassador had someone with him just then, but that he was anxious to meet her and would she be so kind as to wait a few minutes.

Melli sighed a small sigh that she hoped was inaudible to the ears of the Orian secretary and found a comfortable-looking chair. She was determined not to stare, though talking person to person with someone who looked a lot like a big-headed pussy cat gave her a funny feeling. Of course he was rather large for a pussy cat. The tips of his big ears came level with her nose and would have been higher except for the slightly forward posture balanced by the long, swinging tail.

She set her package in her lap, dug into her copious purse, extracted a portable tape viewer, and prepared herself for a long wait.

She had spent a great deal of her free time these last few weeks waiting in some office or another—in the Marriage Bureau, the Housing Authority, and lately in the austere surroundings of the Eugenics Council. John had similarly been occupied getting the permits they needed to buy household furnishings, registering their intent with the Department of Internal Revenue, as if it were any of their business, and enduring the endless probing of the Eugenics Council. For two young people who were madly in love and frantic to get married, Melli and John had seen very little of each other for nearly two months. A couple of days ago it had seemed they were finally reaching the end of their ordeal. And then came this new snag, which had brought Melli to the ambassador's office.

Even though *Violet X7* was her favorite of all the programs in Romance Publications, Inc.'s computer and usually produced stories she liked, she had difficulty concentrating on the book in the viewer. She found herself going over a passage several times without having caught the sense of it. Her attention kept wandering around the room. She was feeling a little disappointed in her surroundings.

The extensive grounds and real trees she had passed on her way into the embassy had suggested splendid luxury to her, but the embassy building itself was rather small, and such rooms as she had the opportunity to see were simple and unornamented. Not that they were shoddy, exactly. There was a sense of skilled craftsmanship about the place, and it looked well kept, and it had a Spartan kind of comfort except that it was too hot. But it lacked the awe-inspiring symbols of power, the vast halls and echoing chambers, the gilt and the crystal, the elaborate furnishings, and the bureaucratic barriers to progress one expected. Embassies were supposed to be posh places, at least Melli supposed them to be so, full of busy, important people with important things to do. She almost felt as if she had invaded a private house by mistake.

The only thing luxurious about the room she was in was the marble floor. The secretary's desk was strictly utilitarian, and the only other furnishings, the chairs and small table, could have come from any department store.

The secretary looked up as a door opened, and Melissa followed his gaze to a small, dark creature crossing the room. Though she had heard of them, she had never seen a Kazi before, and she reacted with a typically human dislike for many-legged things. Controlling a shudder, she fixed her eyes on her viewer. The Kazi's legs rattled against each other, and its feet made small scratching sounds against the floor.

"Will you come this way, Melissa Larkin?" The secretary pronounced her name as if it were all one word. Hurriedly packing away her viewer and picking up her parcel, she followed him to a door of beautifully polished wood.

He guided her into some sort of anteroom, a tiny space between doors.

"I ask your indulgence," the secretary said. "I must look at your parcel and into your purse. I must also ascertain there are no weapons on your person."

"I went through all that at the gate," Melissa protested.

"I know. I am sorry. There is much political tension these days. We must be very careful. It is necessary. Please?"

Melli shrugged and surrendered the items she was carrying. She held her arms away from her body and allowed the Orian to brush his furry hands, long-fingered paws with the claws clipped blunt, over her. He seemed as reluctant to touch her as she was to be touched, but they went through the ritual anyway. He was thorough but as dispassionate as an aged physician, and left her feeling less molested than the guard at the gate had done. The guard had been quite human, and enjoyed his work.

The formalities over, the secretary escorted her through the second door.

The office was no more elaborate than anything else in the embassy. The ceiling was low and painted white. The walls were an unornamented sandy color, broken only by one small, high window. There was a large desk and two or three upholstered chairs, some shelves against one wall, a Tri-D tank in a corner, and a Com/Com link beside it. Melli tried to remember what she had heard about the Communications/Computer system as it applied to the Oriani. It seemed to her that they had had something to do with supplying the technology that had supplanted videotex. But she wasn't technologically oriented, and what she chiefly remembered was hearing about videotex technicians picketing the legislature because they were being put out of work.

When the Orian behind the desk acknowledged their presence by looking up, the secretary said, "Ambassador Talan, this is Melissa Larkin." Then he slipped silently away and left her face to face with the object of her pilgrimage. She had expected a long time of journeying from office to office, of being put off and turned away and being told to come back tomorrow, and so she was unprepared. She discovered that she didn't know what to say. Her confusion manifested itself in an undignified flush and stumbling words.

The ambassador moved from behind the desk and guided her gently into an inner room of more intimate setting, with a low table and half a dozen open-backed chairs built to accommodate the Orian tail. He offered her coffee and gave her a few moments to compose herself.

"It's very kind of you to see me," she managed to say at last.

"I am most pleased to meet Bill Anderson's granddaughter," he answered. "Your grandfather was one of the first Terrans I knew well. His death grieved me."

"I know," Meili said. Oh, no, she thought, that sounds terrible. She tried again. "I mean, I know you knew him. My grandfather. You see, that's why I just had to see you. You're the only person I could reach who did know him. You see, Mr. Ambassador, I'm planning to get married soon."

"Indeed?" The word hung on the air between them. From without, the sounds of the ceaseless traffic intruded in spite of the muffling trees. Holding the delicate cup in both hands, Melli sipped her coffee and watched the Orian over the rim. Though he must be a busy man, he looked now as if he had all the time in the world for her. Leaning back, relaxed in his chair, he regarded her with grave yellow eyes, waiting for her explanation of what she was doing there.

The coffee was good, hot and aromatic, so different from the insipid stuff she had to stand in long lines in the cafeteria to get. The ambassador did not, it seemed, find coffee appealing. For himself, he had poured a draught of mauvish fluid into a tall glass. It smelled to Melli much like raw hamburger.

"Mr. Ambassador, I need your help," she said, conscious that this was perhaps not the best way to start.

"My name is Talan," the Orian said. "I am not overly

fond of awkward titles. How can I help you, Melissa Larkin?"

Fascinated by the way the highlights on the ruff around his neck moved as he spoke, Melli caught herself wondering if the Oriani groomed themselves like cats. The thought of the ambassador licking himself clean was absurd. Melli stifled a giggle that was more than half nerves. Fifty-five kilos of highly intelligent being with long fangs that hung down below the line of his mouth like ivory daggers was nothing to giggle about.

"My mother died recently."

"I'm sorry to hear that."

"Thank you," Melissa said. She indicated her package, which now rested on the table. "I found this among her things. It's a manuscript or something, handwritten on paper, by my grandfather. It came with the rest of my mother's personal possessions. I guess she's had it all this time, but she never said anything about it. I didn't even know it existed.

"We have been able to verify my grandfather's handwriting, but nobody seems to know if this—whatever it is—is true.

"The thing is, you see, if it is, my grandfather had a serious medical problem."

"I can see you are disturbed by your suspicions. Am I to understand it has some significance for your forthcoming marriage?"

"Yes, yes, it does," Melli said more emphatically than was necessary because she was surprised the Orian didn't understand. "For the Eugenics Council, don't you see? If my grandfather had heart trouble, it may be I won't be allowed to have children. Bill Anderson spent most of his adult life on Orion. We have no medical records past the time he was thirty-one years old. I need some evidence to present to the Eugenics Council of his good health, or I won't be able to have any children."

Ambassador Talan took a moment to compose his reply while Melli fidgeted with her coffee cup. "I cannot be reassuring," the ambassador said. "Your grandfather did suffer problems with his heart." Melli felt her hopes shrink inside of her. "However," Talan continued, "it would seem your mother did not find this an insurmountable difficulty."

Melli's despair sounded in her voice. "Maybe not. But there wasn't any Eugenics Council in those days." She hesitated a moment before flinging her last, frail hope to the wind. "Mr. Ambassador, was Bill Anderson's sickness genetic? Couldn't it have been the result of an injury or something?"

"I couldn't say. I am not a physician." He nodded toward the package on the table. "It is undoubtedly not my place to say so, but if this manuscript is the only indication that Bill Anderson was less than physically perfect, and since it is not officially known, why bring it to the attention of the council at all? Would it not be simpler and more expedient to ignore a problem which possibly does not exist and in any case cannot be proven?"

Melli was shocked, really shocked. To think a senior diplomat would suggest such a thing to her! It was not only against the law, it was against all conscience. Her jaw dropped, and when she picked it up again she was angry enough to have acquired some courage.

"I would really like you to know that I agree in principle with the concept of the Eugenics Council," she said. "There are definitely too many of us human beings. It's only reasonable that in controlling the population, the genetically weak strains should be bred out, as any farmer could tell you. If my grandfather was genetically deficient, I want to know it. I don't want to bring defective children into the world."

Talan accepted this outburst without any sign of having taken offense. "Can you keep a small secret?" he asked.

Not expecting confidences, Melli was put off balance yet again. She swallowed hard to try to regain her equilibrium. "Sure. I guess so."

"Personally," Talan said, "I am not certain the Eugenics Council does your race a service." He hesitated a moment and then went on. "I am not sure you can breed out madness without also breeding out genius. There is a certain danger in reducing the genetic variation in a species, as any farmer will tell you. As to what characteristics are deemed desirable for continuance, this seems to be as much a matter of whim as of science."

Seeing the flush come to Melli's face, the ambassador's eyes dropped to the table. "Forgive me. I have no right to speak against human solutions to human problems. I have an unfortunate tendency to become argumentative on occasion. It is an irrepressible fault of mine." He looked up at her again. "You asked me to help you. How can I be of help?"

"Well, I need my grandfather's medical records. I was hoping you could get them for me. I could go through the regular channels, but it takes so long."

Talan considered her request. "It is unlikely the Medical Center would have retained Bill Anderson's records beyond the time of his death unless they were of clinical interest. I will inquire. If the records are not available, perhaps a statement from the healer who attended Bill Anderson would serve. I believe he is still in Owr-Lakh." The name of the city, pronounced by the Orian, sounded like a growl. It took Melli a moment to realize what it signified.

The ambassador misread her hesitation. "This is not adequate? You need something further?"

"Well...uh...actually, yes. A...uh...psychological profile."

Talan waited for her explanation.

"The manuscript, fact or fiction, shows some... um...antisocial tendencies." Melli thought she detected skepticism on the ambassador's part. "I'm a psychology major at the university, Mr. Ambassador. It's not just my imagination."

"I see. Antisocial tendencies would also be considered a fault?"

"Yes," Melli answered firmly.

"Very well," Talan said, standing. "I will do what I can to get the information for you as quickly as is possible, since I detect some urgency in the matter."

Melli had not expected that kind of understanding from an alien. She felt a surge of warmth for the person who just a moment before had outraged her. She was

scarcely aware of being guided back into the ambassador's office and then into the outer office as Talan told
her, "If you would be so kind as to leave the manuscript
with me, I will guarantee its safe return in no more than a
few days' time. I would appreciate the opportunity to
read it, if you would permit."

Melli turned the heavy parcel of paper over in her
hands. It was all she had of her grandfather. No family
legends, no childhood traditions held any sign that he
had ever existed.

She surrendered the manuscript to the ambassador
with no misgivings.

Talan laid the book on his desk and spent a moment
merely looking at it. The thick volume was bound in the
preserved skin of an animal, which gave Talan a queasy
feeling. It had been dyed dark green, but had worn to its
natural color at the corners. The covers were held together by a lockable metal clasp, which was not locked.
Nothing on the outside of the book indicated what was
within.

It was odd, very odd, that Bill Anderson could have
written this without Talan's knowledge. Talan tried to
imagine the man he knew in the role of either author or
historian. Neither hat seemed to fit the memory very
well. It would be easier to believe Bill Anderson had
been keeping records with a view toward blackmail—
that would be more in keeping with his character. And
typical of him that he would make all the preparations
and then be unable to carry through. As Talan remembered him, Bill Anderson had had a taste for the fruits of
villainy but lacked the stomach for villainy itself. Against
his will, he had been a decent man.

And we used him badly, Steven Black and I, Talan
thought. It would be a kind of rough justice if his mem-
oirs came back to haunt me just at this crucial time.

He lifted the cover of the book. The first few pages
were blank. Then the ambassador came to the date written at the top of one. Immediately his thoughts sped
back fifty Terran years to a time of pain and ugliness as

clear in his mind as if it had happened only a moment ago.

The secretary came in. "The representatives of UBI will be here in a few minutes," he said, yanking Talan back into the present. The ambassador's tail wagged slightly in annoyance. The secretary pretended not to notice.

"Must I?" Talan complained.

"They are coming at your invitation," the secretary reminded him. "You did say that the Universal Brotherhood of Intelligence was perhaps our only ally on Earth. And their numbers are growing, in spite of adverse publicity."

"What do they want?"

"I understand they are seeking permission to promote their philosophy on Orion."

"That should prove interesting. I wonder if they realize how little patience our people have with fanatics. And how little we are inclined to gather in groups."

"I doubt it. In spite of their claims on the universe, all the present members are Terran."

"I see. Do they also see the Kaz as potential brethren?"

"I have not heard."

"Have someone find out, will you? Preferably a Terran. Preferably one who can be persuaded that it is best that we not be associated with the inquiry."

"Very well." The secretary placed a Tri-D record the size of a thick coin on the desk. "I thought you should see this."

"What is it?"

"A current affairs broadcast. Recorded this noon."

"How long?"

"Ten minutes."

"Very well, put it on. Then we will welcome our universal brothers."

The tape started with the end of a story about the opposition by an environmental protection group to a proposed new dormitory complex. A young woman was protesting to the newsman. "You think grass and trees are just decoration. They're not, you know. If this keeps going on, one of these days the inner cities are going to suffocate."

"But," the newsman said, "still, people have to live somewhere."

"Yeah," the environmentalist agreed. "And they have to eat something. Our best farmland is under concrete. Now they want to take some more of it." The picture cut away from the girl's agitated face to a field of ripening wheat. But her voice continued. "You can't keep doing that, don't you see? You can't keep doing that."

"This is Nick Wenkowski for CKRL News."

The scene shifted back to the studio and the network anchorman. "In Berne today, world leaders met for the third straight day to discuss increased support for the Interplanetary Community. After meeting for several hours, the leaders announced through their press agency that they had failed to ratify the Orian proposal which would make our planet a full-fledged member of the Community. The failure was due, they said, to strong opposition by several governments. As spokesman for the opposing group, the Foreign Secretary of the United States, Michael Goldman, said later that the United States 'feels strongly that any further support by our nation of the Interplanetary Community would seriously erode the sovereignty of the United States.' Orian officials declined comment. For your comments, here's our man in the street, Aldon Monk."

Talan reached over to shut the machine off. The secretary stopped him with a gesture.

The camera cut to the exterior of a shopping center, where Aldon Monk was trying to elicit the opinions of busy shoppers. The first two he accosted said things like "I don't know anything about that" and "I guess those guys knows what they're doing." But on his third try, he got a live one.

"What do you think about the American Foreign Secretary's statement that any further support of the Interplanetary Community would seriously erode the sovereignty of the United States?" Monk asked a tired-looking man in grubby coveralls.

"Damn right. He's damn right."

"Why do you say that, sir?"

"There's plenty of people right here on this Earth that need looking after," the man answered. "We should be solving some of our own problems instead of trying to look after a bunch of aliens who God knows what they're up to."

"You don't think we need the Community?"

"What for, I'd like to know. Maybe they need us, but we got along for a long time without them." The man looked square into the camera. "Hey, am I on the Tri-D?"

"Yes, you are, sir."

"Hey, how about that."

"Tell me, sir, what you think of the Orian contention that the Community would be of benefit to all peoples?"

The man got a good solid hold on the microphone. If Monk wanted it back before he was through, the newsman would have to wrestle him for it.

"Now, you see, that's just what I mean. They're not people at all; they're furry sons-a-bitches. They're all over the place, trying to take over—furry ones, scaly ones, long ones, round ones, and some with nineteen legs. I tell you, mister, I like my people to look like people. And that's all I got to say." He relinquished the mike, waved at the camera, and strode off.

The tape ended. The Tri-D tank went blank.

Talan leaned back in his chair and closed his eyes. It was a long moment before he spoke. "I don't understand them. How have we failed so completely to communicate?"

"The UBI will be arriving."

"Yes. We have to keep trying, don't we? Please greet them and make alcohol and coffee available while I go over the brief. I will join you in a few minutes."

The secretary left. As Talan turned to the Com/Com link, his arm brushed the book still waiting for him on the desk.

We could talk to one another, Bill Anderson, Talan thought. Yet in the end, we did not understand each other very well. What is lacking here, between your kind and my kind? What am I doing wrong?

I am a poor diplomat, Talan thought, because at that moment the manuscript held far more interest for him than did the history of the Universal Brotherhood of Intelligence.

Interesting or not, it was late at night before Talan's duties permitted him to return to the book.

When Bessy Breckenridge came into his office that evening, the ambassador's secretary sighed inwardly, though he kept all sign of dismay carefully to himself. He didn't actively dislike humans, but he had never quite become reconciled to the fact that aside from himself and two junior aides, all the employees of the embassy were Terran. Knowing the limitations of interplanetary travel, he could have accepted the situation in better grace if the humans didn't take such a proprietary interest in the ambassador. Bessy Breckenridge, so-called supervisor of the custodial staff who came in at night to do the cleaning in typically human slapdash fashion, was pointing at the door behind him with a plump, red finger, completely ignoring the fact the secretary had work to do. She talked nonstop, not even hesitating when one of the aides came in and told the secretary that the starship they had been expecting from Orion was now overdue and hadn't been heard from since passing the Centauri Colony. Certain beyond any shadow of a doubt that Bessy Breckenridge understood nothing of his native tongue, the secretary wasn't concerned about her presence. He just wished she would go away.

The aide left and Bessy Breckenridge talked on. "I tell you, the poor man didn't sleep at all last night. I seen him, walkin' the hallways, silent as a ghost, he was. He's always got a word for me, you know. I don't think he even saw me. He's workin' too hard, you know. He should be gettin' his rest."

The secretary kept his attitude blandly neutral. "I think you are unduly alarmed. Ambassador Talan is quite capable of taking care of himself. But you have a good night's work ahead of you yourself, Bessy Breckenridge, before you can get home to your family."

"Eh, that's right enough," the woman agreed. "And

me with four little ones waitin' on me." She smiled broadly, displaying large, flat, metal-filled teeth. "No rest for the wicked, they say. Well, you look out for him just the same, you hear? He's a good man, but he works too hard." She went out, finally, and left the secretary trying to envision by what stretch of her limited imagination Bessy Breckenridge could see herself as wicked.

But in spite of the apparent lack of concern with which he had greeted Bessy Breckenridge's news, he was just a little troubled by Talan's behavior of late. The ambassador was a man of reasonably regular habits, taking as good care of himself as was consistent with his interests and his duties. Lately, however, the ambassador had been eating little and, it seemed, sleeping less. The secretary didn't like that; it smacked of an emotional involvement. The embassy could ill afford to have its ambassador descending into primitive patterns of thought at this crucial period in Orian–Terran relations. He debated the wisdom of bringing his concern to Talan's attention. But he had very little evidence, really: one unimportant appointment set aside, which was not all that unusual an incident, and Bessy Breckenridge's overwrought gossip. Talan might very well suspect that the secretary was the one who was becoming emotional, and he would be hard pressed to defend himself from that suspicion.

Besides, Talan's interest in humans wasn't new. His long-standing fascination with the hairless ones was well known. Once, the ambassador had confided some of the reasons behind it: "They're half savage, half civilized, and have managed to come to terms with themselves. We could learn from them."

The secretary settled himself to the task of preparing for the next day's appointments, but the news about the late vessel niggled in the back of his mind. He consulted the log on the Com/Com link and discovered that while he had been listening to Bessy Breckenridge's chatter, a broken transmission had been received. The Orian starship had been fired upon. It was damaged, but the captain was confident that they could reach LunaPort, limping along at sublight speed.

That was something else to worry about. Talan would have to be told if he ever was released from the wrangling going on among the sainted darlings of the UBI. Already the meeting had gone on far longer than it had been scheduled to. The secretary marveled at Talan's endurance. The Brotherhood professed to be ready to honor intelligence wherever they found it, but they seemed to have great difficulty getting along with one another.

Earth turned slowly on its axis. The days were long, and the secretary's internal clocks were set to a shorter diurnal cycle. Long hours before planet night, he felt sluggish and ready to sleep. He pushed himself to continue, annoyed with his inability to adapt. Talan came in and walked straight through to his own office. Wearily the secretary rose and followed him.

Talan leaned his head back and stretched, beginning with the muscles of his head and neck and ending by fully extending the long claws of his feet.

"You are due at the Department of Interplanetary Affairs reception in less than an hour," the secretary reminded his ambassador.

"So soon?" Talan said with surprise. "I seem to have lost track of time."

The secretary was enough of a diplomat himself to suppress his astonishment at this unheard of occurrence, but he could not help asking "You are feeling well, Talan?" He was certain that in the congested cities of Earth, matters of sanitation could not possibly be properly attended to and that among the warm, damp, hairless, close-packed bodies, every conceivable type of disease must freely breed.

"Quite well," the ambassador answered.

"You haven't eaten."

"I will get something later. If, that is, our ever-solicitous Terran employees will allow me into the kitchen."

The secretary wagged his tail in appreciation of the small joke, but the bitterness in it disturbed him.

"Would you tell Brian McInnes," Talan said, dismissing him, "that I will be ready in half an hour, that this is a wholly nonhostile, social assembly, so we will not need

his army of security people, and that I think arriving by
private vehicle will appear somewhat ostentatious in
light of the fact that the local government has announced
yet another cutback in fuel rations."

When the secretary had gone, Talan closed his eyes
for a moment, trying to prepare his mind for the strain of
the forthcoming reception. A man of his people, he was
not comfortable in large groups. Yet he could not deny
the value of these gatherings. The mixing of peoples in a
relatively informal setting, shielded to a degree from the
prying eyes of the publicity makers, lubricated with alcohol or whatever minor stimulant the various races fancied, had on more than one occasion provided
information available from no other source. Talan still
wished for a different way. He could not feel happy
about the need to attend another such function,
crammed in close with a hundred other people of maybe
thirty different shapes and sizes, with thirty different
smells and thirty dialects.

It's time to go home for a while, he decided, to get
away from this crowded place, to walk among the gardens of the Polar Park until the smell of humanity leaves
me, and to spend some time in the vast empty spaces of
the Western Desert that soothe the spirit by their very
emptiness.

In the Western Desert, he and Bill Anderson had been
young together, young and full of high ambition and
youthful confidence. On the desk, Bill Anderson's book
still waited for him. Talan picked up the heavy volume,
turned it in his hands once, and then tucked it into a
drawer.

The office door opened and Brian McInnes burst in
without ceremony. "What the hell are you talking about
'ostentatious'? What are you planning to do, get on the
bloody subway? You think you're going to be inconspic-
uous in a crowd or something? Like a Great Dane in a
poodle show. You'll get mugged, for Christ's sake."

His agitation carried the security chief to lean across
the desk toward Talan, who regarded him with a steady,
thoughtful gaze.

McInnes was a big man, perhaps twenty-five centimeters taller and twenty kilos heavier than the ambassador. Talan had to look up to meet his eyes.

"It's good of you to be concerned," Talan said.

"It's my fucking job to be concerned, damn it. You want the interplanetary incident to end all incidents, just get yourself killed, why don't you? You're nuts, you know that?"

"Mad though I may be, I had not seriously considered the subway. I did think that since most of the alien embassies are within a few blocks of one another, we might use a common vehicle. A small gesture from the diplomatic community, I grant you, but one that would possibly be appreciated by the populace. However, you have made your point rather forcefully, Brian McInnes. I bow to your most vigorous objections."

"Oh." McInnes' face flushed and he stammered a little. "I—I—uh, guess I overreacted some."

Talan said nothing. The security chief grew uneasy in the silence. He's expecting something more from me, Talan realized, but could not imagine what it was. As McInnes' embarrassment faded, it was replaced with resentment. But over what?

"I feel you are angry," Talan said, "but I don't understand why."

For a brief moment some of the lost fire returned to McInnes' eyes; it faded quickly. "Ah, it's nothing. You be ready in fifteen minutes?"

For Talan, a creature who neither wore clothing nor shaved, and who did not adorn himself, getting ready involved activities primarily mental, reviewing the guest list and deciding what bits of information he could safely yield to whom in return for the information he wanted. But thoughts of Brian McInnes and the misunderstanding between them kept intruding. For Talan, the inability to control these stray thoughts indicated a lack of discipline. He did not consider this a good sign.

But he remembered to leave a note on the Com/Com link for his secretary. The new round of fuel rationing had brought something to mind that might help the Orian cause.

If Earth had adequate supplies of energy, perhaps other worlds would not seem so remote. If Earthlings realized how much energy could be made available, perhaps they would find the threat of the Kaz not quite so distant and unrealizable—if they could be prevented from first using the power in an orgy of self-destruction.

The secretary returned to the office after Talan had left. There was one more chore he would attend to before retiring.

He would allow none of the staff, however efficient or well recommended, to enter the ambassador's office. Aside from problems of security, and with the Orian form of open diplomacy such problems were few, long years of close association had made the secretary familiar with the way Talan liked things done. So he made it his habit at the end of each day to slip in and tidy up. There was usually little to do. Talan was a tidy person.

He found the message on the link and transferred it to his own unit without bothering to find out what was in it. Morning would be soon enough. There were two letters on the desk. Strange how humanity clung to its paper, never believing contact had been made unless a piece of paper moved from one place to another. The letters, one from the Union of Soviety Socialist Republics, one from Eurocom, could have been more quickly and surely transmitted via the Communications/Computer Network.

Though slightly different in tone, the letters were much alike in content, warning the ambassador that association with the group of dissidents/agitators known as UBI was not well thought of and would not serve his government well. He opened the desk drawer intent on putting the papers away, and saw the book. Picking it up to slip the letters underneath until he was sure Talan had seen them and they could be filed, he held it for a moment, feeling the weight of it. More paper, that's all it was. More paper.

He started to put it back. Then he lifted it out of the drawer and set it on the desk. Fully conscious that curi-

osity had always been the curse of his race, he opened
the book at random.

The script was strange, bearing only the faintest re-
semblance to printed English, but he could make it out
when he thought about it for a while. Ignore the con-
necting strokes. Read the long loops as lines. It started
to take form.

"It doesn't paint a very flattering picture of Orian society, does it?"

The secretary started guiltily. Engrossed with what he
was reading, he had not heard Talan return. With quick
motions, he closed the book and put it back into the
drawer while he attempted to recover his composure.

"I really couldn't say," he answered.

"Come, now," the ambassador said impatiently. "You
must have formed some opinion."

"It seems to me to have the usual bias and dramatiza-
tion of events that Terran writing often has. I don't think
anyone would seriously consider it an accurate represen-
tation."

"Except perhaps other Terrans. A strong opinion from
one who a moment ago professed to have none," Talan
chided. "How much damage do you suppose it might do
to our already battered image if it were made public?"

The secretary shifted uneasily. He was not comfortable on the wrong side of the desk and he was acutely
aware of having violated the ambassador's privacy. Furthermore, he had some notion of the circumstances surrounding the events he had been reading about, and if
that part was any indication of the whole, reading the
journal must be keenly painful to Talan.

Personally appalled at the thought of Talan participating in those events, and by nature scrupulously honest,
the secretary, left to his own devices, would have said
nothing at all. But Talan was waiting for an answer, and
so he had to make one.

"I cannot see it being accepted for fact. Perhaps as a
work of fiction . . ."

When Talan did not reply at once, the secretary

snatched the opportunity to change the subject. "Did the reception go well?" he asked.

"As well as could be expected. I am convinced the secretary-general of the United Nations sees the need for a shift of power to the Interplanetary Community, but many of the leaders of the so-called sovereign states do not. Without their support, the secretary-general can do nothing. I am beginning to believe we will have to swallow the niceties of manners and actively promote transfer of authority from the little political subdivisions to the planetary government, if we are to have any hope at all of getting Earth and her followers into the Community. It could be a very long term project."

"Did the Kaz give any indication that they are going to do more than verbally oppose the Community here?"

"The Kaz did not see fit to send a representative."

Though he gave no outward sign, the secretary winced inwardly at Talan's flat statement. He himself had become involved in diplomacy almost by accident, and in Terran politics reluctantly at Talan's request. He found it difficult to understand the Terran habit of judging a race's politics by every characteristic of that race other than its political policies. But he did not doubt that Terrans had a crude shrewdness and that they would not miss the significance of the absence of a Kazi: They might deal with the Oriani or the Kaz, but not both.

"But you are not seriously considering interfering in Terran domestic affairs? We would face censure within the Community."

There was an empty moment before the ambassador answered. "Perhaps it will not be necessary. Perhaps we can play the Kazi game. I have been thinking about the wisdom of supplying Earth with mature fusion technology—it will be many years before their own develops adequately. In return, we could insist that Earth break off all relations with the Kaz. It is not the way we prefer to do business, but it might be effective."

"That's dangerous. The Kaz could turn around and offer exactly the same deal."

"Yes. Except that Kazi technology is not so readily adaptable to humans, they could indeed. We would have to gamble on the fact that the Kaz are a little uneasy about Terrans and their aggressive tendencies."

"And we are not?"

"We are, or the offer would have been made long ago. It is frightening to think of humans in control of as much power as they could find a use for."

Although touched by the heat of Talan's words, the secretary did not hesitate to use the time the ambassador was distracted to get around to his proper side of the desk.

"But would it work?" More comfortable now, the secretary was more willing to argue. "We thought improving the communications system would help bring the nations together, but so far it has served only to allow them to argue faster."

"Yes."

"And the whole scheme comes perilously close to blackmail."

"Yes."

"If the Kaz were to suspect our intentions, they would dump their technology on Earth without conditions. I don't see how we could get in ahead of them and still maintain control."

"Nor do I. It will take some study."

"Furthermore, I am not at all certain we would be believed. For some reason, Orion lacks credibility in human eyes." The secretary stifled a yawn. "I think we are confused with some sort of domestic animal."

The secretary's weariness did not go unnoticed. "Go to your rest now," the ambassador said kindly. "In the morning, find the nearest Orian vessel and send it home on diplomatic priority. I think we need the advice of the council in this matter."

"It may be some time. The starship *L'rar* carrying the diplomatic courier was fired upon and damaged just inside the orbit of Neptune."

"Fired upon? By whom?"

"We have no details yet. Communications are very poor."

"Were there casualties?"

"Unknown."

"Is there another vessel in the area to render assistance?"

"The merchant vessel *John Taylor Brown* has informed us it is nearby and will get into position to take the passengers sometime early tomorrow morning. Then perhaps we will be able to get some information on the condition of *L'rar*."

"Keep me up to date. I want any news as soon as you get it. Regardless of anything which might interfere."

Alone, Talan sighed a most unambassadorial sigh and dropped heavily into the chair behind the desk. What had happened to *L'rar*? Pirates, or provocation of a type impossible to ignore? If provocation, why? What was to be gained? By whom?

In spite of the absence of all evidence, Talan suspected the Kaz. Perhaps, he thought, he was being unduly paranoid about Orion's traditional enemies. But it was not beyond imagination that the *L'rar* incident was the opening salvo in a new Ellgarth War. He would not like to see Earth and Orion set against one another. Reluctant to fight, Orion would be at a tremendous disadvantage. Without Kazi assistance, Earth would be ill-equipped to engage in such a conflict. Of course, the Kaz would render assistance. The Kaz would not only benefit from such a contest, they could very well be actively promoting it. It was a strategy they had used often, and successfully: set two races against one another, wait until they had reduced one another to ruins, and then step in and pick up the pieces. It might take centuries, as it did in the Ellgarth Cluster, but the Kaz had time. They plotted on a time scale upon which the span of a single life was barely noticeable.

Talan thought that perhaps in his present exhausted state of mind his imagination was running away with him. He knew that he, too, should sleep now, and he knew he should be expending whatever energies he had to spare following the meager leads the reception had offered. The drawer in front of him was partly open, the green binding of the book showing through the crack. He thought of the secretary, ears folded down in embarrass-

ment. Talan had been too hard on him. There was no
excuse for that.

His mind strayed to the manuscript. He had had time
for only a few pages, chosen randomly, but he found the
account of familiar events distorted by an alien point of
view oddly compelling. Partly because handwritten English was unfamiliar to him, progress was slow. But that
was not the whole of the problem. The work itself
was disquieting. The words of an ancient Terran poet
had come to mind while he was reading, words he had
learned long ago in school when he was studying that
barbaric and yet strangely moving language called English:

> To see ourselves as others see us
> Would from many a fancy free us
> And foolish notion.

The words came back to him with new force and
meaning.

Visions of loneliness and confusion stared up from
this manuscript. They also were disturbing. Talan believed that he had known Bill Anderson as well as it was
possible for one intelligence to know another, but it
seemed there were aspects of the man's character that he
had never touched. Oriani were instinctively solitary. It
was their nature to leave others alone unless a pressing
need demanded they do otherwise. Loneliness was a
thing Talan realized he understood poorly. He had no
concept of it driving a man as it seemed to have driven
Bill Anderson.

Perhaps more important, Talan thought, the manuscript was giving him new insights into the problems of
his homeworld. As did most of his people, Talan had
always accepted the view that the lesion that was the
port city outworlders called Orion Space Central fes-
tered on his planet because of the presence there of un-
ruly and unprincipled aliens, and that it could not be
cured, only contained. Could it be suppurating, as Bill
Anderson suggested, only because of neglect? Orion had
once attempted to disinfect the wound, but the treatment

had been effective only briefly. Steven Black had represented a particularly virulent form of corruption, but removing him had only made way for a proliferation of other kinds.

Talan closed his eyes for a moment, trying to shed the old ghosts of his youth. But they wouldn't go. He took the book out of the drawer, placed it on the desk in front of him, and opened it to the first page.

Bill Anderson had been one of the first Terrans to spend a significant amount of time on Orion outside of the port city. Perhaps this writing was a unique opportunity to understand that strange resentment, instinctive and hidden, which humans bore the Oriani, a resentment that needed only some small excuse to become open and respectable.

It's so easy to find excuses to do what you want to do, Talan thought. Am I merely rationalizing?

The writing absorbed his attention, throwing him back fifty years in time, and he never answered himself.

Outbound

The skipper was new and nervous and afraid of the lumpy gravity well around a tertiary star system. He brought the good ship *Greyhound* out of hyperspace a solid three days out, with a long, slow drag left to planetfall. It would irritate his passengers, he knew, but he preferred to err on the side of safety.

There was no way he could have anticipated the outcome of his caution. All the information he was given said that the pirates who scourged the shipping lanes never came that close to Centauri.

Bill Anderson was among the irritated passengers, although he was less irritated than he would have been if he had been the least bit anxious to reach his destination.

But nothing he had been able to discover about the Centauri Colony pleased him. He had come to the conclusion that nobody went there by choice. The weather was lousy, as one would expect on the planet of a triple star system, and there was nothing much there except a few farmers cultivating one of the local veggies from which was extracted some kind of pharmaceutical. And, of course, the factory that did the extracting. There were also a couple of trading houses, and the government office where he'd be working as official translator. Not a really wild, exciting place to be. And he was going to have to try to live there for three blessed years. He wasn't looking forward to it.

The transfer was Anderson's punishment for telling that crotchety old fool, Alistair Stone, just what a fool he was. That's the trouble with the Civil Service, he thought as he looked from *Greyhound*'s viewport at the hazy red disc of Proxima Centauri off the port bow. All you need to succeed is endurance. If you can last long enough, you'll make it to the top. Good old Alistair didn't seem to realize that the head of linguistic services was still a long way from the top. He thought he was God. Anderson thought he was an ass. His mistake was telling the man so.

All the passengers were crowded around the viewport. It had been a long time since there had been anything to see. Nobody in prestarship days had imagined that man's great adventure into space would be so hideously boring.

"It'll be such a marvelous adventure, Bill," his mother had said. She was full of enthusiasm for other people's adventures. She was always pushing him to do something for her own vicarious excitement. After thirty-one years, she was still living his life.

"A whole new world. I can't imagine it. And the extra money's nice, too."

He had said, "Yes, Mother, marvelous." But he had imagined it all too well. Bleak and dreary. Remote duty pay would hardly make up for that.

For a while in LunaPort he thought maybe the adventure wouldn't be quite so bad. Half a dozen people in green blazers with "World University Services—Forestry" written in gold thread on the breast pockets had gathered around him at Gate Four, chattering as they waited for the Centauri flight. They seemed pleased enough.

Anderson had picked out a pert young blond girl and said, "Hi."

She had smiled at him politely.

"Are there forests on Centauri?" he asked, pointing to the lettering.

"Not yet," she answered, and turned back to her companions.

That left him with no one to talk to but the Orian.

The alien stood to one side, aloof and reserved. He was also being ignored by the foresters, and by everyone

else. A circle of empty space had formed around him as
if he had some dreadful disease and the perimeter of the
circle marked the limits of the contagion. Anderson
stepped into the circle and said hello. The Orian turned
grave yellow eyes on him and studied him for a moment
before responding. But there was only time to exchange
the most preliminary of pleasantries before they were
called aboard. Then everything was hustle and bustle for
a couple of hours until *Greyhound* got underway.

Anderson thought he had been lucky to catch the fast
packet to Centauri. If he had to go, it was better not to
spend weeks getting there. He'd had enough of space
flight already, with the Earth–Moon passage. One day
accelerating and one day decelerating, with everything
turning ass over teakettle at the halfway point. He decided he liked a planetary surface where up stayed up
and down stayed down where it belonged. Besides, once
he got through admiring the way the little blue ball he
came from hung all alone there in the dark, there wasn't
a blessed thing to do.

The trip to Centauri had promised to be more of the
same, and it was. Nine hours of crushing acceleration
kept the passengers in their seats with their concentra-
tion fixed firmly on breathing. Then there was the gut-
wrenching but momentary experience of dropping into
hyperspace. Then there was nothing for the next six or
seven days. Anderson had explored the little ship in no
time. There wasn't much to explore. *Greyhound* had
been built for speed, not for entertainment.

The after half of the slim blunt cylinder was occupied
by the engines, where passengers weren't allowed to go.
Forward was the bridge, where passengers also weren't
allowed to go. The remainder was bisected by the deck,
cargo space below, up to twelve passengers above. Food
preparation and sanitary facilities and a host of re-
minders to conserve resources—note: the Company is
not obliged to accelerate one spoonful of water more
than necessary to meet safety standards—occupied a
small area amidships. In front a viewport extended into a
deep well, presumably so that light, when there was
light, would also reach the hold. A railing around the

well kept the passengers from falling into it. The decor was a uniform institutional gray.

Anderson made another attempt at getting acquainted with the blond forester, but she was thoroughly engrossed with her companions in discussions of the sex life of gymnosperms. So he hung over the rail at the viewport and watched the nothing outside. After a bit, the Orian had joined him there.

"You must have done a lot of this," Anderson said.

"My home star is Omnicron Orionis, approximately one hundred eighty-three light-years from Sol."

"How do you keep from going out of your skull with boredom?"

The Orian didn't answer directly. Instead he asked, "Do you play chess?"

"Yes, as a matter of fact. Do you?"

"I was learning until I was called away from Earth. Perhaps you would be kind enough to take up where my teacher left off?"

So they whiled away the hours at the chessboard the Orian produced from among his baggage. The alien played like a beginner, but he showed a lot of potential and had a way of lashing out from behind a solid defense that was full of sharp surprises. Between games, Anderson had learned quite a lot about Orion but relatively little about the man, except that his name was Talan and he was a diplomatic attaché paying a courtesy call on the Centauri Colony before returning to his homeworld.

The pirate captain had none of the qualms about difficult transits that troubled the *Greyhound*'s skipper. He flung his ship in from between Alpha II and Proxima, using the stellar perturbations to mask his approach until he was almost on top of his intended victims.

There was no question of *Greyhound* putting up a fight. The pirates had an old military vessel of Rigan design. It might have been an antique, but the little unarmed packet didn't have a prayer against it. *Greyhound* surrendered without argument. The young skipper tried to keep the quaver out of his voice while he informed the passengers.

"Stay calm," the Orian advised, but Bill Anderson found that advice very difficult to take. His nervous hand upset the chessboard and his knees lost all their strength. When the outlaws came back into the passenger compartment and started herding everyone up to the bridge to join the crew, he could hardly walk.

The crew was already on the bridge, of course, looking white and shaken. The skipper had blood dripping down into his collar from a nasty, bruised cut just under his eye, and Anderson's stomach did flip-flops every time he looked at the man.

The pirates pushed them all together in a bunch and looked them over, disappointed with their catch. A cargo of tree seeds, half a dozen terrified silviculturalists, and a bureaucrat had little value on the black market. But they also had the Orian attaché.

A few sharp words snapped back and forth quickly developed into a pretty serious-sounding squabble. A scruffy mixture of races, the outlaws spoke a language all their own, about twenty percent standard Terran dialects, with smatterings of two or three other languages Anderson recognized and lots he didn't.

"What's happening?" the skipper asked him. "Can you understand them?"

Anderson could get the gist of the argument. He didn't think knowing was going to make the skipper feel any better.

"This bunch," he said, "is a tad nervous about our Orian friend and want to dump the lot of us overboard and run for it. The other group seems to think the Orian is a pretty valuable commodity and the rest of us ought to be worth something, and maybe they could at least cover their expenses if they held us all for ransom."

The skipper bit his lip. "I wish I knew which side I was pulling for," he said.

The pirate captain was one of those things with horns from Brodenl that Anderson had only seen pictures of until that moment. He did not seem to be in very secure control of his men, so he let them argue it out and when they finally decided on ransom, went along with it against his better judgment. But after all, as one brigand pointed out, dumping was something they could always do later if things didn't proceed as planned.

The blond forester couldn't take the strain. She had counted quite a few Terrans among the pirates, and she was looking at a bad time ahead.

She broke from the group and charged the pirate captain, screaming at the top of her voice, arms flailing. What she thought she was going to accomplish, nobody ever knew. The captain had nothing more than a monetary interest in her. He raised his weapon and shot her dead. The skipper looked as if he was about to take up where she left off until the muzzle of the pirate's gun turned on him.

It was an effective demonstration both to his men and to his captives that the captain's temper was short. Everybody was much more subdued after that.

The outlaws ransacked *Greyhound,* picking up anything they could find that they thought might be of value, and rifled the passengers' personal effects. Then, with much snarling and shouting and waving of weapons, the terrified prisoners were transferred to the pirates' vessel and dumped like so many sacks of flour into the hold. *Greyhound*'s engines were spiked and she was left to blow herself to atoms.

When the detonation rocked the pirate ship, the skipper let out a groan that came from his soul and then went back to the business of trying to get everyone huddled together to keep from freezing to death.

"You got any idea where we're going?" he asked Anderson.

"Epsilon Indi, I think, for safekeeping. They've got some kind of stronghold there."

"Blast. That's a hundred years from anything." He studied Anderson's face with genuine concern. "You going to be all right?"

About then Anderson experienced his first attack. It came like a hammer out of nowhere and slammed into his chest, turning his world into ashes. For a few moments overwhelming pain radiated down his arm and into his belly from the nova where his heart had been. He had time to realize he was dying, to sense the surprise and terror and the stupidity of it, and then he slipped into oblivion.

There was a passage of time, some blank pages in the book of his life. Then there were a few minutes of near lucidity, with the Orian bending over him. Talan had found water somewhere and was forcing it between Anderson's clenched teeth. The Orian looked tired. People crowded around, murmuring and shifting restlessly. A vile stench filled the air. And pain.

This sequence repeated itself randomly. All that marked the changes was the growing weariness he could see in the yellow eyes watching over him and his own increasing desire to have it finish, to end the futile battle for life. To give up. But something of iron determination just beyond his understanding would not allow it.

Epsilon Indi

The thin dawn broke and Dr. Thomas Yaeger of the World University Services Forestry Division pushed his way through the crowded bodies to the frame around the door and dug his fingernail into the soft wood as he had done every dawn for the past—how many? He counted the notches. Thirteen. If he were superstitious, he would have considered it a bad omen.

The day before, in a rare moment when the Orian was resting from his labor over Anderson, the alien had told Yaeger that twelve notches represented approximately twenty Terran days. So thirteen was close to twenty-two —if the Orian knew what he was talking about.

Yaeger had no idea why it was so important to him to keep track of the time. The days were all the same. He wondered how long they could continue. The food was scarce and very bad. The sanitation facilities were worse. The atmosphere in their tiny room held a stench he couldn't get used to. It was a miracle that no one except Anderson had yet become seriously ill. But their luck, if that's what it was, couldn't hold out forever.

Now he had forty hours to put in until it was time to make another notch. He made his way through the people once again, ignoring the irritated grumbling, to where the skipper was sitting with his back against a wall.

Intellectually, he couldn't blame his fellow prisoners for grumbling. They had nothing else to do, and with eleven people crowded into a bare space not much bigger than a tract house kitchen, everyone got on everyone else's nerves.

Just the same, he felt barely able to restrain himself from bringing his fist smartly into contact with Maria Sanchez' nose. Her high-pitched complaining whine was the least tolerable thing in this intolerable place. He couldn't believe that at one time he had considered her an attractive woman.

He eased himself down beside the skipper and stared into the same corner the skipper was staring into.

"Think they'll feed us today?" Food was the only subject that held any real interest anymore. Yaeger considered the hollow place where a nice round gut had not so long ago strained the buttons of his shirt.

"Don't know."

Yaeger nodded at the Orian laboring over Anderson. "Why doesn't he give up?" he asked, because it was something to say. The skipper shrugged. This topic had been exhausted long ago, as had every other topic of conversation anyone could think of. Never was a group of people so well acquainted with the details of one another's lives as this one was. "He must be nuts," Yaeger added. He was disgusted with himself when he realized how much he resented the way the Orian had commandeered more than his fair share of the space and more than his fair share of the water to look after a man who should have been dead by now.

Back in the beginning, when Yaeger had still had enough energy to care, he had asked the Orian what he was doing and if he needed help. The alien had been quite brusque.

"I am attempting to preserve a life. I will be best able to do so if I am subjected to a minimum of interference."

How the preserving business went on, Yaeger was unable to figure out, but Anderson was definitely still alive, stirring weakly. The man was obviously weaker even than he'd been a day earlier. As time went on, Anderson's periods of consciousness became briefer, and he seemed less alert in them.

The Orian brought water and insisted that Anderson swallow it. Then he sat back on his haunches and closed his eyes. He swayed slightly and caught himself.

The fellow's exhausted, Yaeger thought. The robust

young man had become a rack of bones with dull, matted fur and eyes that seemed to have grown enormous. And he's become quite rank, too, Yaeger added to himself, wrinkling his nose. But then I guess we all have.

"What do you think it would take to get them to at least open a window?" he asked the skipper.

"Not very damned much. A minor irritation, I suspect. There's no air on this world."

"Oh."

The door slammed open. All heads turned that way, hoping that food had arrived.

While a third man stayed in the doorway, two of the outlaws marched in, weapons at the ready, one of them carrying a recorder. Shoving and kicking people out of the way, they went directly to the Orian and pushed him around to face them. "Listen to this," they said in plain English.

The Orian listened.

"What're they saying?" one of the outlaws demanded.

"The Orian government is asking what conditions are to be met in order to secure the release of your prisoners."

"That's all? That's a lot of growling for one question."

"They are inquiring after our health, asking for the names of those who are being held, and requesting a prompt reply."

"Yeah? It's about time." The outlaw switched the recorder back on. "Okay, tell them."

"What would you like told?"

The outlaw dictated and the Orian translated. Yaeger thought the pirate had a lot of faith in his ability to adequately intimidate a prisoner. There was no way the outlaw could know if he was getting an accurate rendering. But at least there was hope. It finally started to seep into Yaeger's numbed brain that someone was actually doing something to get them out of the mess they were in. A swelling murmur and a wave of restlessness spread through the room as it dawned on one after another of the prisoners what was happening.

Getting nervous, the outlaws backed out of the room

and slammed the door shut. The prisoners all heard the *clack* of the lock engaging.

The Orian made his way to where the skipper was sitting, squatted down beside him, and rested his hands on his thighs. "Orian Security is mounting a rescue operation," he said. "We will not be here much longer. The negotiations are intended only as a distraction."

"Are you sure?"

"Yes. My government does not bargain under duress. This is the only possible explanation."

"My God," Yaeger said. "They'll get us all killed."

"Unlikely. Security is quite expert in these matters."

"You've got to stop them. We'll all die. Don't they understand? It would take nothing to make those yahoos decide we're not worth the trouble."

"Hush, Doctor," the skipper said. "What can we do to help, Talan?"

"Any further distractions you might devise would be of value. Any sort of disturbance to divert our captors' attention. Perhaps if Dr. Yaeger were to have a fit of the screaming terrors, that would be sufficient. I must get back to Bill Anderson, so I will not be able to assist you."

The skipper waited until the Orian had returned to his corner.

"Start screaming, Doctor," he said.

When the bulk of the planet lay between Orian starship *Tigit* and the pirates, the Orians dropped a shuttle into a shallow, gliding path that brought it to a point just beyond the horizon from the outlaws' installation. Fifteen members of the Security Service in full environmental gear left the shuttle and began the march overland. Though cautious about moving over the rocky, frozen ground on a hostile, airless world and aware that their orbital maps might hold less detail than they would like, the team members were nonetheless conscious of the need for speed, and they made reasonable time across the rough terrain.

Meanwhile, *Tigit* scoured the region for the pirate ship. In time, they found the old Rigan cruiser in the shadow of the planet's minor moon. After that they held their position and waited for word from the ground forces.

Negotiations continued only as long as it took the surface team to reach the pirate stronghold.

Within the stronghold, the Brodenli outlaw leader was having problems. Some sort of minor riot was developing among the prisoners. He had already threatened to blast the lot of them to ashes if they didn't settle down, but in truth, he was reluctant to do so at this stage. After all, the Oriani had finally deigned to take notice, and it would be too bad to blow away his assets after waiting so long. His captives obviously understood this all too well. They ignored his threats and continued with the quarreling and shouting and banging on the door.

More serious was the Orian negotiator. In spite of the Brodenli's demands that they use another language, the negotiator insisted in working in his native tongue and there was no one among the pirates who understood it. For all he knew, the Orian didn't understand him, didn't know what he was asking for. He couldn't even argue. This was something that had to be solved.

After sparing a few choice words to describe an unlikely miscegenation that he suggested had given rise to the Orian race, he sent a couple of his henchmen to bring his captive member of that maligned breed to the communications room.

The men went and came back in a few moments to tell him that the Orian didn't want to leave the sick man.

For a minute, for the first time in his life, words failed the Brodenli. "Maybe if you ask him pretty please," he snarled at last. "Or drag him out by the bloody tail."

They went again and returned, with the Orian between them, just as a burst of noise came from the speakers: the pirates could barely make out the voice of the head of the skeleton crew that had been left aboard their vessel. The ship had been attacked and was breaking up. Then they heard nothing but static.

Realization dawned on the pirate captain just as a small muffled explosion rocked the building. He experienced a moment of panic when he thought the structure had been breached and their precious air was leaking out into vacuum. It took him that moment to realize that breathing was still possible.

Then he found more Oriani around him than he had ever wished for.

He yelled at his men to stand and fight. The battle was brief and one-sided, as the pirates soon realized they could not win and they had no place to hide.

For his own part, the Brodenli decided on one last act of vengeance. If the thrice-damned Oriani were going to play a dirty game, at least they weren't going to get their precious hostage back. He leveled his weapon at Talan. He would cheat them out of that if it was the last thing he ever did.

It was the last thing he ever tried to do. He was shot down before he could fire.

The Medical Center

Bill Anderson spent a long time just lying there in a box full of dried aromatic grass or something like it, looking at the ceiling, listening to the quiet and absorbing the comfort and solitude. It was great. Marvelous. So peaceful.

Gradually he became aware of the activity beyond the walls, and then of the wires and tubes attached to his body and leading off to a place behind his head that he couldn't see.

A massive bandage circled his chest.

He lay stark naked on his bed of grass. The room was too warm.

He had no idea of place or time. He might have been anywhere in the galaxy, or out of it, as far as that went. He really couldn't work up a lot of concern. He was alive. He could be satisfied with that for the moment.

The room was tiny and sparsely furnished—his bed of hay, a panel of instruments attached to the wall above his head, and off to one side of the bed, a small, short cupboard whose top was serving as a table. A little farther off there was a door, closed.

Through the window in front of him, furious, nearly white sunlight poured down. Nearby, a few green growing things waved in a stiff breeze, but most of what was visible through the glass was desert, stretching out to the horizon, with a haze of blowing sand near the ground.

Then an Orian came in and looked first not at Anderson but at the monitors and dials over his head, and things started to make sense.

As soon as he saw the newcomer, Anderson figured the Orian was a doctor, furry tail notwithstanding. Every doctor he'd ever met had that same air of harassed impatience and bustle. Doctors had always responded to him as if all his concerns were silly and groundless and everything were fine and normal and he had nothing to worry about but he wouldn't understand the explanation if they had time to give it to him. This one looked to be no different.

The doctor said something to him in a language Anderson didn't understand. Anderson produced one of his more brilliant witticisms.

"Huh?"

It made him feel outstandingly clever.

The doctor vanished and returned in a few moments with an interpreter, a delicate young female who translated for him in heavily accented English.

"He wants to know how you are feeling."

"Fine."

"He wants to know if you have pain."

"None."

"It is good so."

While the doctor poked and prodded about his person, Anderson asked the interpreter, and the doctor through her, the obvious questions, such as Where am I, and How did I get here, and What day is this. The girl told him he was in the Medical Center in Owr-Lakh, on the edge of the Western Desert, on the continent of Berewanith, on the world whose Orian name Anderson felt sure he would never be able to say, but which the interpreter gave him to understand was Omnicron Orionis V. The place Earthlings usually called Orion, as if there were no other populated worlds in the entire constellation.

The interpreter said her name was Ee, and pronounced it exactly like a softly voiced scream.

"What happened?" Anderson wanted to know.

"You had a heart attack."

"What?"

"This is wrong?"

"Damned wrong. I'm a young man, for crying out loud."

Ee cocked her head and looked at him, then consulted with the doctor. After a bit, she turned back to Anderson.

"The muscle was dying, what you would call a-trow-feed. But there is no need for crying loudly. It has been repaired."

There followed, with much discussion between the two Oriani, a long, technical explanation about regenerative surgery, but between Ee's difficulty with the terms and Anderson's lack of medical knowledge, most of it went right over his head.

But there was one point he wanted to be absolutely certain he had straight. "I am going to be all right, healthy, when this is over?"

"Surely."

The doctor left, in a hurry as doctors always are, but the interpreter stayed with Anderson to answer his questions. He came to admire her patience, for he had a lot of questions.

It had occurred to him that his mother would be worried because she hadn't heard from him, that the Colonial Office would be pretty upset because he hadn't arrived as scheduled on Centauri, and that the Department of Linguistic Services would be in convulsions wondering where he had gone and who was scrubbing his little brain clean of all its assembled motes of sensitive information.

The image wasn't entirely displeasing. There was nothing like a lot of high-level flap to make a guy feel pretty important.

No doubt various Secret Service agents were stumbling all over themselves trying to find out what had become of him. They worried a lot about translators. Translators, interpreters, and coding clerks—low-ranking folk privy to all too many high-ranking secrets. More than one administration's clandestine plans had been brought into the bright light of day by a disaffected coding clerk. The Secret Service itself courted the translators of rival governments with enthusiasm and no small success. So of course they worried when one of their own was missing. All the governments on Earth would breathe a collective sigh of relief when someone finally got a computer to do a translator's work.

Fortunately for the continued existence of Anderson's job, no one had achieved outstanding results in programming computers to translate one Terran language to another, never mind alien tongues based on entirely different concepts. He had fooled around with the idea himself on those rare occasions that he could get access to one of the big government computers. But nobody took his hobby very seriously. He was a translator, not a computer expert, and in the eyes of the bureaucrats, never the twain would meet—which might have been part of the problem.

None of that had much bearing on the troubles of the moment. Anderson had more pressing concerns.

He told Ee that he had to get home, back to Earth, and made a valiant attempt to get out of bed. He got his head up. The room did one and a half turns and then fell in on him.

When he recovered consciousness, the doctor was back, looking at the dressing on the incision in his chest. The doctor said something and Ee translated.

"He says you have some courage but very little sense."

"Tell him I have to get back to Earth. People will be worried."

While he checked the tubes and wires and studied the instruments, the doctor relayed the bad news. "I would not stop you, if that is what you want. You are to decide. However, it will be some time before it would be wise for you to travel. I must also tell you that the repairs made to your heart are not forever. In time, the new tissue will a-trow-fee and die, just as before. With medical help and more treatments when they are needed, there is no reason why you cannot live out the rest of a lifespan normal for your species. However, this cannot be done on Earth. The knowledge for this work is not there. Without it, with care, you can expect a time equivalent to five, or perhaps six, standard Terran years."

"But you said I would be healthy when this was over."

"You will be so. You will need help to stay so."

"I can't stay here."

"As you wish. I do what I can now. What is to come is not in my hands."

Numb, Anderson nodded his understanding and the doctor left him to his thoughts.

Ee said something about informing his government of his whereabouts, but Anderson had lost interest in his picture of Stone trying to deal with the wrath of the upper echelons. Half of him was disbelieving, as if as long as he didn't admit that it might be true, it wouldn't be; and half of him was furiously angry, raging without an object. Beneath the bandages his heart bumped a regular rhythm, growing stronger with every beat. It couldn't be true, but he knew it was.

Ee went out, and Bill Anderson was alone. Very much alone.

So here I am, he thought, the kid voted most likely to succeed by the class of '03, the scourge of the Translation Division, Alistair Stone's personal nemesis, neatly trapped by my own body on an alien world, lying on a pile of hay, staring up at a blank white ceiling, trying to convince myself it's not just a crazy nightmare. He rubbed the beads of sweat off his forehead with the back of his hand.

To spend a lifetime on Orion. The implications sunk in slowly. In his conversations with Talan on the ill-fated *Greyhound*, Anderson had formed a mental picture of the place, and the picture he had formed was the Sahara writ large. The fifth planet from the primary, the only biogenic one in the system, Orion was a hard, dry, hot world. Less than half of the surface was ocean. The sun looked small, but it burned fierce and white in an almost green sky. Talan had told him that the sky had that odd color because there was so much dust in the upper atmosphere. The seasons were long; the days, short.

What wasn't there? Practically everything. Football.

Nancy Bremner, who made lots of promises and kept
none of them. Steak and lobster tail. Aleathea, who
never would give him the time of day. Jazz. Bowling. His
mother. George Montgomery's sloppy sandwiches at the
Saturday night poker games. Girls on the beach. The
beach. Beer. Comic strips in the newspapers. Newspapers. An endless list, a whole world long.

If only he could afford to commute. All he would need
was a couple of million credits. Was that too much to
ask?

He tried to imagine himself as an invalid, but couldn't
build a very convincing image. Invalids were always the
distant friends of someone dimly known, whose names
come up briefly between the second and third drink at a
cocktail party. "Did you hear about poor Bill?" an acquaintance might ask before going on to discuss the
antics of some Tri-D personality or some couturier's latest collection.

Glass in hand, he would say, "Too bad," and move
quickly to more pleasant topics of conversation.

He felt strangely disoriented, more so than when he
had first awakened not knowing where he was, for he
had felt the cosmos shift so that he was no longer at its
center, the favored child of a benign and indulgent universe. He had discovered that he was just a man like any
other, and that the universe could get along fine without
him. But for the wildest kind of chance he would have
been dead already, and all the world, the worlds, would
be carrying on, unperturbed. Of course. Naturally.
Everyone knew that. Except that nobody ever believed
it until the point was driven firmly home.

How does a man reconcile himself to a thing like that?

He couldn't brood on it any longer, because another
Orian strode in and growled at him as if he should know
what the fellow wanted. The newcomer was big for one
of his kind, and his fur was long, and he didn't understand Anderson any better than Anderson understood
him. But he had a way of pushing and pulling the patient
around, demonstrating what was to be done and declin-
ing to acknowledge refusal. He could only be the physio-
therapist Ee had promised would come. Anderson

labeled him Hairy. He saw quite a lot of Hairy in the next
few days.

As he began to get over the shock, to gain strength
and take more interest in his new surroundings, Anderson grew curious about the man to whom he owed his
life. He asked Ee.

She told him that Talan was being treated in the same
hospital.

"What for?"

"The way for keeping one alive," she said, "takes
large expenses of energy. It is very hard to do for so
long. Many could not. Talan has lost much mass, twenty
kilos, and he is very weak. But the healer believes he
will probably recover health."

"Probably? What do you mean, probably?"

She looked at Anderson for a moment. "I mean, it is
most likely to happen this way."

Talan himself would make better sense. "I want to see
him," Anderson said.

"Looking at one has some value?"

"Visit? Meet? Hold a conversation?"

"This is needed?"

"No, wanted. Desired."

"I will inquire." She started away at once to make her
inquiries. With Ee, there was never much hesitation between the saying and the doing.

"Ee?"

She stopped and turned to him.

"This way for keeping one alive, how is it done?"

Ee thought it over, head cocked to one side. "It is
difficult to say. Your language has not the words."

"Try."

She was quiet for so long that Anderson began to
worry that he had inadvertently given some obscure,
Orian-type insult. He was about to start apologizing
when Ee asked, haltingly, searching for words, "Do you
know of a thing, a power of life, a compulsion for living?"

"Do you mean a life force, the will to live?"

She thought about it for a while. "Perhaps."

"What about it?"

"It is this thing, badly named, which is transferred, one to another."

"But how?"

"It is a work of the mind. Mind to mind. I do not know how to explain further. It is like speaking of sounds to one without hearing."

"Can anyone do it?"

"I think you cannot."

"I mean any Orian."

"Most can. Some are more able than others. This use, it is a thing taught, as what you would call primary assistance."

"You mean first aid?"

"Perhaps. As a way to sustain life until proper action can be taken."

"Oh."

"You are disturbed?"

"Mm. I'm not sure I like the idea of someone poking around in my mind."

"Do I understand, you feel a privacy has been invaded?"

"Something like that, I guess."

"No, Bill Anderson. Talan is not Rayorian, to read thoughts as if a book. What is possible is contact on a much lower level. Empathy? Empathic? It is sufficient for this. It is not what you fear."

He felt somewhat reassured.

Anderson remembered Talan as a dynamic person fairly radiating competence and bursting with good health. But when the Orian came into Anderson's room, he looked terrible, weak and dull-eyed, ears drooping slightly at the tips as if there were not enough vigor to hold them erect. Walking was an effort for him.

Ee brought him a chair, which made Anderson's little room crowded, and they spent most of the morning talking. Anderson suspected that Talan was as bored with hospital routine as he was.

Talan recounted the story of the rescue, ending with the information that the Brodenli had been killed and one scientist was "slightly damaged." The pirates' landing facilities were destroyed and their communications equipment confiscated. Their sanctuary had become their prison.

"You guys took some terrible chances with other people's lives. We might have all been killed," Anderson protested.

"We were not," Talan said superfluously.

Anderson thought the pirates' stronghold was going to be a rough world to live on without access to modern conveniences. The Oriani did exhibit a nice sense of the ironic.

"I always thought Oriani were pacifists," he said.

Talan thought that over for a moment, either chewing over an unfamiliar word or looking for a diplomatic answer. "We're not above defending ourselves," he said finally.

Talan was, Anderson discovered, a diplomat, no doubt about it. He had said that he was destined to diplomatic service before he was born. Anderson didn't know whether to take that literally or not. He couldn't tell if Talan was making a joke and he had no idea how Oriani chose their careers. Maybe some central authority did decide, for example, that more grocery clerks would be needed in thirty years' time, so all the babies born in the next two weeks would be raised as grocery clerks. It didn't seem likely. If Talan was an example, Oriani were pretty independent minded. But how could an outsider tell?

They got off the subject of pirates and onto Anderson's personal problems, and Anderson found himself telling Talan all his worries about his health and his finances, how he was going to have to do something about earning a living and that his work with Linguistic Services hadn't suited him for much more than furthering a doubtful career in the bureaucracy.

"I have a pretty good idea of whose apple to polish and whose ass to kiss, who to invite to dinner and whose head to step on," he said, "but I don't think it's going to be of much use to me in a place where I don't have the foggiest idea how the bureaucracy works."

Talan mulled that over without comment.

"I don't know what I'm going to do about the hospital bill," Anderson added. "I don't know much about the relative values of things on Orion, but this kind of medical care has to be expensive."

He wished he'd had a recorder with him because he figured that on another day he wouldn't believe he was accurately remembering Talan's answer.

"In your present circumstances," Talan said, "there is no question of payment for medical care. The doctor has but done his duty and the facilities of the hospital are intended for those who need them. In case your circumstances should improve, you would be expected to make a contribution to the facility according to your ability to do so and according to the needs of the moment."

Anderson took a moment to digest that. "That's just ducky. Suppose I never decide I have a contribution to spare?"

"I don't think I understand the question," Talan said.

"Never mind," Anderson said. "I'll worry about it later. I have another question: Why me?"

The Orian studied Anderson with head cocked slightly to one side. "Forgive me. Once again, I do not understand the nature of your inquiry."

"Look, I'm nothing to you, or Orion, for that matter. Not that I'm not grateful, but why didn't you just let me die? I really want to know."

Talan looked truly puzzled. "Who or what you are is in no way involved. It would be the same for anyone with the same need, insofar as it is possible. It is understood?"

"I think I would be happier if you said you had recognized my irreplaceable genius, but yes, it's understood."

"Your point about a suitable occupation is a valid one," Talan continued. "I will be at my mother's house in the city for a time. Come to me there when you are ready and we will discuss the matter. It occurs to me that until then, a linguist might put his idle time to work learning the local language."

Ee was overwhelmingly enthusiastic about teaching her Terran patient the Orian tongue. The next thing Anderson knew, his small room was filled to overflowing with records and tapes and a baffling array of teaching machines brought there at her request and stacked one atop the other for want of space. She spent much of her free time helping, and she insisted Orian was an easy language to learn. It was Anderson's experience that everybody thought that about his own language. He discovered that written Orian required seventy-one characters and thirteen diacritical marks. It wasn't all that easy. And he would always speak it with something like a lisp, for it included sounds his physiology simply could not produce.

Anyway, the studying filled up the empty days. After about three weeks—he wasn't all that sure of the time, for the days were short and his time sense, built for a different system entirely, had never been all that strong —they let him out of the hospital. He never, before or since, had felt so completely at a loss, so damned helpless, so lonely and homesick.

Owr-Lakh

At the time that Bill Anderson unwillingly landed on Orion, humankind had accumulated fifty years or so of experience with the Oriani, and that experience included precious little about Orian culture, system of government, activities, or aspirations.

Oriani were perceived by humanity to be shrewd traders and sublime diplomats, which might well have been two manifestations of one facet of character. It was known that they did not encourage tourists, although neither did they actively oppose them. Sociologists and anthropologists came away more puzzled than enlightened, saying only that the Oriani had a strong sense of privacy, and offered no help whatsoever to people prying into what they considered private matters. Psychologists were in even worse straits. Oriani would not discuss their sex lives at all, and no amount of undercover work had elicited evidence of any. Although they spoke of their adult children with normal parental pride and sense of achievement, young children were referred to with something akin to embarrassment, and no human being had ever even seen an Orian baby.

The political scientists collected odd bits of data like loose beads and found no underlying principle upon which to string them. Historians found Orian history open to them, but they could not find the thread that tied ancient to modern times.

Onto this blank page, Bill Anderson was unceremoniously dumped and expected to make his way. He had no point of reference.

The morning the doctor told him there would be no need for him to stay in the Medical Center any longer, he had been glad to be free of hospital routine. The next morning he stood in the doorway of his new home and wondered what he was going to do with the rest of his life.

With Ee's help and that of some social agency or something, he got a place to stay in the city and the basic necessities of life. More or less. There were a few things they didn't think of, such as clothes. All he had was what had been on his back when he left the *Greyhound*. After all, why would folk born wearing fur coats worry about clothes—or a razor?

Ah, well, he decided, it was too hot to wear clothes anyway. Except that if he was going to go outside at all he'd need them to keep the sun from burning him to a crisp.

And he'd become more or less used to the beard in the hospital. But he'd have to say more less than more. He wouldn't have been too unhappy to have the means to get rid of it.

The house wasn't exactly what Anderson expected from a technologically advanced culture. One low story, it was an irregular hexagon in shape, with stone walls about a quarter of a meter thick. The roof, slanted to catch the sun, consisted almost entirely of solar panels. The windows were small and high under wide eaves.

The design seemed sensible, given the Orian climate. But it lacked a little something in the comfort department.

The space inside was just that: a space. The ceiling seemed a bit too close to the ground for Anderson's liking. He kept feeling as if he should hunch down a bit. Against one wall there was a solar cooker and some cupboards forming the rudiments of a kitchen. The cupboards were stocked with local cuisine, which definitely lacked appeal. He'd had enough of local cuisine in the hospital, but when he had asked Ee about a steak, she'd looked at him as if he were demented.

There was a hay bed in the house, and a Com/Com

link, a couple of chairs, and a small table, also too low to
be quite right.

And that was it. Anderson was quite convinced there
existed Stone Age societies with more elaborate dwellings than the Oriani had. Ee told him it was assumed that
the tenant would finish the interior to suit himself. But
she didn't say how that might be accomplished.

The house was set on rather extensive grounds and
separated from its neighbors by half-wild plantings of ex-
uberant and thorny vegetation. For quite some time, Anderson was not even sure he had neighbors.

Ee kept him sane those first few days. She had volun-
teered to continue with the language lessons and she had
the language lab materials sent from the hospital. That
filled up some of the empty space in the house, and Ee
filled up some of the empty space in Anderson's days.
She and her equipment were the only halfway familiar
things on the planet.

In between times he brooded and walked.

Among all the other instructions that Hairy had con-
veyed through Ee had been the order to walk. At first Ee
walked with him, but she soon became impatient with his
slow pace and his need to stop and pant. She seemed to
think that sweat was amusing or, perhaps, slightly ob-
scene.

After the first few days, Anderson went out on his
own in the evenings when the sun was low and the air
had cooled a little. But he tried to get home before dark,
because Owr-Lakh had no lights and Orion had no moon
to speak of.

Eventually he grew confident enough to wander a bit
beyond his own neighborhood. He had a feeling that
sooner or later he would surely find something familiar
somewhere. After all, the cities of Earth were much like
one another: The centers of Paris, Chicago, London, and
Vancouver all looked and felt quite similar.

Not so Owr-Lakh.

For one thing, there was hardly anyone on the streets.
For another, there weren't many streets.

The Oriani had located their cities on ground that

wasn't useful for any other purpose, well away from waterways that might suffer from close proximity to dense populations. So there wasn't any landmark, any natural center. Though Orian architecture was probably as diversified as any, to Anderson the structures had a similarity about them that made it hard for him to tell one from another. Like his house, most homes were of stone, hexagonal in shape, with flat roofs of solar cells slanted to catch the sun, small, high windows, and wide eaves.

Owr-Lakh was small by Terran standards. In his peregrinations Anderson found an industrial region of ceaseless activity, largely mechanical, but he never found out what they did there. Another area he thought might be a business district. The residential area lay in a crescent around the north and west sides of the city. It looked like an overgrown garden with houses randomly scattered in it, and he wondered where all the water came from to keep that vegetation green.

Beyond the perimeter of the city there was nothing but sand.

There were no apartment buildings in the Orian city.

There were no theaters, no galleries, no sports stadiums.

There were no restaurants, no nightclubs, no video arcades.

Anderson was enormously curious to know what Oriani did for fun. He couldn't make Ee understand the question.

Huge roadways penetrated the industrial core, but not the residential region, where no provision for surface traffic had been made at all, and flyers were rigidly excluded. To get around, one either walked the rambling pathways or tackled the complexities of the underground transit system. Anderson walked a lot those first days. Hairy would have been pleased.

He got lost a lot, too, not that it mattered, since he wasn't going any place in particular. Once while lost he discovered that there was one point on the southern perimeter where, if he strained his eyes, he could just make out the spires of a spaceport shimmering in the heat rising over the desert and occasionally catch a blinding glint of sunlight from a lighter making its way to or from the starships hanging in orbit above.

He found it harder and harder to conceive of any kind of future in Owr-Lakh.

He felt like the lion down at the zoo.

The lion and the zoo were in Antwerp in another life. He had been in Antwerp waiting on the pleasure of the American and Soviet trade commissions. For three days he had sat right next to Ivanova Mikoyan and told the Americans what the Russians were saying while she told the Russians what the Americans were saying, and they had not passed the time of day between them.

Some ideological point came up—Anderson no longer remembered what it was—and the result was that all the delegates walked out of the meeting in a huff and left the two translators with nothing much to do for the afternoon.

He'd gone to the zoo for no particular reason except that he'd heard about the famous zoo in Antwerp, and it was too early in the day for much more interesting entertainment. He had stopped beside the lions and idly watched them while the old patriarch on the other side of the bars stared back, not at him but through him, off into the distance as if to catch a glimpse in his mind's eye of some better life. Chances were that his ancestors for twenty generations had been born in cages, yet some feral instinct told him that this was not proper for his kind.

Anderson had no idea that Ivanova Mikoyan liked zoos and lions, too. He only found that she was beside him. They had watched the lion together until the old boy put his great head down on his paws and closed his eyes to dream of zebra. Then they walked around the rest of the zoo and later went to a beautifully decadent capitalistic night spot together, dined on wonderfully rich, decadent, capitalistic food, watched a totally decadent stage show, and did what they could to cement American–Soviet relations in a small hotel room that was merely decadent.

But all of that was long ago and far away. He couldn't go there now.

His cage was planet sized, but he know how the lion felt.

He wondered if the Oriani kept zoos.

He thought about the spaceport a lot. It was the open door through which he could not pass.

He talked to Ee about it, bringing it up in the middle of a lesson one day by asking for the Orian term for such a place. She told him.

"How far to the spaceport, Ee?"

"That's a concrete concept. Why are you using an abstract form?"

"Because it seems abstract to me just now."

"I think you are not ready for such subtleties. The mixture of forms is quite humorous."

"Feel free to do whatever it is Oriani do when amused. Tell me about the spaceport."

"There's nothing to tell. It's not a very nice place. Perhaps another subject . . ."

"Are there any human people there?"

"There are some."

"I want to go there."

"No."

"Yes, I do. Tell me how to go to the port."

"You have no need to go to the port, Bill Anderson. It's a dirty, noisy, ugly place."

"But if there are Terrans there, I want to go. Don't you understand, I'm—" Anderson hesitated, realizing that he had no Orian word for lonely. "I'm in need of the company of my own kind."

She looked at him as if, abstract or concrete, this were a concept utterly beyond her ken. "People die in Space Central," she said after a moment.

"People die everywhere."

"Not so much. Not so violently. Not by killing one another."

"Why would anyone want to kill me? That doesn't make much sense."

"Why? How could one know? Why do apparently

sane beings attack one another? Because one has too much money, or not enough. Because another has fear or envy. For reasons I cannot begin to imagine."

"I still want to go, Ee."

"That is foolish, Bill Anderson. If you are restless, you should go to Talan. He may have some useful activity for you."

She was right. That's what he should have done. But he said, "Why would Talan bother? It's nothing to him."

"It is his duty."

"What duty? He doesn't owe me anything. It's the other way around, if anything."

"He does. It is required that he make the life given you worthy of acceptance."

"That's a weird idea."

"It is our way."

"Well, it's not my way. Anyway, I can't. I haven't any idea where in the city his mother lives. How will I find him?"

"Try the Com/Com Net, Bill Anderson," Ee said dryly, and then she left for the day.

Anderson couldn't have said exactly why he resisted the idea of appealing to Talan. Partly it might have been plain inertia. Partly it was his nutty pride, which made it very hard for him to ask a favor. The heritage of living half his life poor was an abiding suspicion of anything that vaguely resembled charity.

He had fiddled around a bit with the Com/Com link. But it couldn't understand his accent. It just kept asking him to repeat himself. So he brooded and stared out into the distance and prowled around Owr-Lakh.

When he thought he had the transit system figured out, he decided to try to get to the port on his own. Ugly or not, he thought at least there might be some action there and someone to talk to.

He discovered that he didn't have the transit system figured out. He kept winding up in front of some kind of machine shop whose proprietor stared at him with frank curiosity but made no move to assist.

Ee was worried for a while, but there was one advantage to being the only human in a pussy-cat city. He couldn't get very lost for very long, even if he wanted to.

After that, Ee told him if he was that determined, she'd show him how to get to the port, but if he went there, he'd be completely on his own. She'd have no part of it.

Orion Space Central

The transit system dropped him in front of the IP Trade Center. After the relative coolness underground, the heat on the surface, reflected back and forth among tall buildings, hit him like a breath from hell.

For a while Anderson was content to stand there, squinting in the sunlight, staring like any openmouthed tourist while streams of busy people flowed around him.

The IP Trade Center building itself rose forty stories into the air. He crooked his neck to look up at it. Its glass front reflected the narrow, crowded street where busy people of all shapes and sizes hurried to and fro, competing for space with endless lines of ground freight vehicles grumbling along. Anderson had never seen so many kinds of beings together in one place. Rough-hided Rigans towered above the crowd. The bright robes of their small, fine-boned cousins, the Roothians, made spots of vibrant color. The midnight-black Agralese, who never went anywhere except in clumps of six or eight at a time, were great obstacles that traffic flowed around as if they were rocks in a stream. A hundred races rubbed shoulders—or the equivalent.

Then he saw mirrored in a window a human being, a man in a wide-brimmed hat to keep the sun off. Turning from the reflection to the reality, Anderson bumped into a massive individual of a race he didn't recognize, who growled furiously at him before continuing on his way.

Bouncing off the big one, he almost stepped on a small Sgat. A youngster, he supposed. It squeaked and, rearing up until only half a dozen legs were still on the ground, stretched its vermiform body to peer at him.

"Hi," Anderson said.

The Sgat collapsed and skittered off, weaving its way with considerable skill among the legs of taller creatures.

The human had vanished into the crowd. Anderson let the flow of pedestrians carry him along the bottom of the concrete canyon whose walls were tall buildings of a hundred dissonant styles of architecture crammed cheek by jowl against one another, and whose rims drew jagged lines enclosing a narrow strip of Orion's green sky.

At the corner at the end of the street the flow of traffic faltered around a Terran and an Lleveci who were shouting at each other at the tops of their respective voices, which in the case of the Lleveci was quite a large number of decibels. Neither one, it seemed, could understand the other. The Terran's uniform identified him as the captain of a merchantman. The Lleveci's red-and-blue face, which made her look like an irate turkey, identified her as a very angry Lleveci.

They had collected a considerable audience that seemed to be cheering them on. The ring of onlookers had expanded until it brought vehicle traffic on one side of the street almost to a halt, and the curses of angry drivers were added to the din.

Anderson got the gist of the argument when he was still half a block away. When he came up to them, he shouldered his way through the spectators to the sounds of irritation and told the captain that the Lleveci was complaining that the shipment was supposed to be boron hydride, not elemental boron.

"You understand him?" the Terran asked.

Anderson didn't bother to point out that the Lleveci was more or less female. He just nodded. He felt conspicuous inside the circle.

"Mind your own business, Earthling," someone called in heavily accented English.

"Tell him the manifest says boron, the hold is full of bloody boron, and boron is what he's going to get," the captain said.

In somewhat more polite terms, Anderson relayed

this to the Lleveci. She thought it over for a moment
while her color gradually faded, then said she would look
in her files and would the captain check back with her in
an hour or so at her office in the IP Trade Center.

The captain agreed to do that. The group of spectators
was breaking up, their fun spoiled. Anderson started
away, but the captain held him by the arm. "Stick
around, boy," he said. "I need you. Do you know what
it's costing me to keep my ship in orbit while we yell at
each other?"

Anderson didn't feel overly anxious to continue the
association, especially after being called "boy."

But before he could protest, a terrible screaming snarl
had commenced that made any other sound impossible,
and when it got so bad that it couldn't possibly get any
worse, it was capped by a tremendous flat boom that left
Anderson with a pounding heart and the feeling that his
heels had been driven an inch into the pavement.

The captain was grinning at him. "New here?" he
asked.

Anderson nodded dumbly.

"Shuttle going up." The man pointed at a thin flame
climbing into the sky. "You'll get used to it."

"Yeah?"

"Yeah. Look, boy," the captain said. "I'll pay you for
your time. Just stick with me until we get this settled.
I'm Alphonse Pettigrew of the freighter *Alicia*. Come on,
I'll buy you a drink while we're waiting. It'll help me
forget about demurrage."

A drink sounded good, especially after he'd gone so
long without, and the easy company of another human
being was also welcome. Pettigrew seemed to know the
city well, and led the way to a door crammed between an
office tower and what might have been a warehouse.

The pub was long and narrow and dim and close, and
a bar ran the full length of it. Like the rest of the city, it
was a busy place, and conversations in a variety of languages made a background hum. Overhead a couple of
wide-bladed fans flopped around in a desultory fashion
and moved the thick air a little. Pettigrew ordered
Roothian beer for them, which, if it wasn't cold, had a

clean, slightly sour taste that was refreshing. They spent a pleasant hour talking about home and all the reasons it would be better to be there than where they were.

By the time they arrived in the Lleveci's office on the fourteenth floor of the IP Trade Center, the Lleveci had returned to her normal sandy color and welcomed them effusively. Her profound apologies were tendered; she had made a grievous error. Captain Pettigrew was entirely right. She would be glad to accept the boron if Captain Pettigrew could see his way clear to accept her regrets for the trouble her error had caused.

"What was that all about?" the captain asked as they were leaving.

"Reading between the lines," Anderson answered, "I'd say she found where she could turn a profit on the boron."

Back on the street, Pettigrew handed over a couple of credits. No fortune, but real money. Anderson started to take his leave, but Pettigrew held him once more.

"Just a minute, boy. How many of these crazy languages do you know?"

"A few," Anderson replied, trying not to bristle.

"How about Orian?"

"I'm learning."

"Come with me." Pettigrew started off, accustomed to having people follow where he led. Anderson followed, elbowing his way through the traffic and sweating with the effort to keep up, down a narrow winding passage to a small bistro wherein a number of ships' officers were gathered. This was a brighter, cleaner place than the bar they'd just left, but it had a much less homey atmosphere.

"Eric, this fellow might be able to help you out," Pettigrew said to a harassed first mate seated at a small table on which an official-looking Orian document lay surrounded by a number of empty beer glasses.

"I hope so, Al. The old man's fit to be tied, and I can't make anything out of this. Sit down, mister, and tell me what it's all about. What're you drinking?"

Anderson sat down and gave his newest language a

workout, surprising himself that he didn't have much difficulty with the paper.

"Basically, it's a request from the Port Authority for some details about your ship, registration number, master's name, crew list, passengers if any, engine type and capacity, gross and tare mass. I guess it's something they ask about any ship when it first comes into Orian space. You can put it on the Com/Com Net. They don't need the paper back."

Eric smiled. "Is that all?" He looked relieved. "You're a marvelous man. I think I'm in love. What do we owe you?"

So he earned another drink and another couple of credits. Anderson was beginning to see how he might be able to make a living. Not exactly steady employment, he knew, and it didn't look to pay all that well, but it would be a start. He returned to Owr-Lakh feeling more confident than he had in a long time.

He was back in the port in the morning.

Right from the start, he felt much more comfortable in Space Central than he ever had in Owr-Lakh. The port was more Earthlike, more like downtown Hong Kong. It had streets and tall buildings, and other things he hadn't even realized he'd been missing, such as streetlights and shops. It had thousands of shops, selling everything in God's bright universe, with the shopkeepers standing in the doorways under their awnings, exhorting the crowd. The port was noisy and bustling, and something was always happening.

He ate a hamburger and talked to a human female. His digestion was better for not knowing what the hamburger was made of, and his ego for not knowing the girl.

He let a clothier entice him into his shop, where he committed the rest of his tiny fortune to the purchase of a new shirt, and earned some of it back interpreting for the shopkeeper when a Roothian came in looking for something special in the way of the long robes that were its racial dress. The shopkeeper told him about the Portside Cafeteria on the next street where people of all races gathered and where he might find gainful employment. Anderson spent the rest of the day there, and returned to Owr-Lakh in the evening with money in his pocket.

Those first few days he commuted. He slept in the serene safety of his hay box in Owr-Lakh. There were two reasons for that.

First of all, Space Central was obviously a tough town, and he wasn't sure he wanted to spend the night there until he knew his way around a little better. The Oriani didn't police the port or have much of anything to do with it at all. It was the small piece of desert they had given over to the sticky business of dealing with other cultures, and they absolutely refused to have it spill over into any other aspect of Orian life. Aside from the port officials, Anderson rarely even saw an Orian there. Orion provided and maintained the facilities needed for cargo handling and navigation, and the Port Authority handled traffic and saw to the safety of ships in Orian space. Otherwise, the station was left strictly alone. One could do anything one was tough enough and ruthless enough to get away with.

And there were plenty of tough and ruthless people around. The deaths of kin or kings could be bought for a few credits. The barroom brawls were often deadly. From time to time passenger lists had to be revised to strike off the names of the deceased. The only mortuary was a busy place, catering to a variety of customs.

Anderson sat in on negotiations where military and industrial secrets changed hands over a coffee table. He translated when the Llevec commissioner of police offered the captain of the *Bon Homme* a consideration of silver to ignore the orders of the Port Authority and give him passage on an already overcrowded vessel. Any number of people, some scruffy-looking, desperate characters, others pretty well turned out, offered Anderson the contraband of twenty worlds in the streets, including the local narcotic rystl, which was reputed to offer the sweetest dreams of any in the galaxy, as well as being one of the most rapidly addictive. Trade in it was strictly forbidden. Nobody gave a damn.

In spite of all that, he felt quite secure. Foolishly so, when the time came to think back on it.

The way he had it figured, once he had committed his few hard-earned credits to the government bank, he had absolutely nothing of value, so it wasn't worth anybody's trouble to murder him in an alley. And he was still thin and pale from being sick so long, which would probably keep him from being shanghaied until he learned his way around. Just the same, there was no need to tempt fate. He slept in Owr-Lakh.

The second reason for commuting was lack of a place to stay in town. His inquiries were typically met with wry smiles or offers the Lord High Regent of Riga might have a hard time meeting. The port was terribly crowded. The boundaries had been set long ago and they never had been, and never would be, expanded. The demand for room far exceeded the supply, which led to some strange juxtapositions. The mortuary was housed in the back of a gourmet grocery store. The Seven Planets Brothel shared a building with the Church of the Immaculate Saint of Roo.

Eventually he did find a place, more by luck than good management. It wasn't much, a minute cubicle over a pawnshop on Sundance Street, but it was fully automated so he didn't have to worry about the housekeeping and it had a real bed. The rent was only an arm and a leg.

The landlord was a nervous, irritable Caparan who ran the chaotic shop downstairs. The shop was a terrible muddle, but somehow the Caparan could find anything in it. Once he and Anderson got to know each other, he sent Anderson clients quite regularly; he was less concerned about Anderson's welfare than worried about his new tenant's ability to pay the rent. Anderson was only a little put out by the way the Caparan seemed to think that because he found Anderson work from time to time, he had a claim on the Terran's services whenever he wanted them. Anytime Anderson was around, he might be called down to the pawnshop to help with a customer.

Furthermore, his landlord was firmly convinced Anderson could translate anything to anything. All protests to the contrary had no effect.

Such as the time he had someone—thing—from Beta Ellgarth in. It was the first one of those Anderson had ever seen.

"Talk to it," the Caparan demanded. "Tell it welcome. Ask it what it wants."

If he had met it on the street, Anderson would have thought it a meter-high pile of straw. He couldn't even figure out what part of the thing to talk to.

"I can't talk to it," he said. "I don't even know where to begin, because it doesn't seem to have anything you could call a head. I don't know its language, or even if it's got a language." The only sound the creature made was a soft rustling, like wind blowing through dry grass.

"Talk to it, talk to it," his landlord kept urging. He wouldn't believe for a moment that Anderson didn't have the foggiest idea how to do that. Eventually the thing rustled itself out of the shop again, getting along at quite a clip for a strawstack.

The Caparan waved a number of arms and his voice reached up into the high registers, threatening to climb beyond audibility. "You dumb Terran. What's the matter with you? Is it too much to ask for a little help now and then? What's the matter, you waiting to get paid? The cheap rent isn't enough for you, you couldn't give a man a little help? You think maybe I hang around here for the fun of it? I'm trying to do business. Maybe you could help a little."

He was quick to hostility, like most Caparans. But Anderson couldn't blame him for being upset about missing out on a deal. The cost of survival, never mind living, was ridiculously high. It couldn't be easy for a pawnshop to stay afloat, even with the usurious rates the Caparan charged.

Anderson found earning a living hard himself. Translators were much in demand, but he was pretty well dependent on the generosity of his clients. Some were generous. Some weren't. Some would squeeze every credit till it screamed, and he'd have to threaten to walk out in the middle of a negotiation to get anything at all.

Money came in easily, but went more easily. Everything in the port was expensive. It took time to get used to the relative value of things. Booze was cheap, relatively speaking. Water was dear.

He settled into his new place, then made one more trip out to Owr-Lakh to pick up the few clothes he had collected, and some other odds and ends he wanted with him.

When he got to the house, a message from Talan was waiting on the Com/Com link. The Orian had been trying to reach Anderson to repeat his invitation to spend a few days in his mother's house. Talan's mother, Anderson had learned, was some high mucky-muck in the diplomatic service, and Anderson honestly intended to take Talan up on the invitation, because he thought it couldn't hurt to have influential friends.

He put in the call and was mildly surprised that the link understood him. His accent was definitely improving.

However, all the Net would tell him was that Talan was in Owr-Neg, another city about a thousand kilometers away, and, according to the Com/Com Net, "not receiving." So much for the galaxy's most sophisticated communications network.

After that, he didn't go back to Owr-Lakh at all. He was feeling pretty cocky, supporting himself on an alien world and just as pleased with himself as a kid with his first job.

He found ways to supplement his income. A little bit of information could sometimes go a long way. He got a hundred credits from a Roothian constable for the name and flight plan of a vessel carrying a shipment of Roothian females the policeman had been following, a bit of information Anderson had acquired while assisting with negotiations between buyer and seller. He took another hundred and fifty from the slaver who was moving the shipment for details of the forthcoming raid. The constable, he heard later, was out looking for Anderson with blood in his eye. Anderson stayed out of sight until the

Roothian was off planet. He didn't feel like it was any skin off his nose one way or the other. He was just trying to make a buck.

Then there was the gambling. There was a lot of it in the port; anywhere he turned some game or another was in progress. Most of them were fixed, but what the average tourist never realized is that once a player figured out how a fixed game was fixed, he could use the altered odds to his advantage. All it took was time and some elementary mathematics.

Anderson had all the time he needed, and mathematics was something that had always come easily to him. He started out cautiously because many of the games were unfamiliar, but later came to believe that gambling was universal in form, varying only in detail, and he got bolder.

In time, he became good enough at it that he came to the attention of some professionals. But he didn't know that.

The Blue Moon

In his apartments above the Tradex Interplanetary warehouse, the largest building of its kind in Space Central, Steven Black placed his considerable bulk between the girl and the door just as Samantha was leaving.

"Stay home tonight," Black said. "I want you here when I get back with Anderson."

"Up yours, Steven. You don't own me," Samantha said.

"Yes, I do. Don't you forget it, lady. Don't for a minute forget it. You need me a lot more than I need you. After all, you aren't the only beautiful broad in town and all you've got going for you is your looks. If you should happen to lose them, I don't know how you'd get along."

She looked at him as if she had just seen a particularly repulsive bug, but all the rebellion went out of her. He only had to remind her from time to time where she stood. She knew from past experience that he didn't make idle threats.

Black turned her toward him, took her face between pudgy hands, and stared into the gray eyes. They almost came into focus.

"Do try to keep what little wits you've got about you, will you? No booze. No pills. This is important."

She pushed his hands away, and he let her. "What's so important about it?"

"We're about to recruit a new man. You'll like him. He's not too awfully bright, but he's pretty."

"Anderson?"

"Mm. You weren't listening when I explained this to

you, were you? Samantha, you know I'm not a patient man."

"I don't care, Steven. You know that? I just don't care. I hate your stupid business, you know, and I hate you. You're both boring and ugly. So leave me alone, okay?"

Steven quelled the urge to land her a solid slap to acquire her interest. This was her form of entertainment, to see how far she could push him before he retaliated. He let her have her fun. It wouldn't do him any good to let her know she got under his skin from time to time. He went back to his chair, lowered his bulk into it, lit a cigar, and waited for her natural curiosity to exert itself. It was early yet; he had time.

Samantha threw herself onto a couch and sulked at a wall. "What's so important about this Anderson?" she asked after a while.

"I thought you'd never ask."

"Well?"

"My dear girl, Bill Anderson may well be the very thing we need to rid ourselves once and for all of that ill-born agitator and all-purpose pain in the ass Talan."

"Talan? An Orian? What's he to you?"

"You really don't pay much attention, do you? He's the one who's been trying to talk the Planetary Council into sending Orian Security in here to sweep all us un-principled aliens out into space. He's got influence and he's got status, and he just might succeed in the long run. If we don't do something about him, you and I may wake up one morning and find we have nothing to stand on. Anderson is the thing we're going to do."

"One 'not too awfully bright' Terran is going to influence the Planetary Council? You're nuts, Steven."

"You think so? It just so happens that this not-too-bright Terran is culturally bound to our Orian friend in a way Talan's not going to find easy to disregard. These cultural obligations are a big deal with the Oriani, don't you know? Of course you don't, you dimwit. Never mind. This is a long-term project. You'll figure it out before it's done. And I repeat, it's important. So you be here, and be on your best behavior when Anderson arrives."

"It'd be a laugh on you if he decides not to come."

"He'll come. It's all arranged."

Black made the half-block journey on foot. If Anderson had known about it at the time, he might have been flattered. Black rarely went anywhere on foot. He rarely went anywhere. People came to him.

At the end of Schats Street—that's what the locals called it, though it was more like a narrow alley—in one of the very few single-story buildings still surviving in the port, there was a nightclub cum gambling hall that the uninitiated often passed by, thinking it was a private house. No sign over the door marked it, and the light falling from the street-side window had a warm, domestic glow. Only the constant flow of people coming and going might alert a thoughtful person to its actual function.

The club was called the Blue Moon, which was a strange name since Orion's moons were tiny, scarcely visible to the naked eye. Some Terran wag had suggested that the name referred to the odds against any patron of its games of chance coming out a winner. The furnishings were lush, the wine the best available locally, and, in truth, Dame Fortune was no more seriously compromised there than anywhere else in the port. It was a popular spot among those who knew about it, and it was always crowded.

By midevening when Black arrived, Anderson was showing a nice profit on the night, playing *Noulla,* a Llevec game he found to be similar to craps except the dodecahedral dice made the arithmetic more involved and the game easier to rig. The Lleveci playing against him was annoyed at being beaten at his own game, and the bettors who ringed the table were enjoying the contest. They egged the Lleveci into wilder and wilder risks, and cheered boisterously when they failed.

Anderson became aware of the corpulent Terran across the table who hadn't joined in the cheering but who was watching him with some interest. He realized that the man had been following his bets for the last few rounds. This was not in his best interests. He glared.

The fat man responded with a nod and part of a smile. He was a good hundred kilos on a frame not much over 175 centimeters; he had little pig eyes and stubby, plump hands encrusted with rings.

He was working his way around the crowded table and had reached Anderson's side just about the time Anderson noticed he was being noticed by an aggressive-looking Rigan who was beginning to drift his way from across the floor. Patrons parted respectfully to let him through.

A lot of gambling establishments employed Rigan muscle. Rigans were big enough and thick-skinned enough to be immune to almost any kind of abuse an irate customer might employ short of a blaster. Further-more, with the features of snub-nosed and grouchy alli-gators, they had a tendency to keep people on their best behavior just by being around.

Another thing that recommended them to club owners was that Rigans rarely, if ever, hesitated to wade into the fray and break up disputes, which they commonly did by breaking up the disputants. A lot of disputes seemed to occur around big winners, and the winners always came out of it poorer, if they came out at all.

The Lleveci was beginning to show quite a lot of color. Anderson realized that he was about to become the center of a dispute.

"Watch it, chum," the fat man said as he left the table. "We've pretty well worn out our welcome."

Anderson checked the progress of the Rigan and de-cided that the fat man was right. He left the table also, and pushed himself into a knot of merrymakers, sailors and sailor's friends who were on their way out of the club, using them to cover his exit. His ruse worked fine as long as he was inside—Rigans weren't known for quick thinking—but once they were out on the street the group dispersed, leaving Anderson to his own devices.

He walked fast, trying to get clear of the narrow alley quickly without drawing attention to himself by giving the appearance of undue haste. The lighting was poor, but he caught a glimpse of a big silhouette crossing the mouth of the alley.

Back in the days when he was still returning to Owr-Lakh occasionally, Ee had warned him, "Many people have walked out of gambling establishments with their pockets full and simply vanished." At the time he remembered it because he wondered what concept of pockets she could possibly have.

Now he remembered it because he was about to vanish as scheduled, unless he could work a miracle or suddenly develop the ability to scale solid ten-story walls at a single bound. The sweat running down his back wasn't all due to the heat radiating from concrete walls that had spent all day absorbing sunshine. There were a few people about, not enough to hide among, and he didn't think there was much chance that any of them would offer assistance if he got into trouble. He was scanning the buildings on either side of the alley for some sort of sanctuary when a hand tugged at his arm.

He jumped and brought his fists up, ready to make whatever feeble effort he could in his own defense.

"Cool it," a thick voice whispered. "Come on. This way."

Feeling that he didn't have a lot to lose, Anderson followed the shadow through a door in the side of a building that opened to the other's voice.

They were in a warehouse, he decided. He was led along dimly lit aisles between stacked crates, up a long, winding flight of stairs, and finally through another door, which gave onto a bright and luxuriously furnished apartment.

And it was cool. That was what Anderson noticed first. He had grown so accustomed to being hot and sticky that he shivered in the more Earthlike temperature. Somewhere an air conditioner muttered, and he wondered how many credits' worth of energy it burned up in a day. And he wondered how one got into a position to afford a thing like that.

The place was decorated in modern Terran style, and it took a few moments before the significance of that sank in, until Anderson started calculating what it would cost to transport one sofa-type thing, which must have weighed close to two hundred kilos, from Earth to Orion. The room was full of big, heavy furnishings, massive lamps, statuary, and bric-a-brac. They must have been made locally to specifications—that was the only explanation that made sense. But there was a lot of wood, and where would anyone get wood on Orion? The boreal forests were more carefully guarded than Aunt Agatha's virginity.

The only thing that actually looked as if it might have been made on Orion was a business desk, isolated in one corner and separated from the rest of the room by a partial screen of open metalwork. The walls were covered with draperies alternating with paintings, and the art ranged in age from one he was sure must have been a Picasso to some as modern as DeLeon.

"Sit down," his rescuer said. "And put your feet up. I think you could use a drink about now." He turned and called off stage, "Samantha!" then turned back to Anderson. "My name is Steven Black. And I know who you are. I've seen you around. For a fellow in such a dangerous line of work, you're pretty careless, eh?" He threw himself down onto an air-cushioned lounge, letting the cushions billow up around him until he was nearly hidden by them. "Sit," he insisted, "Sit. Relax. You're among friends."

Anderson recognized Black as the fat man who had been following his bets in the casino. Mumbling his thanks, he sat down on an immense chair and sank so deeply into it that he was momentarily concerned that he might never be able to extricate himself.

A woman came in carrying a pair of frosty glasses. She had a sulky, feline grace of motion. In a long, glowing gown of many layers of sheer fabric, she looked a great deal more undressed than some of the naked women Anderson had seen. She spoke not a word, but put the glasses on a low table in front of the men and continued out of the room with nothing more than a flip of her thick, black mane of hair.

Anderson's eyes followed her as if they had a will of their own, and it wasn't until the door closed firmly behind her that Steven Black could again claim any part of his attention.

"...at least get yourself a weapon," he was saying.

Anderson picked up one of the glasses. Ice tinkled pleasantly inside, more squandered energy. The man must be made of money.

"There aren't any on the market around here as far as I know."

"Well, now," Black said. "I imagine one could be found, if you were willing to pay."

Anderson took a sip of the drink, savoring it. Alcohol is brewed by many peoples and comes in a fascinating array of colors and flavors, and in the port Anderson had the opportunity to sample a good many of them. But he had never found anything to compare with the taste of a good grade of scotch. It was one of the things from home he really missed.

"I guess, Mr. Black, if you know as much about me as you seem to, you also know I'm not a wealthy man." Anderson put the glass down. "Anyway, I'm not sure I want one. I'm not handy with guns. Some mugger would only take it away from me. I'd rather avoid trouble as much as I can."

"And when you can't?"

"I guess I'll have to trust my luck. It's been holding up pretty well."

Black put his own glass down and busied himself with getting a cigar ready. "Tell me," he said. "How long do you intend to stay on Orion?"

"Indefinitely," Anderson answered. "Why?"

Black had the unlit cigar stuck between his teeth and talked around it. "Oh, I just thought a young fellow like you would be getting a bit homesick by now. And finding Orian society a bit dull. You in trouble at home?"

"Look," Anderson said, struggling out of the chair with some difficulty. "Maybe I owe you something for your help, but I don't see how this is any of your business."

Black waved Anderson back to his seat with a languid flap of his hand. "Take it easy. I'm asking because I thought if you were going to be here for a reasonable length of time, I would offer you a job. I could use a bright young fellow like you."

Unwilling to be caught again by the copious cushions, Anderson perched on the edge of his chair and resumed his scotch. "What makes you think I'm looking for a job? I'm doing all right on my own."

"Are you?" Black paused to light the cigar and puff up a nice little cloud of smoke around himself. When he resumed speaking he was twisting away at one of the many jeweled rings he wore on sausagelike fingers. Anderson didn't know how Black dared to go out on the street with them. A variety of people in the port would have gladly cut his throat for any one of them.

"You're making enough to keep yourself in booze, all right," Black said, "as long as you're not fussy about the kind. But how long would it take you to save enough for a trip home? Or pay off your debt to the Oriani? A hundred years maybe."

Anderson frowned. Black knew enough about him to be scary, more, obviously, than he would learn from casual interest. For whatever reason, Black had looked into Anderson's background quite thoroughly.

"The Oriani never asked me for anything," he said.

"No, but you still feel you owe them, don't you?"

Anderson said nothing.

"Don't be embarrassed. They do that to people. Okay. I'm ready to offer you three hundred a week to start and when you're worth more, you'll get more."

Three hundred a week was lot of money. It opened up all sorts of possibilities. But why would Black be handing it over to someone he just hauled in off the street?

"That's a very generous offer," he said. "Too generous, but—"

"You don't have to make up your mind right now," Black interrupted. "Go home and sleep on it. Let me know tomorrow or the next day. Good night."

Anderson was ushered out of a different door from the one he had entered through, and he found himself on the street about a block away from the Blue Moon, staring into the night with the heat pressing down on him again, realizing that he hadn't had a chance to ask Black what he was expected to do that would be worth such a handsome reward. ·

He wandered around for a while, mulling over the potential of Black's offer. With three hundred a week, a little judicious investment, and frugal living, he should be able to afford a round-trip ticket home in, what—ten years? A long time to wait, but better than never. And Black did hold out the possibility of more at a later date, which could shorten the time considerably.

Eventually his idle wanderings brought him, as such wanderings seemed to do quite often, to the Sississin Bar, where Issith the Roothian served a better quality of goods than did most of the gin mills around him. Sississin prices were a bit steep, and the decor was lousy—a few stiff plastic plants representing uncertain species— but it had a quiet, relaxing atmosphere hard to find in the vicinity, and besides, Anderson rather liked Issith, a man forever caught between his pious upbringing and the expediencies of running a pub.

The Sississin was quiet that evening. At the tables that occupied the back two-thirds of the place, a morose, solitary Terran, obviously in pursuit of insensibility, invited no company. A respectful distance away, a pair of Llevecis huddled over a board game with all the intensity of human chess players. At the L-shaped bar in front there were half a dozen patrons, none of whom Anderson recognized.

He had taken to drinking Rigan firewater. Although the stuff tasted pretty much like turpentine, it packed a quick and substantial wallop. In twenty minutes, near the end of a second round, he could be comfortably separated from sobriety.

In such a state of something beyond mild intoxication, he became aware of the woman who had hitched her hip onto the stool next to his.

"Hello," she said in a low, husky voice that matched her appearance perfectly. She had changed into a form-fitting black jumpsuit. Somehow she managed to look fresh and cool. She regarded him with pale, pale gray eyes, as if she and Anderson had known each other a long time.

"I'm Samantha," she said.

He recognized her. She wasn't one he was liable to forget right away. "I saw you at Black's," he said.

She smiled slightly.

"You're a long way from home," he said.

"Aren't we all?"

"Can I get you something?" he offered.

She pursed her full mouth a little. "I don't think I could handle what you're drinking," she said.

"Name it."

"A sparkling wine, something light?"

She accepted the glass from Issith, tasted it, and tried to disguise a face of disapproval. She caught Anderson watching.

"I'm sorry," she said, "but it's never quite right, is it, this local stuff?"

"Maybe you'd like something else?"

"No, thank you. This will do." Then she leaned toward him like a conspirator. She had a warm, female smell. Maybe he was missing a few things from home even more than he was missing scotch.

"I'll tell you a little secret. What I really miss from home is good French champagne."

"Then it is champagne you should have, my lady," Anderson replied.

"It's a lovely kind of madness you have, Mr. Anderson," she said.

So, he argued with himself, it's a crazy thing to do. Maybe a man deserves to be a little crazy once in a while. Strange things had already happened to him that night. Besides, there was the beautiful, sexy girl and the dark, warm night and the nearest goddamn moonlight worthy of the name was close to two hundred light-years away.

He called Issith. The Roothian stood across the bar from them, regarding them with his unblinking reptilian stare.

"Don't be silly, Bill," Samantha whispered. "You can't possibly afford it."

"Issith, my friend, do you, by any chance, have

tucked away in your back room an honest bottle of real, genuine champagne?"

If this was an unusual request, Issith gave no sign of it. "You got the money?" he asked.

Anderson pulled a couple of handfuls of his crap-table winnings from his pockets and dumped the money on the bar. Issith took off with most of it and returned shortly with a dusty green bottle.

"Issith, it's warm. It has to be cold."

"Ssure, Bill," Issith said, unmoved. "Sso, you make it cold."

"Come on," Anderson told Samantha. "Let's find a more suitable location." They moved from the bar to a corner table under an impossibly green pretend tree. "This is a palm tree," he said, indicating the plastic foliage. "And this—" his hand swept an arc indicating the room "—is Waikiki Beach. Out there," he said, pointing through the window, "is the ocean. All the tourists come here because it's such a beautiful spot."

"You really are crazy," she said, and she laughed, and maybe that laugh was worth the price of the champagne.

"How did you know my name?" he asked when they had each had a taste of warm champagne.

"I took the trouble to find out."

"That's very flattering."

Samantha grew suddenly serious, and the expression added years to her face. Anderson realized that she was five, or maybe six, years older than he was.

"Don't feel too flattered," she said quietly. "I'm really not a very nice person."

"Is that supposed to be intriguing?"

"Not particularly."

"Well, it is."

She shrugged and gave her attention to the champagne.

They didn't say much after that, except a desultory remark or two about the weather, which was hot, as always. Each of them was wrapped in private memories evoked by the wine, which, despite being warm and slightly flat and too long in storage, still smelled and tasted of all the good things of Earth.

Samantha reached over the table and put one slender finger under his chin as if to raise it. "Hey, now, it's not supposed to make you feel bad."

"I'm sorry. I was thinking of home."

"Me, too."

"Have you been away long?"

"Yes, a long time."

"You must be lonely, too."

She didn't answer but gave him a wistful little smile. "You're a nice man, Bill Anderson, do you know that?" She twirled the glass in her fingers and kept her eyes fixed on the glass. "You should go home. To Earth, home. Really, you should."

Great, he thought. I'm such a nice man, women can't wait to send me home. But before he could recover from his surprise to protest, she was gone.

Just like that. Gone.

Leaving a trace of perfume and a small sadness where she had been.

Issith, making his endless rounds of his establishment, stopped at Anderson's table and settled for a moment in the empty chair. Though he didn't often sample his own wares, he accepted a glass of wine.

"You know thiss Ssamantha?" he asked.

"No. We just met."

"You be careful, Bill. Iss plenty ssmart, plenty bad lady. Iss Ssteven Black'ss girl. Iss a danger, yess?"

Anderson told Issith not to worry. He said he wasn't interested. That was a bald-faced lie, and he guessed Issith knew it, but the Roothian didn't say anything. Anderson tried to get him off the subject of Samantha and onto the subject of Steven Black, but Issith said he was too busy and couldn't spare the time.

So Anderson went to his humble apartment, got on the Com/Com Net, and called the library in Owr-Lakh.

He discovered that the Oriani hadn't taken any great interest in Black, except for once. That once would probably have been enough for most mortal men, but Black had managed to squeeze out of it, in a manner of speaking.

Added together, the dry library files made an interest-

ing story. Some years ago, it seemed, Steven Black had
made a short foray into the real estate business, which
seemed on the face of it a very bad idea on Orion where
nobody actually owned any land. Nonetheless, Black
negotiated the sale of considerable tracts of Orian agri-
cultural land to a group of visiting Rigan aristocrats. The
Rigans were incensed to discover that the Oriani, indi-
vidually and collectively, considered Black's deal to be
in no way binding upon them. The judicial body of the
Interplanetary Community agreed. Furious, the Rigans
threatened to claim their property by force of arms if
necessary, and had to be restrained. All of which re-
sulted in an awkward interplanetary incident, and because of it, relations between Orion and Riga were still
what would be called in polite society "uneasy."

Black escaped the legal penalties for his actions by
staying in the port where Orian Security had no jurisdiction. But they'd nab him the instant he stepped beyond
the boundaries. Oriani don't forget, and there was no
statute of limitations to fall back on. The Orian system of
justice being what is was, they would turn Black over to
the injured Rigans, who also were not forgiving.

Anderson switched off the link, went to the window,
and looked down at the street. The restless populace of
the port paraded beneath.

The information the library had offered had not been
reassuring. Black was a crook, and trapped here as much
as Anderson was. If he couldn't help himself . . . Still, the
more he thought about it, the more convinced Anderson
became that Black would be his best chance to get off
Orion. Maybe his only chance.

All the soul-searching he did during the night didn't
produce any other answer.

Next morning, braced with enough ersatz coffee from
the NeverClosed Cafe next door to the pawnshop to produce a modicum of alertness after his sleepless night,
Anderson went to find Black. He wasn't all that sure he
remembered where the place was, but he needn't have
worried. Black's fortified apartments above the ware-

house of Tradex Interplanetary were better known than most of the pubs.

He gathered that Tradex belonged to Black.

When he got there, he found a lot of big, intimidating people standing around wearing guns and ugly faces, but none of them made any effort to stop him. Black was expecting him.

He was seated at the desk, chewing on a cigar.

"Okay," Anderson told him. "What do you want me to do?"

"I need a local manager," Black said. "I want a fellow I can understand, who understands me, someone I can trust. There are some things you just can't turn over to aliens, who think around corners. In due course, I expect you to do that job. For the time being, I want you to interpret when I need you, carry messages and maybe goods sometimes, run errands, and be a sort of general handyman. An apprentice, if you like the name. All you have to do is stick close to me and do what I tell you to."

"That's fine with me," Anderson said, "as long as you don't tell me to kill someone." It was only half a poor joke. There was an air about Black that made such a request seem credible. "But I can't see where it's worth—"

"You let me be the judge of that, Billy boy," Black said. "I want you paid enough that you won't be tempted to do anything foolish. The last man who had this job got a bit too ambitious."

"Where is he now?"

"In cometary orbit about Capara, I believe."

"That's not very reassuring."

"It wasn't meant to be." Black watched Anderson to see how he was going to respond.

"Okay," Anderson said with more confidence than he felt. "On one condition."

"Oh. What's that?"

"You stop calling me Billy boy. I hate it."

"All right, Sir William, I guess I can go along with that."

Black had a sarcastic streak in him, and Anderson couldn't see where he was ever going learn to like the man. But he had a feeling that there was more to be had from an association with Black than just a big fat salary. The mere mention of his name gave folk in the port city the shakes.

After Anderson left, Samantha came around the screen into Black's office space.

Black looked up from contemplating the ash on the end of his cigar. "Get out of here, Sam. I have work to do, and so do you. You're supposed to be out there, cementing our boy's loyalties."

"Leave him alone, Steven."

"Eh, what? Do I hear the voice of dissent?"

"Leave him alone. He's a basically nice person who's gotten a bit desperate. He hasn't got a clue what he's getting into."

"I'm sure he doesn't. Let's try to keep it that way, at least for the time being."

"Can't you get somebody else?"

"What for, when I've got him?"

Samantha left and Steven went back to studying his cigar. He was waiting for an important meeting, and waiting wasn't one of the things he did well. Also, he was a bit nervous about the meeting, and he had grown unaccustomed to being nervous about others, a feeling he now had difficulty acknowledging, even to himself. These meetings always left him with the notion that he had bitten off just a little more than he could comfortably chew.

He heard the Kazi, its feet scritching against the floor, before he saw it.

The Rigan at the door stepped respectfully aside to let the diminutive creature pass. The massive bodyguard deferring to the meter-high, twenty-kilo visitor afforded Steven a passing moment's amusement, but only a moment's. This was serious business. Power came in small packages.

The Kazi climbed Steven's desk and ensconced itself on the top, crouching on its many legs to bring itself eyeball to black, faceted eyeball with the human. This posture was meaningless to it, but it had learned that this person paid more attention when it was face to face with its audience. It had a hideously ugly, rigid, blank face. Steven suppressed a shudder.

Lacking an acoustic language, it communicated through an intricate device it carried on a strap about its almost nonexistent neck. The mechanism had a metallic, uninflected delivery that somehow always sounded menacing.

"We have not had a report in some time," the thin, tinny voice said. "We are not pleased with your progress."

The hair on the back of Steven's neck prickled. He couldn't honestly say he understood his reaction. Though by no stretch of the imagination an athlete, Steven felt confident he would be able to take the Kazi apart with his bare hands if need be. Yet its displeasure was worrisome. Perhaps it was the sense of forceful intelligence that surrounded it. Perhaps it was the sure knowledge that if any harm came to it, the hundred or so of its brood kin would see it avenged. The brood looked out for its members. They would plot and scheme and work until all safeguards were undone and their revenge was complete, however long that might take.

"But I am making progress," he protested. "I've found the weapon. It's only a matter of time."

"Good. Not too much time, if you will. Interference by the eaters of eggs is damaging our schedules."

The Kazi often referred to the Oriani as "eaters of eggs," though Steven didn't know why. As far as he knew, Kaz eggs formed no part of the Orian diet. "Don't worry. There isn't going to be any peace conference. I guarantee it."

The Kazi, for its part, was tempted to explain, to make an experiment. Though the study of humans was new, scarcely begun, already much was known. Humans were passionate creatures, and their passions were written on their faces, those soft malleable faces whose parts moved relative to one another with seeming ease. As with this one before it now—curiosity inscribed upon the features.

But the broodmaster had told it no, it was too soon.

Better to know the humans and how they would respond, lest the mistake of the Rayorians be repeated, lest
the empire again lose credibility among those who found
hate-mongering the greatest of crimes. Such races existed. How this could be so, the Kazi did not understand.
But it was so.

So it said only, "Indeed, on the basis of such a guarantee you received support in the first place. Failure would
not be pleasing."

Samantha

Anderson peeled Muffy off his arm and wished the baron would come and reclaim his woman. They suited one another better than either suited him. But the self-styled peer of God-knew-what realm, who was nominally Anderson's host, had vanished into the smoky, dimly lit melee of the apartment, and Anderson had not seen him for a considerable period of time—time made more considerable by the unwelcome attentions of Muffy.

"Quit that, Muffy," he said. "It's too hot."

Not that Muffy was that unappealing, but she was only slightly more than half his age, and she had a wheedling, whining voice and a one-track mind, a track he didn't particularly care to be on.

She clung to him like some sort of man-eating vine. She wanted to get laid, and Bill Anderson had been chosen to do the honors. Why, he didn't know. He might have been flattered if he thought her mind was in gear, but her eyes were wide and blank, and the hand she brought up to pat his cheek affectionately missed by half a meter.

All other things aside, there was the baron. Anderson didn't feel unduly fond of the pretentious kid he had only just met. Quite the contrary. He thought the whole performance overdone and childish, based primarily on some hophead's drugged dreams. However, if the boy wanted to go around pretending to be a long-lost Terran nobleman snatched from his cradle by evil alien forces and abandoned among the stars, and if those he called his people were willing to let him get away with it, why argue? And if Muffy didn't like being designated consort, let them settle it between themselves. Anderson wanted no part of intrigue within a sham peerage.

And even more than that, he didn't want to fight with Sam.

He disengaged himself one more time, left his post against the wall, and pushed his way among the other guests to find Samantha. What he did want, very much, was to get out of there.

"You're a positive tesseract, Bill Anderson," Muffy whined. It took him a moment to make the connection. Tesseract: a four-dimensional cube, which was a three-dimensional square, which was an archaic term for a rigid, inflexible person opposed to modern trends.

Maybe Muffy was right. This certainly wasn't his kind of party. He'd never been all that keen on chemical happiness. It made for wholly boring conversation. Bodies draped on furniture and sprawled on floors, each totally engrossed in whatever internal visions the drugs induced, lacked conviviality. These people were being alone together. They groped at one another but never made contact.

Anderson felt he was all too able to be alone all by himself, without pharmaceutical assistance.

He stepped carefully over outspread limbs and eased his way around groups of people clutching one another. Many of the limbs he tried to avoid were not human, and with the smoke and the heat and the occasional curses and groans of protest, the whole scene might have been a medieval painter's vision of hell.

He found Sam in a corner of the bedroom, sitting on the floor and propped against the wall. The baron was sitting beside her, small snores marking his slow breathing. Sam was half undressed and was staring into the corner as if she had forgotten what was supposed to happen next.

Anderson should have been furious, outraged, but he couldn't conjure up the strong emotions. Instead he felt a combination of pity and resignation, as he might have felt for a child who persisted in getting itself into trouble it couldn't get out of. He put his shoulder into Samantha's armpit and half carried, half dragged her to the bathroom to the sound of muffled protests from the scattered flesh they bumped over.

He got her into the shower and turned the cold water on, taking some small satisfaction in what it was doing to the baron's utility bill. Water wasn't the cheapest commodity in Space Central, and the Port City Utilities Company had a captive market, which it gouged unmercifully.

He let the shower run until Sam started to splutter and complain. Then he went to see about getting her home.

That Samantha filled more than a physical need for him was something he had come to accept reluctantly. She was his companion, as petulant and unsatisfying a companion as she might be, the one person with whom he felt free to discuss his work and his life and to complain about the strictures of being in Steven Black's employ. In many ways, when she had her wits about her and her friends were elsewhere, Sam was nice to be around. She was capable of great enthusiasms and unrestrained enjoyments.

She was also capable of fits of black brooding, and that was when she would look up her funny friends and their illicit pharmacy and their strange parties.

Anderson's work for Black left most of his evenings free. He had planned to spend them fruitfully, picking up the same kind of work he had been doing before. But once people started to associate him with Steven, they were afraid of him. As time went on, there was less and less demand for his services. Except from his landlord. The Caparan didn't seem to care. Samantha took up a great deal of this nominally free time.

They got along well together at first. She had become demanding only gradually. When she first announced her intention to move in with him, Anderson had been apprehensive.

"What's Steven going to say?" he had asked.

"Nothing. He won't care."

"You sure about that?"

"Bill, it's not like that between us. Believe me."

"Oh. What is it like? What are you to Steven?"

She had answered him with a cold, flat word that made him flinch. "Property," she had said.

So he had agreed, out of embarrassment, or pity, or some other emotion, and wondered if he would live long enough to regret it.

He laid Samantha out on the bed. He couldn't get her awake, so the only thing to do was let her sleep. But hanging around watching her do it wasn't too exciting, so he went downstairs to spend the rest of the evening with his landlord, the Caparan with the unpronounceable name.

They sat in the back of the pawnshop at a desk that held an ancient incandescent lamp casting a yellow glow over the small space kept free of the racks and stacks and boxes and piles of things that filled the rest of the shop, and they discussed the state of the worlds over a couple of liters of Roothian beer. Anderson liked the Caparan. He was an excitable guy, and a discussion of almost any subject would get him worked up, his voice rising up the registers until it finally got out of range, and three or four arms waving to make his point. It would have been easy enough on casual acquaintance to dismiss him as a spaced-out neurotic, but underneath all that nervous agitation there was a good, mean mind.

Anderson was sitting with his back to the door, the Caparan facing him so he could watch the shop. All at once the Caparan's eyes bugged out. He was quite bug-eyed to start with, so it made a truly startling display of surprise. Anderson craned his head around to see what had caused it.

Anderson's own eyes bugged out a little, because the last person he had ever expected to see in a pawnshop in Space Central was Talan.

Talan spoke a few high-pitched syllables in the landlord's native tongue, and the Caparan skittered away to the front of the shop and busied himself there. Talan took his place facing Anderson.

"You are well, Bill Anderson?" he asked.

"Fine."

Talan looked Anderson over very carefully, almost as if he were trying to memorize the Terran's appearance. Anderson found it unnerving to be the object of such intense scrutiny, and offered Talan a beer to cover the growing warmth in his cheeks. Talan declined with elaborate politeness, and Anderson got redder. He had forgotten that Oriani had no taste for alcohol, and it seemed at the time to be a bad breach of etiquette to have made the offer.

"I didn't expect to see you here," he said.

"Reasonable of you. I did not expect to find an occasion to be here."

Apparently satisfied with his inspection, Talan shifted his eyes to take in the surroundings. Anderson became acutely aware that "dingy" was the word that best described them.

"Why are you here?" Talan asked.

"Why not?"

"Reasons exist."

"Name one."

"You have embarked on a most perilous enterprise, Bill Anderson. And you have divided me against myself. In part, I hope you know what you are doing because I believe you have bought more trouble than you bargained for and more than you can handle. In part, I hope you do not know what you are doing, because the only moral justification I can imagine is ignorance."

Something about the way he said it made Anderson mad.

"What moral justifications? Whose morals? And who do I have to justify myself to? And what the hell are you talking about anyway?" His words came out sharper than he meant them to, but he wasn't all that unhappy about the tone.

Talan chewed it over for a moment. "Whose morals? A good point. Morality is somewhat subjective, is it not?" He didn't wait for an answer, but started off on another tack. "How much do you know about Steven Black?"

"Enough."

"This I doubt. If you will permit, I will relate a brief biography."

Anderson didn't say anything. He wasn't feeling too warm toward Talan just at that moment. At the same time, he was eager to learn anything he could about Steven.

"Steven Black," Talan began, "was born in the Centauri Colony in 2177, Terran system of dating. He did not care much for the rigors of frontier life and ran away from his home at the age of seventeen to join the Merchant fleet, lying about his age to obtain a position as a common sailor. He worked his way up through the ranks during a stormy period in the history of the Merchant Service, a time when the fleet was being periodically decimated by the activities of pirates. He was a competent sailor with obvious leadership qualities, and he was commissioned just prior to his twenty-ninth birthday.

"He proved to be a capable, if occasionally erratic, officer. His people were proud of his progress. He was engaged to the daughter of a distinguished Centaurian. He brought pleasant trinkets to his mother from distant places and, all in all, if I understand the vernacular correctly, was a fine example of a country boy made good.

"Then a senior officer of the *Outbound,* the ship in which Steven Black was serving, discovered a quantity of controlled drugs in Steven Black's possession. The ensuing investigation showed Steven Black to have been a regular courier for a large smuggling ring for some years. The investigation uncovered some hints that the ring had Kazi connections."

"What's this Kazi?"

"The Kaz are our common enemy, Bill Anderson.

"Steven Black did not await the outcome of the inquiry," Talan continued. "He fled, and arrived sometime later on Orion. He was subsequently involved in a fraudulent lands transfer incident and seriously damaged relations between Orion and Riga, which brought him to the attention of Security. He fled once more, to the sanctuary of Space Central. There he was absorbed into the underworld to emerge as the leader of a gang of mercenaries, what I believe you would call hired muscle. He was very effective in this role and has expanded it until he is virtual dictator of Space Central and all its activities, licit and illicit. Only the Port Authority remains free of his influence. All others must accept his domination and pay his levy.

"It is a most dangerous man you have allied yourself to, Bill Anderson."

"I'm not 'allied.' I just work for the guy. And why not? The work's not hard and the pay is good."

"I cannot protect you in this place."

"Nobody asked you to."

"It is not understood that I have this responsibility?"

"Not by me."

Talan's ears flattened almost as if he were in pain. It was a moment before Anderson became aware of the snarl of the shuttle rising. He watched the Orian and saw him flinch when the sonic boom hit, the sound only slightly modified by the walls of the building.

"Shuttle," Anderson explained.

"Yes."

"You get used to it."

"Indeed?" Talan went into his staring mode again, which was followed by another lateral change of subject.

"What do you know of the Midway Conference?"

"I know there is one. A bunch of do-gooders trying to talk Turgorn and Beta Ellgarth out of their war."

"There is a possibility the conference will succeed. The signs have been favorable."

Anderson shrugged.

"I do not comprehend your lack of concern."

"Those two worlds have been potting away at each other for roughly a thousand years. If they quit, good for them. If not, I don't see how it's going to make a whole lot of difference to the rest of us."

Over the edge of the desk, Anderson could see the end of Talan's tail twitching. Obviously he wasn't happy with that attitude. But Anderson couldn't, in all honesty, work up a lot of excitement over a bush war going on eighteen light-years away.

"Steven Black has expressed an interest in the conference." It was about one-half flat statement, one-half question; Anderson couldn't tell if Talan were asking or telling.

"Yes," he said because it was an answer that would work in either case.

"He has not been noted previously for his accomplishments in public affairs."

"Steven is interested in a lot of things. You'd be surprised."

"Indeed I would. I can see no legitimate reason why Steven Black should involve himself in affairs at Midway."

"I don't suppose Steven wants to interfere. I guess he'd just like to know what's going on. I guess there are times when you diplomats get in the way of his business."

"What business has Steven Black on Midway?"

"I don't know."

"I see." Talan sounded more than a little skeptical.

"I really don't. Steven doesn't take me into his confidence any more than he has to. You only get to know what you have to know to do your job. Steven's like that. He plays his cards close to his chest."

"Cards?"

"It's just an expression. It means he doesn't trust anybody very much."

"I see," Talan said with more conviction this time. "And it does not bother you to work under such circumstances, for one whose avowed purpose is subjugation and exploitation and whose methods include bribery, terrorism, and murder?"

"Yeah, just like any other government."

Talan hesitated. "I have some difficulty seeing Steven Black fulfilling the role of government even by its widest definitions."

"Yeah? Well, what other government have we got around here? What government doesn't threaten its citizens with dire consequences if they don't obey the rules? And what community can survive without rules? The Oriani don't want to get their hands dirty dealing with Space Central, then they bitch about the fellow who's willing to do the job."

"You have given the matter considerable thought."

"I guess I have."

"Such an elaborate rationalization suggests to me you are not entirely comfortable with what you are doing."

"Are we getting back to morality again?"

"Perhaps we are."

"Well, quit it. I don't need a mother. I got your point. You don't like me working for Steven. I don't see how it's any of your business."

"I am bound, Bill Anderson. It is my business."

"I don't think so. So drop it."

"As you wish," Talan answered.

In time, Anderson learned that Oriani said that a lot. It usually meant that they thought the wishes in question were particularly stupid.

Talan left. Anderson leaned back in his chair and fought down all the old doubts Talan had raised anew.

He had to suppose the Orian meant well. Talan was a good man in a stuffy sort of way. But it wasn't as if Anderson had been doing anything particularly evil. Far from it. Mostly what it was was dull.

Given Black's reputation in the port, Anderson had originally thought working for Steven Black was going to be an interesting, if not traumatic, experience.

But he had been doing strictly clerical work, collecting information. He talked to people, having a small advantage in that department, at least until word got around that he was working for Black. Steven had warned him to work fast, before an epidemic of amnesia overwhelmed the populace with utter forgetfulness. The rest of the time he spent with the computer, collating what data he'd collected, and searching records.

Exciting stuff, worthy of Talan's attention.

Anderson felt that he'd been through an awful lot just to get back to where he'd started. Steven Black was a little meaner and a little crankier than Alistair Stone ever was even in his fondest dreams, but the work wasn't that much different. If he hadn't been king of Orion Space Central, Steven would have made a superb civil servant. He loved fiddling detail, the finer the better.

Some of the data Anderson was collecting did in fact

concern the Midway Conference, but he had been entirely honest with Talan in telling him that Black had not explained why the conference interested him. Anderson had tried to promote an explanation by telling Black that it would be easier to get the kind of data he wanted if he knew what it was for. Black told Anderson only to get on with the work and stop bothering him.

It was hard to see Steven Black with political ambitions, but what else could he want with Midway? At that time, nobody had ever heard of it except a few astronomers and perhaps some students of interplanetary affairs.

Curious, Anderson had queried the library on Owr-Lakh. What he learned didn't go very far toward explaining Steven's interest.

Midway was in the Ellgarth Cluster, the lone, frozen, dark companion of an ancient collapsed white dwarf. It would have been a planet singularly unknown in galactic history if it weren't for the fact that the populated worlds of two other stars in the cluster, Beta Ellgarth and Turgorn, as they are known on Earth, began, with their first ventures into space, a violent and enduring struggle for control over the region. The dwarf's companion had the misfortune to lie almost exactly halfway between the two warring systems, and was considered by both belligerents to be an essential base.

There was just a chance that, after centuries, the war might soon come to an end. The Orian name for the contended planet translated roughly as Midway, and Midway in all its battered glory was about to become host to a delegation of diplomats from six neutral worlds who were trying to negotiate an end to the conflict.

Very admirable of them, Anderson thought at the time. But what could it possibly mean to Steven? Samantha said she didn't know. Anderson wasn't sure he believed her. There were times when he felt certain that she was less than completely honest with him.

When he went upstairs, Samantha was awake and waiting for him in front of the Tri-D, sitting cross-legged on the floor within the folds of his bathrobe. She was not a very big girl, and the robe fit her like a blanket. She had tidied herself up a bit, combed her hair until it lay like a fall of black water over her neck and shoulders, and got some food sent in, which Anderson thought was a blessing since Sam couldn't cook worth spit. She had a plate in her lap and she was picking at the contents.

"I thought you were never coming," she said. "I've eaten practically everything, and that's not fair. You know I have to watch my figure."

She was much more alert than Anderson had expected she would be, and somewhat more cheerful. He had hopes that she might be getting over this round of depression.

He told her Talan had been in the shop, and that if there was any figure-watching to be done, he wanted to do it; he reached for the belt of the bathrobe to begin doing just that, but she covered his hand with hers and held it.

"What did the Orian want?" she asked.

"Nothing much," he said, hoping that Talan wasn't going to interfere in yet another part of his life.

"You know who he is, don't you?"

"Yes, of course I do. I've known Talan a long—well, I guess it isn't actually all that long, but it seems like a long time."

"He took a chance coming here."

"How so?"

"Ambassador Meela's son Talan has been speaking to the Planetary Council—that's the local version of the United Nations, if you can imagine the UN with some teeth in it—trying to drum up support for his plan to clean up Space Central. That's us. He wants to start over with a proper Orian facility under proper Orian control. Steven wouldn't be the only one to cheer if Talan suddenly disappeared."

"Don't say that, Sam. I owe Talan a lot. Everything. My life."

She tugged his hand, urging him down to her level. "Then I'm grateful to him, no matter what."

He squatted beside her and pushed the robe away from her shoulders. She smiled up at him, but worry still clouded her eyes. He planted a kiss on each of them to erase it, then buried his face in the still-damp abundance of her hair.

Locking her hands behind his neck, she pulled hard, until he overbalanced and fell on top of her.

"Hey, who's ravishing who here?" he asked.

"You have to guess," she said. She had her hands up under his shirt and she ran her fingers along the scar on his chest. "Did they really cut your heart out?"

He shook his head. "It's still there. Can't you feel it?"

"Hey, it's really going!" She sounded delighted, as if it came as a surprise.

Later, when they got their breath back and had showered and dressed and ambled over to the Sississin in the last cool hour before the dawn, Sam got back on the subject of Talan's visit.

"How did he find you?" she wanted to know.

Anderson tried to be reassuring. "The Communications/Computer Network, of course. If the Com/Com Net can't find you, you probably don't exist."

"But why? Why would he go to all that trouble and take the risk?"

Anderson told her he and Talan were friends—and wasn't that reason enough?

"No way, Bill," she said. "No Orian ever called a human being friend. He must have had some other reason."

If she was so sure of that, she knew more about Orian psychology than Anderson did.

"What damned difference does it make what he calls me?" he asked crossly.

"You know what I mean."

"I don't."

"Well, I'll tell you. Oriani don't make friends. Not even with one another. You should know that by now."

"What do you know about it, anyway?"

"I know enough to know that. Everybody knows it."

"Have you even talked to a real live Orian?"

"That's not the point."

"What is the point?"

"The point is why he came." She flapped a hand at him to forestall the repetition of his argument. "I know, you're friends. You keep saying how you're Talan's friend. But what does Talan say? Did it ever occur to you to ask him?"

"Who knows?" he said. "And who cares? He came, and it was nice to see him. He's gone, and it's no big deal. What's bugging you, Sam?"

"Why after months, Bill? If you're such great friends, why did he wait so long?"

Anderson said he didn't know and promised to ask Talan the next time he saw him, but that only made her mad. He could not figure out what the devil she wanted. When she started on "What did he say and what did you say?" he gave up and left her. After all, he had to go to work.

Steven had a few things to say about muzzy-headed help and how people who came to work late could at least try to be alert when they got there.

Later in the day, Anderson couldn't find Samantha in her usual haunts. She didn't come home in the evening. And when she did finally straggle in in the small hours, she was in another universe entirely. She wouldn't talk to him at all. And he couldn't find a flower on the whole benighted planet with which to make a peace offering.

If Talan had come a few days later, Anderson could have answered his questions about Steven's interest in Midway, although it was quite probable he would not have cared to do so. If the Orian knew what Black was up to, he'd have the whole planet in an uproar.

Two days after Talan's visit, Black called Anderson into his office and told him he was being sent along as supercargo with a shipment of arms to Turgorn. He was to join the already laden *Star King* just outside of Orian space. That was how he learned of yet another of Black's activities.

An angry diplomat might say that Steven was selling arms without discrimination to both factions, but that would be the wrong way to put it. Steven was very discriminating, taking great care to see that neither side received a significant advantage in weaponry.

"Balance of power, Bill," he said, chewing a cigar butt to death. "That's what it's all about, my boy. Balance of power. We only stay in business as long as nobody wins."

So of course he was unhappy about the Midway Conference. Peace negotiations were not in Steven Black's best interest.

Galactic history might have been quite different if the leaders of Beta Ellgarth and Turgorn could have observed Steven huddled over his calculations like a malevolent spider. Perhaps they would have seen their war in a different light, not so much a glorious and noble enterprise as a straight business proposition from which other people were making tremendous profits. Steven was very, very careful, taking into account not only his own sales but the manufacturing capabilities of the planets and the sales of every other arms merchant as well. Sometimes the calculations would totally occupy the computer for days.

The conference had Black worried, although at the rate the negotiations to merely have a conference were proceeding, Anderson felt confident that no one then living would be around to see the time the conference actually commenced, and that if the conference itself moved apace, perhaps his grandchildren would know the outcome.

Steven agreed that this was possible, but he was willing to leave nothing to chance. So one of Anderson's duties on the trip was to sound out the Turgorn attitude.

"How am I supposed to do that?" Anderson wanted to know.

"Try asking them," Steven said.

"Now, wait a minute. I've picked up a few elements of the Turgorn language around the port, but not enough to embark on any subtle dialogue."

Steven shrugged, a tremor in a mountain of lard. "You'll manage."

In some ways, Steven was a lot like Anderson's landlord. He was even less inclined than the Caparan to be-

lieve there were limits to Anderson's linguistic expertise
and he tended to put some force behind his rejection.

Not that Steven would be pleased with the compari-
son. There was a streak of xenophobia in his makeup,
which expressed itself as a general contempt of all things
not human.

Anderson protested, and Steven told him to go and
pack.

He didn't protest too hard. Even given the impossible
task, he thought the trip would be interesting. He was
ready for a change of scenery.

It was too damned bad Steven didn't have any traffic
with Earth.

Sam came out of her sulk long enough to wish Anderson a good trip and immediately got into another one
because he was going to be away over a month. "What
am I supposed to do with myself while you're running
around making like a traveling salesman?" she wanted to
know.

He told her to do whatever she had done before he
turned up.

"Oh," she said, and made it sound like a threat.

Later she came to help him pack, all fuzzy around the
edges. It made packing interesting. She put stuff into his
bags and he took it out, until she got exasperated and
went to sleep it off in the bathtub. Limited to twenty-five
kilos and twenty cubic decimeters, he couldn't afford to
take along pillows or a large number of shoes. When he
was ready to leave she was still out, snoring gently, like a
cat purring. With her clothing bundled up and her
makeup smeared, in the unkind light of the bathroom
panels he could see that she was going to make an ex-
traordinarily common-looking matron when those round
cheeks sagged and the hint of a second chin expressed
itself more fully. He picked her up and put her on the
bed. He wanted to say good-bye, but he couldn't rouse
her and he had to go. Time and starships wait for no
man.

Turgorn

Even from *Star King*'s parking orbit, Anderson could see the effects of the ages-old conflict in which Turgorn was engaged.

He had been told, to ease his apprehension, that the planetary defenses were good. They must have been good or Turgorn would have long since been battered into oblivion. But they weren't perfect. The planet's surface was pocked with massive craters in which the luxuriant growth normal to Turgorn no longer flourished, giving it the look of a world ravaged by some hideous disease.

Turgorn proved to be an overwhelmingly depressing place. The journey from the spaceport to the capital was made in an aging groundcar over broken, decaying roads. In fragments of a dozen tongues, his driver told Anderson that Turgorn had been a beautiful world once.

It was no longer beautiful. A soft blue sky still arched overhead, and low, rounded mountains still gave onto gently sloping plains with wide, meandering rivers. The very oldest people, the driver said, knew stories of a better time, of abundant food, elegant gardens, high-rising architecture, and the leisure to bask in the rays of a warm and temperate sun. The old people spoke almost as if they had known such things, though no one of them was old enough to remember a time without war. But, the driver said, now the young didn't even know the stories. And the gardens and the towers were no longer built.

Wandering around the capital in search of answers for

Steven, Anderson came across one of the old, prewar buildings. It was a graceful construction of stone, with airy spires and arches that were a delight to the eye, vaguely reminiscent of Earth's Angkor Wat. Miraculously, it had survived almost untouched, but it was falling to centuries of neglect. Neither time nor effort could be spared on Turgorn for the preservation of old artifacts. The forlorn derelicts sheltering under its arches paid no mind to the priceless murals they rubbed against, and neither knew nor cared that the fumes of a nearby munitions factory were eroding the stone.

The capital was a city of old people. There were few juveniles about, and almost no one in the prime of life, except for one small group of soldiers prowling the empty, decaying city in search of the remnants of the way of life they fought to protect but that was long since dead.

All activity revolved around the war. People were starving in the streets to buy ammunition. Whole generations, many of them, had grown up, raised their children, cuddled their grandchildren, and died knowing nothing but war. Little groups of broken folk huddled in the shelter of broken buildings, guarding their few possessions with shoulders hunched toward the sky as if they expected destruction to rain down on them at any moment. And why not? Destruction from the sky had been their history and their expectation for centuries.

The Turgorn had a tradition of militarism. They still celebrated ancient tribal battles, and the city was studded with monuments to famous soldiers. Their everyday dress included an obsolete personal weapon. But by the time Anderson was making his inquiries haltingly through the language barrier, even the hidebound, tradition-riddled elders who formed the civilian government had realized that there was no military solution to their conflict with Beta Ellgarth.

Long before *Star King* was unloaded and refueled for the return journey, Anderson knew he had to go back and tell Steven that the Turgorn were favorably disposed toward the Midway Conference, asking only that their interests be protected. He didn't feel easy about that chore..It wasn't unknown for Steven to vent his rage regarding some message upon the messenger.

He saw a Kazi for the first time on Turgorn, and he could understand why people didn't like them. It looked too much like a bug to attract much sympathy. Besides which it smelled, a musty odor of dark, damp places.

He couldn't find out what it was doing there. No one was willing to say much about it. It probably wondered equally about him. Tourists weren't all that common on a world that was chronically short of food and had zero luxuries. There were happier places to go. The Kazi and Anderson were undoubtedly the only outworlders on the planet.

The trip back to Orion was uneventful. After Turgorn, Orion's hot, dry, Spartan comforts were abundantly welcome. But Anderson didn't have time to do much more than draw one deep breath free of the worry of an imminent outbreak of shooting before he was whisked off to Steven's apartment.

Steven's reception was milder than Anderson had expected. It could be he had anticipated the answer. He paced heavily around the room, puffing up a smoke screen on a big cigar, fiddling with his rings, and listening without interruption while Anderson told him what he knew.

"What about Beta Ellgarth?" he asked when Anderson had said his piece.

"I wasn't there. I don't know."

Steven puffed and walked and rearranged objects in the room. "Any opposition? Anything organized we could use? A political action group, the army, something like that?"

"I don't think so. The Turgorn don't look to me to be all that political. Mostly, their government seems to hold power by default, and nobody pays it all that much attention. I talked mostly to an old, disgruntled general who was quite sure he would soon be out of a job. There might be a few more like him, but they're isolated individuals. I can't be sure."

"You have to be sure," Steven said, his annoyance flaring up.

"Right. We're talking about a whole planet here. I'd bet there were as many differences of opinion among the Turgorn as there are in any other race. But one thing I am sure of. Their race is dying. There aren't any young. If this war doesn't end soon, there won't be enough Turgorn left to sustain a civilization. And your market will go to hell anyway, Steven."

Steven threw himself down on his cushions to sulk. Anderson went to his own place to unpack and get his first shower in twenty-nine days.

Sam was waiting for him there, not quite sober, but close.

"Good trip?" she asked when he came in.

"Okay," he said without much expression. Something of the tragedy of Turgorn had returned while he had been talking to Steven.

Anderson had his own notions about where the line fell between what was justifiable and what was not, and it had nothing to do with legality or morality or anything else he could put a name to. For a while, in the ruins of Turgorn, he had had the uncomfortable feeling that he had wandered onto the wrong side of the line. It had been easy enough to push the feeling aside. But it came back.

"Steven satisfied?" Samantha asked.

"As much as ever. You know Steven." He punched up the makings of a drink on the autobar and looked questioningly at Samantha. She shook her head.

"You're not very communicative," she said. "What's the matter with you?"

"The war has to end, Sam. They just can't continue."

"So it ends. There'll be another. Don't feel so bad. It's not the end of the galaxy."

Anderson looked at Samantha and couldn't think of any way to answer her.

"You can't do much about it anyway," she said.

"I know that."

"Well, then, forget it. You've been gone a month. I've been waiting."

"I bet you have."

"Boy, are you sour. Travel doesn't agree with you, you know that?"

Anderson turned to the window and looked out. The street below seemed a thousand miles away and the bustling people ludicrous in their haste. "Samantha," he said. "Would you go away, just for a little while? I need to be alone for a while."

"So much for greeting the weary traveler," she said. "I bet you didn't even bring the fur."

"Fur?"

"You promised me a tagat fur from Turgorn."

"Christ, Samantha, there's all the fur you want right here."

"Don't act so dense. You know what I mean. Real fur. Off of an animal."

"An animal? There's no ammunition on Turgorn to spare on animals. All the guns are pointed toward Beta Ellgarth. Besides which, what do you want with fur in this climate?"

"Bill...honestly..." Exasperation stole her words. "I think I will go. Maybe I won't come back."

"Sam, wait a minute," he called after her. But the door had already closed behind her.

Anderson showered and changed and brooded around the apartment for a while thinking how incredibly well he had handled Samantha. Then he walked over to his office in the Tradex building and tried to catch up on a month's work. But his heart wasn't in it.

There were a lot of odd bits of data lying around that didn't seem to relate to anything. Steven had been spreading his nets wide, talking to sailors, traders, anyone who by virtue of training or travel might give him a clue, trying to snare the vital piece of information he needed to show him how to shaft the Midway Conference.

More out of habit than anything, Anderson took all that stuff in one big, ugly lump and shoved it into the computer without even bothering to weight it according to source, and told the machine to look for common factors. The project had to be at an end anyway. At least, he hoped he'd convinced Steven to give it up, but whether Steven was convinced or not, conference or no conference, Anderson was certain Turgorn was finished.

While the machine ground away, he went down to the Sississin, thinking Issith's melancholy old face would suit his mood perfectly just then.

He heard Sam's laugh as soon as he was in the door, and saw her accepting a drink from a strange man's glass at the same table under the plastic tree where she and Anderson had shared champagne in the dim past. She seemed to be finding the procedure hilarious.

The man was just a stringy kid with a lot of mouth and a lot of money, a merchant sailor with six months' pay in his pockets and randy as a stud horse. Sam had an arm draped around his shoulder, leaning on him, giggling, her eyes focused on the center of the galaxy. The kid had a stupid, pleased look on his face, as if someone had given him a prize.

Nobody would have guessed to look at him that he spent all his spare time studying martial arts and lifting weights.

Anderson felt quite confident about going over to the table, telling the kid to get lost, and suggesting to Sam that it would be better all around if he took her home.

The smooth movement by which the kid disengaged himself from Sam and got to his feet should have been a warning.

"Leave me alone, Bill," Sam said.

"Leave her alone, Bill," the boy echoed.

"Don't give me a hard time, sonny," Anderson said, and he thought he sounded quite reasonable. "You can see she's stoned half out of her mind."

"Up yours, pop," the kid answered.

Anderson nudged the boy out of the way and reached for Sam's hand. The boy nudged him back and sent him sprawling across the table in a cascade of breaking glass.

From there on, things went from bad to worse. Somewhere along the way, Anderson realized that he was in no condition for barroom brawling. He'd spent far too much time sitting in front of a desk. All those nice hard muscles Hairy had so carefully cultivated while he was in the Medical Center had long gone. Hairy would have been appalled.

It took Issith a while to round up enough big people willing to break up the fight. By the time they got him home, Anderson had a broken bone in his hand that hurt all the way up to his earlobe, a couple of cracked ribs, and a badly damaged ego.

Steven sent round some Llevici who he said was a doctor, along with some choice words regarding the dangers of stupidity coupled with incompetence. As far as Anderson could tell, the Lleveci was nothing but a ham-handed quack. Anderson wanted to go into Owr-Lakh and get proper medical attention, but Steven would have none of it.

Everything hurt, but some things more than others. The Lleveci told him that the pain in his back was from a bruised kidney. Anderson figured it hurt quite a bit more than any bruise had any right to. But he thought enough booze might ease it a little. The Lleveci said that a lot of alcohol was probably a very bad idea just at the moment.

Then everybody left him to suffer in peace. He spent some time trying to figure out why he had suddenly taken exception to the tough young sailor. If he'd been smart he would have walked away, and let the kid pay Samantha's bar bills for a while, and buy the champagne that was dearer than blood around the port. Maybe he would have paid some of her gambling debts, too. Sam gambled so badly, trusting to hunches and charms instead of mathematics.

Sam came.

Anderson told her to get out, and he was in no mood to be polite about it.

"I'm sorry, Bill," she said. "I really am. I never thought—"

"That's for damned sure."

"Look, you don't have to be so hostile. I didn't ask you to fight with that dumb kid."

"What did you think I was going to do?"

She didn't answer. Instead she went to the bathroom and came back with a glass of water and a pair of largish white pills.

"What's that for?"

"It'll help with the pain."

"Yeah?"

"Try it. It really will."

He was ready to try almost anything. The alleged doctor had offered him no relief. Still, knowing the repertoire of pills to be had among Sam's funny friends, he hesitated.

"For goodness sake, Bill, are two little pills going to kill you?" Sam asked impatiently.

"I don't know."

Sam took his hand and slapped the pills into his palm. "Swallow the blasted things, will you?" she asked, and stalked out, not waiting to see if he was going to do it.

They did help. In a few minutes the pain had receded to some vague place in the background, and he was groggy and half asleep and things did seem easier. Not good, but easier.

And then it was morning again, and Sam was there.

And then it was evening, and Sam was there.

It developed into a comfortable, dependable routine. Sam came twice a day, dedicated to her role as nurse, bringing food he had no interest in and the pills.

He had a sense that she was unhappy, but he didn't care. Half the time she looked as stoned as he felt. It didn't seem important.

The days passed.

It wasn't so bad a way to live, really. Once in a while he would get a sense of the days of his life dripping away through a hole in time. Once in a while it bothered him that this was happening. But mostly he didn't care. He lived inside a bubble all his own, into which the rude world did not intrude. He felt safe in there. There were no demands on him in there, no necessities, no decisions to make. All he had to do was dream.

He dreamed of being loved, of being respected, of being important. They were quiet dreams, in which nothing much happened beyond the feeling he had, a warm, comfortable feeling of being right and good, and trusting in the universe.

Occasionally in the beginning he heard alarm bells

going off in distant recesses of the inner chambers of his mind. But it was easy to quiet them. He had only to relax and close his eyes and pretend they weren't there, and they weren't. And he would smile because it was so easy.

It was so easy. That was the whole lure and the charm of it. It was so easy.

The gods have never been that kind. He should have known it wasn't going to last. And it didn't.

Sam came late. When she arrived, Anderson was stripped down to his shorts and sprawled on the couch sweating his way through a particularly hot day, not asleep but not awake either. She stood for some time leaning her back against the door, watching him. And when it sunk into his head that the routine was disturbed, that something was amiss, he roused somewhat and sat up on the edge of the couch, rubbing a hand over bleary eyes and a grating stubble of beard.

Sam didn't move. She looked as if she was anticipating the need for a fast getaway.

"I can't get the pills anymore," she said.

That was the one thing she could say that was guaranteed to get his attention. In spite of the close warmth of the apartment, he felt a chill descending.

"You have to," he said. A thin worm of fear struggled up through the fog in his brain.

"I can't."

"Why not?"

"I just can't, okay?"

He was on his feet now, worry giving him energy. "It's not okay, damn it. I need them."

"I'm sorry."

"Sorry? What the hell good is sorry going to do me?" he asked, his voice rising.

"Steven has some."

"Well, get them from Steven."

"I can't. He won't give them to me. You have to go."

"What for?" he shouted.

She cringed from his anger. "I don't know. Maybe he doesn't trust me."

She was lying and she knew he knew it, and she was nervous about what he was going to do. It was in his mind to take her by the shoulders and shake the living daylights out of her until she started making some sense, so he turned away and went to the window and looked down at the crowds on Sundance Street below with the sun pouring down on them as if Omnicron Orionis was determined to fry every living thing on the whole benighted world.

He didn't want to go to Steven. He really didn't. Steven was a gloater. He'd slop down into a chair and grin around his cigar and rub his hands together making the rings click on one another. He'd smile and make Anderson squirm for what he wanted. It was the kind of situation Steven enjoyed. Anderson firmly believed that Steven deliberately maneuvered people into situations where they'd have to come to him for favors. Steven liked to see folk humble and asking his largesse.

"I'm sorry," Samantha said in a small voice.

"Yeah, sure," he growled without turning around.

"What are you going to do?"

"Don't worry about it. I'll get by."

"Bill . . ."

"Get out of here, Sam, and leave me alone."

Sam went. Anderson threw himself back down on the couch and stared up at the ceiling for a while.

Telling Sam he'd get by was one thing. Figuring out how he was going to do that was quite another. He got a crawly feeling on his skin just thinking about it. He got up and paced the small space in his apartment and considered his alternatives. All he got for his effort was sweaty. In a very short time he was feeling restless and irritable and generally miserable. Shades of old aches and pains showed up. His head started to hurt.

To distract himself, he went down to his office in the Tradex building. He hadn't been there for a long time, and, strangely enough, Steven hadn't been nagging at him to get back to work. That might have alerted him if he had been thinking straighter.

The poor old computer was still waiting, the ready

light still on. He activated it to let it get its last job off its mind.

"Computer readout," the machine said in its flat monotone. "Re data set one hundred thirty six stroke ten stroke zero seven analysis of common factors presented in order of statistical probability factors of less than point one probability omitted . . ."

It burbled on about its method and then began the list. The first items were pretty obvious, then a phrase caught Anderson's attention.

"Computer stop. Define 'Merchant Security Force.'" Anderson had never heard of such a thing.

"Insufficient data," the machine said.

"Approximate."

"Insufficient data."

"Drop dead, you stupid machine."

"Query is this intended as instruction if so please refer to programming manual for correct phrasing and re—"

"Computer stop. Output hard copy of analysis. Instruction ends."

He started to think about how to get more information on the Merchant Security Force. But he couldn't concentrate. So he went to the Sississin instead, to see if he was still welcome and if Issith had forgiven him for all the broken furniture.

Booze didn't help all that much. The unusually boisterous, noisy patrons of the Sississin annoyed him. He didn't want to talk to anyone and they wouldn't leave him alone. They kept telling him he looked terrible and trying to get him involved in their inane conversations. Instead of being miserable, he got drunk and miserable, and it wasn't a big improvement. By the time he was miserably drunk, Issith sent him home.

So he was miserable around the apartment for a while. And the booze wore off and his hands started to shake at about the same time.

He figured he had two choices. He could go to Steven, or he could go out on the street. As the lesser of two evils, he chose the street.

Anderson told himself this was going to be a short-term thing. He had no intention of spending the rest of his life in this condition, but at the same time, there was no need to suffer any more than he had to and it would be smart to taper off gradually.

He knew the city well enough that he had no trouble finding the young Gnathan. The kid typically hung out among the street sellers' stalls in Peddler's Lane or in the shadows of Red Alley.

The Gnathan took one look at Anderson and doubled his prices.

The drug he bought might have been pure strychnine. Anderson didn't think he would live.

By the time he could raise his head again, the Gnathan was dead. Steven had had him shot. Then he'd sent a couple of his muscle men after Anderson and they dragged him into Steven's office as if he were a truant schoolboy. Anderson was furious, but he was still sick, and there wasn't a whole lot he could have done even if he had been healthy except to sputter and fume, which he did.

Sitting at his desk, Steven grinned like the king of the world and rubbed his fat little hands together and made the rings click.

"Well, aren't you in a fine state, Billy boy? Just look at you. What have you got yourself into?"

"Nothing you need to worry about," Anderson said, trying to sound a whole lot tougher than he was feeling.

"Wrong again, Billy boy, wrong again. I'm concerned about my people. I like to see them happy and healthy. It makes for loyal troops."

"Get off it, Steven. What do you want? If you wanted to see me, all you had to do was call. You didn't need to send the goon squad." The two behind Anderson stiffened a little.

Steven's smile slipped. When Steven smiled, he looked like a happy pig. When he didn't, he looked like a cross pig. He leaned back in his chair and actually put his cigar down.

"I wonder," Steven said. "Anyway, you're here. And I have to tell you you haven't been a great deal of use to me lately. So I figure you aren't happy. And it's up to me to make you happy." He reached into a desk drawer and put a couple of white pills on the desk top.

Anderson reached for them. Steven's pudgy hand caught his wrist.

"Sure you want them, Billy boy? You know what they are, don't you?"

Of course, Anderson knew. He'd been around the port for quite a while by then and he was reasonably observant.

"They say rystl addiction is a hard thing to live with. I hope you're up to it," Steven said.

"I'm not an addict."

"Of course not. No one ever is, are they?"

Anderson just glared at him.

"There'll always be some here for you, Billy boy, but not during working hours. You understand that? You scramble your brains on your own time." Steven's expression had degenerated into a tobacco-stained snarl. "You're hooked, Billy boy, so you'd better obey the rules."

"I told you not to call me that." Anderson bristled.

Steven's hyena laugh followed him out of the room.

Midway

The heat of high summer brought daytime activity in the port city virtually to a standstill. Even the roar and the boom of the shuttles was not heard during the day because dockworkers and stevedores refused to work from early morning until late afternoon. The streets were deserted except for an occasional Sgat; those people seemed to be utterly undisturbed by temperatures that kept even Oriani quiescent and on the watch for cool shady spots.

In the evenings activity resumed, with an additional frantic character added as if folks needed to make up for the lost hours melted away by the burning sun. The evenings were hot, but tolerable. The favorite topic of conversation was moving to the polar regions for the summer, but it was just talk. There was no way the Oriani were going to allow it, and besides, no one felt he could abandon his business completely for a season that was typically five months long.

On one such an evening, Kurt Morgen stuck his head into Anderson's office. Kurt was one of Steven's oldest and most favored followers, and looked after Steven's private army of thugs, thieves, pistoleros, and assorted unpleasant charcters.

"Steven wants to see you upstairs."

Steven was lounging in cool, air-conditioned comfort on a couch and admiring a new painting on the opposite wall when Anderson arrived. Anderson rather hoped he had a lot to say, because Steven's apartment was the nicest place in the port to be at that time of year.

But Steven was abrupt. "Pack a bag," he said. "You're going to Midway."

"No, thanks," Anderson said. "It sounds like a pretty dull place."

Steven growled from the depths of his cushions. "Billy boy, I'm not asking you please. I'm telling you. You're going to Midway. The *Star King* leaves tomorrow evening. Find Gangril. Tell him he's going with you."

Gangril Vorb was the Rigan Anderson had first seen coming at him across the floor of a certain gambling club and later as a threatening presence at the head of a well-remembered dark alley. Anderson had been a long time in Steven's employ before he found out that the Blue Moon belonged to Steven Black and that what he had until then thought of as an accident had been no accident at all. Steven had arranged it for reasons of his own.

"What do I need that stone brain for?" Anderson asked. There was no love lost between Gangril and Anderson. The Rigan's presence would only make an unpleasant trip that much more unpleasant.

"Two reasons: one, the job might need some muscle, and two, Gangril is going to look after your pills just to make sure everything goes smoothly."

"What's the matter, don't you think you can trust me?"

Steven snorted.

"You have before. What's changed?" A cold finger of apprehension poked at Anderson's gut.

Steven had pulled himself out of his cushions and stood facing Anderson. He smiled that maddening wax imitation of a smile he reserved for the times he could enjoy a living demonstration of his power.

"Trust you? I guess I can. But not far. And not in some cases. You keep having these little twinges of conscience. I haven't forgotten who bailed the Caparan out when he should have taken his medicine and been a good example to the rest of the citizens."

"He's a friend. Is there anything wrong with that?"

Steven pursed his lips. He walked over to his desk and arranged himself behind it. "It's neither here nor there. I want the Midway project to go perfectly. There shall be no hitches, no second thoughts. I'm buying all the insurance I can. Gangril's going. So are you. So go get ready. Your ship leaves in thirty hours."

"At least tell me what we're supposed to do there."

Steven looked Anderson square in the eye. His gaze held all the warmth of icebergs, the compassion of a wolverine. "Sure. You're going to assassinate the junior member of the Orian delegation to the Midway Conference. You are going to do it in such a way that the Turgorn, or their enemies, I don't care which, will be blamed. That ought to fix the conference. By the time everybody gets past squabbling over ruffled sensibilities, they'll have all forgotten what they were doing there in the first place."

Up to that point, Anderson still naively believed that even in Steven there must be somewhere in his dark, ugly mind some essential humanity, some tiny spark of fellow feeling that could be touched. He was wrong. Steven used people with as little consideration as one might give a garden spade.

Steven crushed his cigar out in an elegant onyx bowl that by rights should have served some more noble purpose, and reached for another. "If everything goes well, I might even give you a couple of days off to drug yourself witless."

"No way, Steven. I won't do it. I told you when we first met I wasn't going to kill anybody, and I meant it and I still mean it."

"Oh?" Steven slammed closed the drawer he had been opening and listened, head cocked, for the confirmatory click of the lock engaging. "Let me know when you change your mind."

"Why me? You've got a hundred professionals you could use. Any one of them could do a better job, quicker and with less chance of it being traced back to you. I'm no killer. You can't make me do it."

"Yes, I can," Steven said with grim satisfaction. "Unfortunately for you, I have to. You see, with the security on Midway being tighter than a Caparan's fist, you've got one advantage over anyone else I could name."

"Like what?"

"This guy knows you. So you've got the best possible chance to get close to him."

Anderson had spent most of his time on Orion in the port. The number of real, live Oriani he knew he could count on one hand. "What's his name?"

"Talan. Talan the Younger, son of Ambassador Meela, petitioner to the Planetary Council, the fellow who's made it his life's work to try to put us out of business. We're going to get two stones with one bird here, my boy."

It was some minutes before Anderson could get out any words at all. "For God's sake, Steven, I owe Talan my life. You know it."

"I know it. Sometimes I wonder if he did you a favor." Steven held up his hands to forestall further argument. "And I don't want to hear about how the war is coming to an end anyway because all the cute little Turgorn kiddies have turned into dust. There's bigger fish in this pond than you know about. Don't give me any argument. You just go away and think it over and come back when you've decided you're going to do what you're told."

Anderson left, staggered.

He couldn't think. The day slid by him. It was in his mind that he should warn Talan. But Talan was on Midway, out of reach. He stumbled around the city most of the night, picking up a drink here, another there, trying to calm his shaking hands with alcohol. It didn't work, of course. It never had, and it never would.

No one on the street would sell him the time of day.

By the time the sun was nearly overhead his resolve had turned to water in the wavering heat. He sat down in front of the Com/Com link and asked the Network to locate Gangril Vorb and relay a message. Then he threw his pride and his scruples into the garbage and went to see Steven.

Steven was sitting at his desk, looking as if he hadn't moved all night. He opened the drawer and took out the two precious pills. "When you've had these," he said, "you're going to feel pretty independent for a while. Just remember, your next dose is on board the *Star King*, outbound for Midway."

Gangril Vorb ducked his head as he came through the doorway into Steven's office. Actually, the movement wasn't necessary: He had a good centimeter's clearance when he remained upright. But it had become a matter of habit engendered by scraping the top of his head on the lintels of a good many doorways. The dimensions of human constructions were just a bit tight for a Rigan, and Orian architecture was even tighter.

"Yeah, Boss?" he asked.

Steven looked up from the desk and took in the massive form. He rather liked Gangril. The Rigan was a nice, simple fellow who would do what he was told without argument and without moral agonizing. He picked the small plastic box containing Anderson's pills off the desk top and handed it over. Gangril accepted it and dropped it into the carryall he wore slung over one shoulder.

"Don't give Anderson too much of a hard time, Gangril," Steven said. "But keep him on track. Sooner or later he's going to try to get out of it, so watch yourself."

"Sure, Boss." The Rigan started to leave.

"Gangril."

He stopped and turned back to Steven. "Yeah, Boss."

"Gangril, I want the Orian dead. I don't care what it takes. And I don't care whether Anderson comes back or not."

A Rigan grinning displays enough teeth to scare a shark. "Okay, Boss. You got it."

Anderson kept hoping, right to the last minute, that something would happen to get him out of the bind he was in, that the *Star King* would develop incurable engine trouble or Omnicron Orionis would go nova, or something, anything, to take the decision out of his hands.

Nothing happened. *Star King* left orbit on schedule. Once on board a starship, there is no place to hide.

The outbound journey was uneventful. Anderson knew from his previous trip that *Star King* was a more

spaceworthy vessel than she looked. She ground her
way steadily along, even though Anderson was still half-
hoping she'd blow an engine and spread herself across
the sky.

Life on board was easy. The crew knew that he and
Gangril Vorb were Steven's men and so treated them
with respect if not friendliness. Gangril delivered the
pills on schedule with a merciful minimum of comment
and only a small delighted grin on his massive jaws.

Anderson hardly appreciated the quiet passage. He
had sunk into a kind of numb despair and spent most of
the time curled up in his bunk doing nothing and trying
hard to think nothing.

Midway was the last word in desolation.

The library in Owr-Lakh had informed Anderson that
Midway had been alive once, that life had flourished
there once, grass and flowers and beasts of its own making, that a mighty civilization had risen and fallen on that
world before Earth condensed out of her primordial
mists. He wondered how they knew.

It was ten million years dead when he got there. The
last exhalation of atmosphere clung frozen to the poles.
Between the scanty polar caps lay bare, battered, black
rock in unrelieved worn angles and eroded planes. A few
long, dry, ancient riverbeds, like puckered old scars,
marred the surface. There was no sign of any construction, or that anything had ever lived there.

Neither Beta Ellgarth nor Turgorn supported societies
advanced enough to attempt planetary engineering on
any great scale. A modest dome covered the few hectares made habitable, and an extension out to a shuttle
dock made the whole effort look like a large, misshapen
igloo. Under the dome, the remnants of the shifting oc-
cupations of Midway huddled in an environment made
barely warm enough to be endurable in an atmosphere
just thick enough to breathe. The rest of the world was
dark, frigid, and empty.

"Even good old Steven doesn't think of everything.
He should have made hotel reservations for us," Anderson said when he and Gangril had explored the possibili-

ties among the few crude, arbitrarily placed, and ill-kept buildings and found them wanting. Gangril looked at him as if he'd taken leave of his senses.

"That's a joke." It obviously did not touch Gangril's sense of humor, if such a thing existed.

They spent quite a while trying to find accommodations among the meager facilities, obtaining, after much negotiation and bribes enough to ransom a minor king, the use of a minute room with a decor of lumpy, unfinished concrete. The room contained a bed, a lavatory, one rough metal chair, and nothing else.

Later—one might almost say in the evening if the concept had any meaning on Midway—they set out to gather what information they could about the conference. This proved to be much easier than finding a room. For the price of a round of drinks for a group of tradesmen relaxing in a pub after a day of last-minute finishing touches on the assembly room, they learned a lot. Most of it was disquieting.

One huge, old storage shed, left behind after one or another occupation by who knew which of the combatants, had been refurbished for the occasion. In this way, housing facilities, catering services, security, and conference rooms were all conveniently under one roof. The talks were scheduled to begin in two days' time as the Turgorn measured it. Most of the delegations, including the Oriani, had already arrived and were settled within the building. There was no reason for any of them to leave it until the conference was over, and no reason to suppose any would. Anderson couldn't quite see the local Chamber of Commerce organizing sightseeing tours. The rest of the community under the dome, the few bleak, gray buildings squatting miserably in a cold light scarcely brighter than that of Earth's moon, offered nothing that might draw them out.

The tradesmen were happily anticipating their release from barren Midway and made pleasant company, but soon Gangril dragged Anderson out into the shabby street and they went to have a look at the conference building itself, following a cracked and rambling walkway that was lighted only by an occasional incandescent lamp stuck on top of a high pole.

It still looked like a warehouse, although it sported what was probably the only coat of paint on Midway. Around it, an electronic force field had been erected that crackled blue from time to time as some errant dust mote entered it. Between the field and the building, a tight guard composed of soldiers from a motley assortment of races prowled ceaselessly. The chances of breaching the barrier looked pretty small.

Anderson felt relieved. If the task was flatly impossible, Steven couldn't blame them for not accomplishing it.

Back in their room, he said as much to Gangril.

"No," the Rigan answered. "Boss says you don't do the job, he don't want you home. He says give you two, mebbe three days. Boss says—"

"The hell with what the boss says sitting on his fat ass safe and comfortable on Orion. He doesn't know what he's talking about."

Anderson's moment of verbal rebellion brought a frown from Gangril that closed his silly little rhinoceros eyes to slits. The Rigan churned it over in his mind, his tongue protruding slightly from between his long teeth with the effort. Finally he shrugged and let it pass.

"All right, then," Anderson shouted at him in despair. "You tell me how. Nobody but nobody can get in or out of there. It can't be done."

"Messengers go."

"They've got passes. They're all Turgorns. I look less like a Turgorn than I look like—like, well, you."

Turgorn was in nominal possession of Midway at the time, so they were filling the role of hosts, supplying most of the support and services required by the conference. They took their responsibility very seriously.

Gangril shrugged again. It wasn't his problem. He was only the baby-sitter. Restless, he went out.

Anderson sat on the edge of the hard bed and looked up at the blotchy ceiling, wondering if there could be any possible reason why Steven might want them to attempt the assassination and fail. He thought about turning him-

self over to the Turgorn Security Service while Gangril
was out of the way, but he didn't think they'd be able to
keep him supplied with pills. He had a hunch they
wouldn't even try.

It was just his nerves, of course, but he would have
sworn he could feel the underground fission reactor that
powered the community vibrating beneath his feet. Fission piles had always struck Anderson as a tad unreli-
able, and with a whole planet to choose from, he thought
the builders might have put it a handsome distance away
from the people. Having it right underfoot made him feel
as if he should tread softly.

Midway turned so slowly on its axis that the march of
its small, dim sun across the sky was scarcely noticeable. But there was so little difference between its black
night and dark day that people there tended more or less
to follow the periods of their home worlds. Gangril was
gone a long time while Anderson dozed fitfully on the
thin comfort of the bed, but there were still many hours
left to planet night when the Rigan came clumping back
into the room.

He had an armload of Turgorn-type paraphernalia,
which he dumped on the floor in front of Anderson. His
collection was pretty complete: the long voluminous,
cowled garment that usually served as the single item of
wearing apparel; the narrow, fringed sash, symbol of
manhood, commonly wrapped around the midparts; a
few items of jewelry; a small green mnemeplast card;
and, of course, the inevitable weapon carried by all mature Turgorn males. It was a thing that properly belonged
in some distant part of their history and served mainly a
ceremonial purpose. The device propelled a small, feathered dart by means of a chemical explosive; a primitive
weapon, but deadly if well aimed at close range. It was
always armed and ready.

"Where's the owner?" Anderson asked. He had uncovered a diplomatic pouch while pushing through Gangril's booty with one foot. There was a letter inside,
intended, as near as he could make out, for some
member of the Llevec delegation. "He's a diplomatic
courier, you know."

The Rigan's perpetual smile deepened somewhat, but
he said nothing. He didn't have to. A few shreds of pale
meat still hung wedged between his fangs.

Anderson tried to hold his stomach down and failed.
Bent over double in the lavatory, he wondered if, should
the boss not want him back, he would also become an
appetizer for that utterly unprejudiced carnivore. He had
met Rigans who were nearly civilized, but Gangril Vorb
was not one of them.

It was easy enough to see what Gangril had in mind.
With the often effective simplicity of his kind, he was
proposing a direct frontal assault. It was a strategy that
his people used often and with sometimes devastating
results, a good enough method even in the complexities
of modern warfare given the willingness to sacrifice a
substantial portion of the assault force.

The hooded garment would adequately disguise as
Turgorn any bipedal being of approximately the right
mass, especially as the settlement was poorly lighted at
best, and the Midway nights were very dark.

No doubt the little green card was meant to take the
unfortunate courier through the force field, so they had
the means to pass the first line of defense.

And after that, what? It seemed it would be mostly a
matter of luck. Anderson had a fair amount of faith in
luck—more, perhaps, than it was reasonable to have—
but he felt certain he would never get off Midway alive.

When his stomach stopped knotting itself and settled
down to a good, solid ache and he could safely leave the
lavatory, he went and sat, exhausted, on the edge of the
bed, watching Gangril's long-drawn breaths and hating
him with all his might. Tired by his hunt and well fed,
Gangril had curled up into a ball and fallen asleep on the
floor. Slow, stentorian snores made the small room rat-
tle.

At one time in his youth, Anderson had been much
impressed with the philosophy of the Universal Brotherhood of Intelligence. It seemed so plausible and so sane
to assume that intelligence, whatever its form, had more
in common with other intelligence than it had differ-

ences, that it was basic to intelligence to respect intelligence. He hadn't known any Rigans then.

He couldn't deny the intelligence of any race that had achieved space flight, yet at times it seemed that Rigans had come into the Interstellar Community by accident. He had believed in UBI once. Still, he couldn't escape the feeling that to embrace the sons of Riga was to take a viper to the breast.

He thought about it some more and decided he'd never have a better chance. He had no idea what he was going to do. There was no place to run on Midway. He didn't think that far ahead. He just picked up the one and only metal chair and brought it down with all the force he could muster onto the back of Gangril's ugly head.

At first he thought he had blown it. The snores stopped abruptly. Gangril's eyes opened and he started to uncoil himself. Reflexes, probably. Then his muscles relaxed and he stared vacantly at the wall.

All Anderson wanted was to get the rystl and get off Midway. He didn't know whether Gangril was dead or alive, and he couldn't honestly say he cared. Even while the Rigan lay there inert, Anderson was afraid of him. Nervously he straddled the still form, searching frantically in the carryall.

Just as his hand closed around the small box, something from just outside his field of vision thumped against the side of his head, throwing him against the wall. When his vision cleared, all he could see were Gangril's yellow fangs gleaming about two centimeters from his face. Gangril's breath was foul, and he was making a low sort of growling sound.

He picked Anderson up by the collar and shook him like a rag doll. Anderson was sure his time had come. Then Gangril dropped him.

Anderson was still clutching the box. Gangril snatched it away with one big paw and delivered a stinging slap to Anderson's mouth with the other. The slapping went on for quite a while, until Anderson passed out.

A little while later he was roused to persistent nudges

from Gangril's foot. Gentle enough from Gangril, but bruising nonetheless.

Anderson's head ached. His face was stiff and swollen. All the teeth on one side felt loose. If there had been anything left in his stomach, he would have been sick. But he wasn't sufficiently damaged to be unable to carry out the task ahead. Violence was something Rigans did understand. They used it with surprising delicacy.

Gangril didn't say much except to issue terse instructions. In his slow way, he got Anderson ready.

Arrayed in the late courier's effects, Anderson was pushed out into the stygian Midway night to go and murder the only person who had been halfway decent to him since he'd left Earth. He had considered the Turgorn weapon and dismissed it as a hopeless case. The dart wouldn't penetrate Gangril's thick hide unless it hit him square in the eye, a ridiculously small target for a relatively inaccurate weapon. All the vengeance Anderson could manage was to hope Gangril had a headache at least as bad as his own.

Inconsequential details fixed themselves in Anderson's mind: the way the dome blurred the stars overhead, and the feel of the coarse, dry soil underfoot, like walking on salt; the roughness of Gangril Vorb's hide as the two of them squatted side by side in a small depression in the ground near the perimeter of the force field surrounding the conference building, in the deep, deep shadows between the yard lights. His brain was in overdrive, but it was just spinning its wheels.

In the lighted area on the other side of the field, the sentries paraded with discouraging efficiency.

Anderson and the Rigan were waiting for the change of guard. Gangril had decided that their best chance to penetrate the building's defenses would occur when, for a few moments, the assorted soldiers would be occupied with one another. It was Anderson's opinion that their best chance was none too good.

Huddled, shivering, against the dirt, he whispered to Gangril, "It's impossible. We haven't got one chance in a million. Let's get out of here while we're still alive."

"With me, you got no chance," Gangril growled.

A flurry of activity within the yard signaled the moment they had been waiting for. "Go," Gangril urged.

Anderson pulled the hood of the Turgorn robe close around his face, stepped up to the scanner as nonchalantly as possible, and inserted the mnemeplast card into the receptacle on the gate post, praying that this was not a sophisticated computer-assisted system that would take measurements of body parameters to compare with a stored list of values appropriate to the official holder of the card.

With a ghostly exhalation as air rushed in where it had been excluded before, the gate opened.

Crouched into a sort of duck-walk to pass below the scanner's range, Gangril slipped in behind Anderson. Snapping and crackling, the gate closed.

Keeping their motion to a brisk, businesslike walk, they proceeded nearly the full length of the walkway before being stopped by a Roothian soldier with drawn weapon.

"Please call the Orian ambassador," Anderson told him, doing the best he could to give a credible rendition of the lilting Turgorn tongue. "This Rigan has information regarding a plot against the life of a member of her delegation." When lying, Steven had told him, always stick as close to the truth as possible. Just the same, Anderson was glad Gangril didn't understand the language. "We must speak to her as soon as possible," Anderson added.

The Roothian stared. Anderson retreated as far as possible into his hood. The soldier held out his hand for Gangril's blaster. The Rigan surrendered it after a tiny hesitation.

"Thiss way," the soldier hissed. "You musst tell the commander."

He led them in through the arched doorway and into a short, narrow hall with a door at the other end. "Sstay here," he demanded, and went to a wall speaker to summon help from a colleague somewhere inside the building. Then he put in a call to his commander's office. While he was turned away, Gangril loosened the fringed sash from around Anderson's waist.

The soldier returned, demanded Anderson's weapon, and then peered once more into the hood, his tongue appearing briefly to taste the air. He was reaching up to push the cowl away when Gangril flipped a loop of the sash over his head, and the Roothian died without uttering a sound.

Another soldier had come in through the far door, but he was a fraction too slow in responding to the situation. In one surprisingly swift, smooth motion, Gangril retrieved his gun and fired. Anderson got the impression that the usual plodding pace of Rigan activity was more a matter of inclination than physiology. The soldier fell in a smoking ruin. Anderson didn't know what species he was.

"Hurry up," Gangril demanded as Anderson struggled to relieve himself of the encumbering Turgorn robe.

"What are we going to do about them?" he asked, indicating the two erstwhile guards. "Somebody's bound to find them in a short time."

Gangril shrugged. He was already halfway through the door. Anderson picked up the little dart gun and followed. He didn't share Gangril's lack of concern and he would rather have had the Roothian's weapon, but Gangril would only take it away from him.

They found themselves in a narrow, well-lit corridor that twisted and branched whimsically and seemingly forever. Doors opened off it every few meters. Anderson tried a few of them cautiously. Most were locked. Others opened onto still more corridors and more doors.

"The place is a maze," Anderson complained. "We'll never find Talan in time. There must be scanners in operation. We've got about two minutes to get the hell out of here, if that's possible."

Gangril had accosted a skinny Turgorn female who had been trundling a cart loaded with cleaning equipment of all shapes and sizes down the hallway. "Where's the Oriani?" he demanded.

The woman twittered, frightened. "I don't know," she said, not understanding. "I don't know what you want."

Anderson translated, more to ease her fears than to aid the Rigan. She pointed down a corridor. "Information, that way." But before they took the indicated direction, Gangril smashed a terrible blow to the back of her neck and left the frail creature sprawled over her mops.

"You didn't need to do that," Anderson shouted at Gangril as he was literally pulled along.

"Shut up. Keep moving," Gangril growled. Somewhere behind them a bell sounded distantly. The alarm had been raised.

Around a sharp bend in the hallway was a wider spot where several passages came together. A semicircular desk was centered in it under a sign that said "Information" in seven languages, although it seemed likely anyone who could find it would be little in need of it. No one was in attendance.

Anderson searched the desk for the information they needed while Gangril continued halfway up the flight of carpeted stairs behind the desk, presumably to get a better vantage point from which to watch for pursuit.

Anderson was blind with panic and half paralyzed, too. He didn't know where to begin—among the papers, some loose, some bound, at the Com/Com console? Where?

"Can I help you?" a gentle Turgorn voice asked at his shoulder. Anderson all but jumped out of his skin.

Where the fellow came from, he had no idea. Just suddenly, he was there.

"Uh—I—the Orian—" Anderson stuttered, then took a deep breath and began again. "I must find the Orian delegate Talan. There's a plot against his life. I must find him."

"Shouldn't you inform the commander of the guard?"

"Yes. He knows." By then, Anderson was quite sure the statement was true. "I must warn the delegate."

Perhaps he had enough wild-eyed and panting dishevelment to be convincing. In any event, the Turgorn came around in front of him and woke the panel to life. "Does the delegate know you?"

"Yes," Anderson said. "My name is Bill Anderson. Please hurry. There's no time to lose."

The Turgorn spoke briefly to the panel as the screen lit up. In a moment, Talan's face appeared there. The image looked past the Turgorn to Anderson. It studied him a moment, taking in the bruises and the panic. "Come," Talan said.

Relieved to have the responsibility out of his hands, the Turgorn indicated the stairs. "Up the stairs, to your right, fourth door on the right-hand side of the corridor," he said in careful English.

Gangril met Anderson at the head of the stairs. He had obviously overheard the instructions, for he started at once down the hall, counting the doors. At the fourth, he stopped.

"The gun?"

"Here." Anderson patted the bulge under his shirt.

"Get it, stupid." Gangril's own blaster was held at the ready. He touched the bell and stepped back against the wall, out of range of the scanner.

The door opened and Talan stood neatly framed in the doorway. His big ears were pricked forward and his yellow eyes were bright with interest. Inside the room three other Oriani sat around a table, their conversation interrupted, looking toward the door. One of them rose and started toward Talan.

Anderson had the little gun leveled. He had only to fire it. He hesitated.

Talan did not.

Without any real concept of how it happened, Anderson found himself on the floor with dust and carpet fibers in his mouth. Tortured air snarled as a blaster was fired and masonry exploded thunderously in the interior of the room. There was another snarl, from within, and Gangril collapsed just beside him.

Talan had one of Anderson's arms pinned against the small of his back with the pressure of his knee. He had two good, solid handfuls of Anderson's hair. With very little effort, he could snap the Terran's spine.

The Dream

Anderson woke from his dream sweating, the sense of panic still with him, the hubbub of the vision still ringing in his ears like the ghosts of spirits.

The dream came often, haunting his nights. It began with a group of Turgorn laborers loading Gangril Vorb's body onto a wheeled cart and trundling it away down a long hall of the conference building on Midway. The sound of the wheels was muffled by the newly laid carpet. Noise, the roar of Babel, issued from Talan's suite, and Anderson was hustled into its midst by rough hands.

The suite was crowded, crammed with the Lleveci officer of the guard and seven of his diverse soldiers, the Turgorn chief emissary chewing his mustachios, and members of participating delegations, including several senior Oriani and two of the dusty little straw-stack folk from Beta Ellgarth who huddled close and were the only quiet ones.

Half the people there didn't understand the other half and, true to the universal irrationality, the less they were understood, the louder they shouted. They did not speak to Anderson. In a corner, with his hands growing numb in their bonds, he was kept under the watchful eye of a soldier whose attitude was less than friendly and whose weapon was large and unwavering.

The argument in progress centered upon who had jurisdiction over Anderson's disposition. Under Orian law, a criminal was considered to owe the victim rather than the state, and since Anderson had essayed against Talan's life, Talan felt he had a claim to Anderson's. The

127

Turgorn, of course, had a territorial claim. They were a people rather inclined to be impatient with criminals and would have liked to escort Anderson outside of the dome and leave him to his own devices with a life expectancy of about two seconds. The Oriani were morally obliged to prevent such an occurrence if possible. Others took sides according to their own beliefs or the political expediencies of the moment. Anderson's fate was bandied about like a Ping-Pong ball.

As the confusion grew, he caught sight of the clerk from the information desk tacking doggedly through the vociferous crowd, making his way toward the Orian ambassador. Bumped this way and that, the man had to make a difficult circumnavigation of an immovable group. His progress was slow, but he was determined. Following in his wake was a gold-braided, brass-encrusted Turgorn soldier whom Anderson took to be the security commander.

The Orian ambassador leaned toward the information clerk, her ears cupped to catch his words, her bright eyes widening. She began asking for quiet, and an island of calm grew slowly around that distinguished lady. When she thought she had a chance of being generally heard, she said, "I believe we have made a serious mistake." She didn't shout. Her voice had a full, rich timbre that fairly commanded attention. All eyes turned her way. "It appears we have apprehended the wrong man," she said.

Confusion redoubled itself throughout the room. In time, a long time, the ambassador reestablished some kind of order and was able to let the clerk tell his story to the others. His facts were essentially correct. It was his interpretation that was wrong. The security commander supported him.

Subdued little groups discussed the matter among themselves. Finally there was a consensus, although some, the Turgorn in particular, still had their doubts.

Begrudgingly, the soldier removed the bonds from Anderson's wrists.

While he was rubbing the circulation back into his hands, the ambassador came to him. In a manner both regal and unassuming, she offered him the Orian salute of greeting, hands raised to shoulder level, palms forward, a humble gesture that failed to reduce her dignity one iota.

Viscous time moved molasses-slow. The dream always repeated itself exactly. Anderson knew what was going to happen. He could not change the flick of an eyelash, the emphasis of one syllable. Dancers in a slow-motion ballet, the players stepped the predestined figures together.

The room was suddenly empty. The ambassador's words echoed slightly. Talan was somewhere near. Anderson couldn't place him precisely.

"We owe you an apology, Bill Anderson," the ambassador said, and Anderson was allowed a luxurious second of feeling flattered. "In the heat of the moment, my son jumped to a conclusion. Regrettable, but understandable, I'm sure you'll agree."

The realization of what had happened seeped slowly into Anderson's understanding. His fate was balanced on the knife-edge of a rare Orian mistake. He was helpless to do anything to make it more secure. The ambassador was still talking. He had to struggle to make sense of her words.

"We would like to make amends if possible," she said. "You will need a place to stay and protection from those who remain unconvinced of your innocence, I think. Would you be willing to remain here for a few days while preparations are made?"

He was helpless to protest. His tongue was numb. His brain was numb. Escorted into an inner room and offered food and drink, he discovered his hands were already shaking. "The Rigan?" he managed to ask.

"He's dead. I'm sorry. There seemed no other way to stop him at the time."

Anderson didn't know who answered. Talan and his mother had become merged in his mind, and sometimes there was one and sometimes two of them. He was never sure.

"He had something of mine."

"I doubt anything he was carrying would had survived the blast. Perhaps the item could be replaced?"

"No," Anderson muttered. "Not here. What am I going to do?"

"There is no need for your anxiety," the Talan/mother person said soothingly. Anderson looked up.

"You are shaking."

He looked at his hands and commanded them to be still. They would not obey. He folded them over the hot place in the pit of his stomach. He discovered that he was alone in the room. The door was closed. He thought it was locked. Near him was a bed, and he was tired. But he heard the sound of muffled wheels and turned to see Gangril Vorb's body being loaded on a cart and pushed down a long hallway. . .

Memenoh

"It is a dream, Bill Anderson. Wake up and see that it is a dream. Get out of the bed now. Get up."

Anderson worked himself to his feet, still half asleep, the sense of dread still strong in him from his nightmare, so that he was startled by Talan's silhouette against the open doorway where the false dawn was just beginning to lighten the sky.

The dream held him by some mysterious threads to Midway. It took long moments and hard thinking for him to remember where he was. Memenoh. He was at Memenoh, in the Western Desert. On Orion. He had been there a long time.

Memenoh was a word from an ancient language. Its meaning had been forgotten. All it meant to modern Oriani was a place of water in the trackless desert. As far back as Orian history could be traced, the place was known. It was marked with special care on maps carved in stone, on charts drawn on vellum and paper, and on maps in computer files, because of the tiny spring that dribbled out of a sheer rock face.

Over the ages, the water had worn a sizable basin in the soft stone, where it rested briefly before wasting itself in the thirsty sand. A few green things struggled for life around it. Otherwise there was little but weathered rocks, their scoured shoulders hunched against the wind. Between the rocks the sand blew, endlessly shifting, moving, streaming toward the jagged black mountains that were the eastern horizon. To Anderson's prejudiced

131

eye, it looked more like Mars than any habitable place and, except for the occasional grunt of some prowling beast in the night, seemed as well endowed with life.

The cabin in which he and Talan were staying had been built in modern times, simply but skillfully in typical Orian style, one room partially divided to provide for a rudimentary kitchen. The main part contained a sizable computer record library, a Com/Com link, and a pair of those boxes full of dried aromatic grasses that the Oriani fancied as beds. Adequately stocked with groceries and roofed over with solar cells to catch the energy that Orion's sun provided in skin-blistering abundance, it was a self-contained unit and one that was familiar to Talan from some other time in his life.

Anderson could not understand the Orian sense of property. The fact that the building was there and Talan had need of it seemed sufficient justification for him to claim it. Anderson wondered what would have happened if another had had the same need. But there was no one else around.

Without firsthand experience, it would be impossible for anyone from Earth with its teeming cities, its few, well-trodden open spaces, and its crowded dwellings to imagine the solitude that was possible on sparsely populated Orion. With only 642 million Oriani, most of whom lived in the towns, the countryside except for the largely automated farms was nearly deserted. The deserts were even emptier.

Talan had taken him there to recover from the drug. A healer had stayed with them for a time. When a flyer came and took her away, there were only the two of them and maybe a million hectares of desert.

The journey from Midway had been swift, the diplomatic packet making the distance in about half the time it took the *Star King*. So Anderson had been told. He didn't remember it too well.

Withdrawal from rystl is not a pleasant experience. No barbarian tribe has ever invented a torture to compare with the one by which the body exacts its revenge for the time of its mistreatment. The stomach knots, the brain shrivels, muscles tremble themselves into cramps.

Nerve after taut, quivering nerve takes up the message until the whole network is acid-etched upon the consciousness. For a long time Anderson's universe encompassed nothing beyond himself and the periodic attentions of the healer with her pneumatic hypo full of Bodramine to ease the symptoms.

Time became meaningless, a river flowing in circles. Anderson remembered only Talan near at hand, deaf to his pleas and enduring in stony silence both his tears and the curses hurled at the Orian in every language Anderson knew. Talan tried to feed him and cleaned him up when he got sick, and held the tormented body against the warm strength of his own to subdue the trembling. The tiny droplets of time Anderson could claim from the first month or so were filled with hating Talan and needing him in about equal numbers.

When the nightmares started, Talan woke him and made him get out of bed and walk, or talk, or sit and watch the desert dawn roaring into day. Talan thought that if the pattern was broken, the dream wouldn't keep coming back. It still came, though not so much. But after the first while, Anderson didn't mind being roused. It wasn't a bad thing to sit in the open doorway of the cabin and talk and watch the desert. Early dawn was the only part of the day that was bearably cool anyway. Most of the time it was too hot to breathe.

The talk was pleasant, too. When Talan had a notion to talk, he was quite interesting to listen to. They discussed Orian lifestyles and human xenophobia. They talked about the morality of eating meat, which the Oriani didn't do. They discussed chess—Talan promised to get a board sent out—and languages, and Anderson discovered that Talan was no mean linguist in his own right. They talked about the Universal Brotherhood of Intelligence, and Anderson told Talan that he had had some second thoughts since knowing a Rigan well. Talan said that his own second thoughts were related to the Kaz. The Kaz came up quite often in these discussions. They seemed much on Talan's mind. Anderson learned, more by hints and inference than by direct statement, that an enmity existed between the two races that had its basis partly in Orion's persistent and occasionally successful opposition to the expansion of the Kazi empire. But there was more to it than that, he was sure.

Anderson left the bed, rubbed the sleep from his eyes, and sat down in the doorway to watch the sky burning red above the eastern mountains. In a few moments Talan joined him there. The morning's discussion began with Talan identifying the various sounds that came on the breeze as the denizens of the desert tucked themselves away for the day, and worked its way to the subject of interstellar politics. Not by accident, Anderson felt sure.

"What do you know of my mother's work?" Talan asked.

"Not a whole lot. Politics has never been my thing."

"I think you are not so ignorant as you pretend, Bill Anderson."

Anderson looked at him, but he had been watching the sunrise, and Talan's face was in the shadow of the doorway, so he couldn't make out the features. "All I know about your mother," he said peevishly, "is that she was involved in the Midway Conference." Then he remembered something else he had learned months or maybe a lifetime ago. "And she's somehow associated with something called the Merchant Security Force."

"You are aware of this?"

"Our—Steven's—computer dredged up the association. But it couldn't define the force or tell me anything about it."

"Steven Black also knows?"

"I suppose so. I left it in the machine. Probably Steven knows more than I do. There isn't a lot Steven doesn't know."

"This is true. I fear for my mother, Bill Anderson."

"The ambassador struck me as a person who could look after herself."

Talan didn't answer. Though outwardly still calm, there seemed to be a deeper tension in the face he turned toward the glowing sky. His thoughts were distant. But as Omnicron Orionis edged above the horizon, he brought them back as though by force of will.

"Listen to me," he said quietly, the command of an Orian teacher to his student. "One could consider the galaxy to be roughly divided into a core and a rim. The populated worlds of the core are for the most part united under the Empire of the Kaz, an empire that has been perhaps a million years in the building.

"In the hot pressures of the thickly populated core, stars were dying before our suns were born. But the forces that bring a star swiftly into being bring it swiftly to its end. The core worlds have learned to read their suns and flee them as they fail. The empire looks outward to the younger, more stable stars of the rim for new worlds for its dispossessed peoples.

"If the rim worlds are to survive enslavement or annihilation at the hands of civilizations older and fiercer than they, they must be at least united in their own defense. We are at a disadvantage. The distances are great, the time scale almost beyond comprehension. We must work without much hope of making a significant contribution in one lifetime."

Talan's voice was flat, as if he were reciting lessons learned in childhood. He was staring directly into the sun, and the nictitating membrane across his eyes made him look blind. It gave Anderson the creeps, and in spite of the fact that the sun was already burning up the air, he shivered in the doorway of the cabin.

There was obviously more to this story, but Talan stopped abruptly. He went into the cabin and started preparing breakfast as if dire threats from the galactic core were as much a part of daily life as eating. Anderson shut the door to keep the day's heat out as long as possible and joined him in the kitchen.

They spent the day the way they had been spending most days since Anderson had become functional again. Talan kept Anderson busy. There was the daily course of exercises, for Talan was determined to build Anderson's damaged body back to health; Talan was far more determined than Anderson was, and it was a source of friction between them. Anderson complained that it was too hot for a lot of physical work. Talan said he had no information that sweat was actively harmful to human beings. And he had a kind of patient stubbornness that was very hard to fight. Anderson was also charged with cleaning things—Talan had a positive obsession about cleanliness —and doing odd jobs to help him with the project he was working on. Anderson couldn't figure out exactly what the project was, but part of it involved tracing the expansion of the empire of the Kaz from the galactic core to its present extent.

Nor had Talan forgotten that his patient was in need of education. Talan had never forgotten anything, as far as Anderson was aware. The Orian returned to his teaching chore late in the evening, from an oblique angle.

Sitting in the doorway again, trying to catch a cool breeze off the desert, they had been talking about Steven Black, and Anderson could see that just the thought of him bugged the hell out of Talan.

"Steven Black is a mote in the eye of my world," Talan said. "He is growing beyond being a mere nuisance. He has become too powerful and his ambitions have become too grand for us to be able to ignore him any longer. More important, he has begun to interfere with the Interplanetary Community. We cannot afford him."

"So get rid of him. Send Security in, pick up Steven and one or two of his lieutenants, and the whole organization will fall apart."

"Steven Black would fight."

"Well, of course."

"Innocent people would necessarily suffer the consequences."

"You can't have it both ways."

Talan didn't say anything for a few minutes; he just sat staring out into the night. It was so quiet that they could hear the endless blowing of the wind and the muted grunts of some beast prowling in the distance.

"One rarely has right and wrong to choose between," Talan murmured almost to himself. "Only degrees of each. Perhaps, as a last resort, some such thing must be done. Evil times make evil deeds. If necessary..." His eyes closed and his ears flattened as if the thought caused him pain.

"But," he said more strongly, "it is our hope, Bill Anderson, that with your help, it will not be necessary."

"Me?" Anderson squeaked, appalled. He couldn't think how he had become involved.

"You are our key to Steven Black's organization."

"Not me. No way. You've got the wrong man. Steven doesn't let anyone get away with crossing him. Besides which, as of the fiasco on Midway, I'm pretty high on Steven's hate list. If he knew where I was, I'd be dead already."

Talan turned away and spoke without looking at Anderson. "Do you seriously believe I am suggesting that I would offer you as a sacrifice? How have I injured you that you believe such things of me?"

"Never mind all that. I know what you're thinking."

Surprised, Talan faced him again. "You do?"

"Yep. You think the Interplanetary Community is necessary to resist the Kaz. Steven is getting in your way, so he has to go. Because I'm a handy, expendable, unprincipled alien, I can be persuaded to do the dirty work for you. The cause will be served and Orian hands will stay nice and clean. Well, no thanks. People with causes scare me. They're generally all too willing to sacrifice friends and neighbors to some distant, greater, capital *G* good."

"It is as much your way of life which is endangered as it is mine."

"I'd rather bow to the Kaz and live than die fighting them."

"If so, you are indeed the wrong man." Talan took Anderson's hand and placed two familiar-feeling tablets in it. He closed the human's fingers over them.

"The drug has been your master for how long? A year by human reckoning? Yet you fight it. Why? Would it not be easier even now to accept your bondage? I think you do not suffer enslavement easily, Bill Anderson."

Anderson could almost feel comfort and tranquility oozing out of the two pills he held. Angrily he threw them with all his strength out into the night.

"You didn't give me any damned choice."

"You have just made such a choice."

"What are you trying to do to me, anyway?"

"I am trying to make you think." Talan put a hand on Anderson's shoulder, a gesture of uncommon familiarity for an Orian. Anderson shrugged him off.

"Leave me alone. You've got no right. Just leave me alone. I don't want any part of your schemes to save the universe, and I don't want your amateur psychology. I got troubles of my own. Just go away and leave me alone."

"As you wish," Talan answered, and he was gone, vanishing like a shadow into the darkness.

He was gone all that night and all the next day and the next night, although where he went was beyond Anderson to guess. There was absolutely nothing for a good 200 kilometers in any direction.

All Anderson could do was wait. He had no place to go, and no way to get there, anyway. Beyond the slash of light spilling out of the open doorway, he could see nothing but the stars embedded in unfamiliar patterns in the night sky. One of them might have been Sol, for all he could tell.

Somewhere out there, he thought, near one of those stars he was watching, there were beaches to walk on and the fragrance of pines. There were ball games and barrooms and crowded, noisy streets, and bright lights, and people he could halfway understand. He wanted desperately to go home.

Anderson had no appetite for Talan's imposed routine when Talan wasn't there. He paced around a bit, got bored with that, and settled down to read, picking a record more or less at random from the library. It turned out to be the writings of some early Orian philosopher. It was involved and difficult to follow, but somehow intriguing.

But his mind was only half on what he was reading. He kept turning over Talan's problem.

He was sure that any other government in the galaxy faced with the kind of trouble Steven was causing would have mounted a policing action forthwith and be done with it. But not the Oriani. They had to find some "civilized" way of handling it. There wouldn't have been a problem in the first place if they weren't so damned fastidious.

What were they afraid of?

Maybe the old philosopher was right: He claimed that the Oriani were afraid of themselves, afraid that if they ever, even for a moment, admitted to their baser natures, they wouldn't be able to recover the facade of totally controlled civility. They wouldn't be able to live with one another.

Though the old philosopher wrote it before he could have known it, it was still true that all the races that had made the hard transition from beastliness to organized society had in common the fact that they were the offspring of some tough, quick, efficient carnivore. All had experienced periods of savagery and tension. With some those periods had been mercifully brief. With others, like the Rigans, endless. All dragged into civilization some baggage that is the inheritance from barbarism.

Perhaps the savage was yet too close to the Oriani for them to be able to get the proper perspective on him. The Orian transition had been fairly recent and quite abrupt. By nature flesh eaters, with the instincts of hunters, killers whose natural habitat was the brutal, unforgiving desert, they knew their newfound civilization to be a frail covering barely hiding a vicious beast, and so mistrusted their own motives.

So Anderson was willing to believe. It made a kind of sense.

He was still reading the old philosopher's record when Talan came back. The writing was quite old, so the language was a bit strange, and the ideas were complicated, but he kept going back to read more. It said things such as: "If we will examine a man carefully and without prejudice, we will soon see he is both a beast and something other than a beast, as a grassy slope is more than the earth beneath. Grass is other than earth; it proceeds from earth. Earth without grass is capable of existence, but grass without earth is not." That was Anderson's first, rough translation. He could see it had lost something.

He didn't hear Talan come in, and when the Orian leaned over his shoulder to see what was on the screen, Anderson was startled, and jumped half a meter. That seemed to amuse Talan.

"You approve of the ancient philosophies?" he asked.

"They've got a damn sight more meat to them than the modern ones," Anderson said.

"You are an unrepentant barbarian, Bill Anderson," Talan answered, but he was not displeased.

Talan had neither forgotten nor given up on his plans. But he had decided on a different approach.

They were sitting at the table in the kitchen having lunch, nibbling away at some of that stuff made out of a variety of cultivated fungus and roasted seeds all glued together with something sweet and honeylike, and dried. Anderson discovered that it was not actually as bad as it sounded, once he got used to it. It tasted a little bit like beef jerky and a whole lot like nothing on Earth.

Sitting with his feet up on the rungs of the chair and his tail wrapped around his ankles, apparently relaxed, Talan said, apropos of nothing at all, "Steven Black believes you were successful in the task he set you."

Anderson was shocked to learn that Talan knew— and that he didn't seem to care. "Huh?" he said brightly and took a beat to admire the quickness of his own wit.

Talan studied Anderson with grave yellow eyes as if he were trying to read not the reaction, but deeper, the reasons for the reaction. He repeated himself exactly, and then went on. "Steven Black has received, through one of his most trusted channels, the news of my death on Midway at the hands of an unknown assassin. My mother goes about with mud smeared on her fur and my friends do not speak my name."

"What the hell?"

"Steven Black has been led to believe that you escaped Midway aboard a tramp freighter bound for Capara."

"You knew all along?"

"Yes," he answered a little wistfully. "If I did not, you have told me several times during your delirium."

"Oh, God," Anderson said. He pushed a shock of sweat-damp hair off his forehead and looked away. In the main part of the cabin, a shaft of sunlight had found its way under the eaves and through the window and lay like a solid rod between the floor and the windowsill. "So, now what?" he asked weakly.

Talan didn't immediately understand the question. He thought it over for a while. "I hold you in no way responsible," he said finally. "I do not believe you were in command of yourself at the time." He got up and stretched himself like a cat, from snout to tail tip. "I have work to do," he said.

"Wait a minute. What's this all about you being dead, then? And why are you telling me about it, especially if you want me to help with this scheme you're cooking up, whatever it is? It only means I could go back to Steven if I want to. If, of course, you ever let me out of this place."

"I have never had any intention of holding you prisoner."

"You could have fooled me."

"Yes, perhaps you would see it in that manner. I wished you to have time, and I could see no other way to give it to you. But time grows short, Bill Anderson.

"Please understand it is not my desire to trap you into anything. If you decide to help, it must be because you choose to do so, because you believe in what we do."

"Christ, you sound more like a preacher all the time."

Cool and remote, Talan looked at him as from a distant place. "I can see that it is not unreasonable for you to be unmoved by the ultimate fate of societies that have not served you well. However, I believe vengeance to be a common motivation among humankind. Perhaps you should consider who has been the author of the agonies you have endured these past months."

"Me, you, Samantha, in that order."

"In what way do you hold me responsible?"

"If you hadn't interfered, none of this would have happened."

"And you would still be an addict. Or do you seriously believe you might have overcome the drug without help?" He paused a moment to let Anderson think it over. "How would it profit Samantha to have you in such a condition? As I understand the situation, it would not be in her best interests."

Anderson had never actually seen an Orian blush—under that fur it would be hard to detect anyway—but he was pretty sure that was what Talan was doing just then.

"Think about it, Bill Anderson. Who would benefit? Who has had need of your unswerving loyalty? Now you must excuse me. I do have work to do."

With that, he ensconced himself in front of the Com/Com link and gave his attention totally to what he was doing there. For a while, for all practical purposes, Anderson was alone.

He watched the day grow long and when he couldn't stand the silence any more, he went to Talan where he was engrossed with the machine.

If the Orian's movement to switch off the link was at all hurried, it could have been only the natural result of his having finished his chores. He looked up at Anderson expectantly.

"You people," Anderson said, "have a notion to ignore anything you don't approve of, like if you don't pay any attention to it, it will go away. So how come, after twenty years, Steven has finally become worthy of notice? And don't give me any garbage about galactic politics. For that you could wait until he died a natural death, even if it took a century."

Talan's gaze was all saffron candor. "There are two more proximate problems. One is my mother's life. Aside from my personal feelings in the matter, our race is not so well endowed with leaders that we can afford to lose them at Steven Black's whim. As the Merchant Security Force becomes more able to protect its members, Steven Black's hold on the port community weakens, and my mother's jeopardy as architect of the force increases.

"The second is one of economics. Economics bind a community more strongly than most other considerations. Steven Black and others like him make trade more expensive than it need be. The spaceports—"

"Are a great place to make a buck," Anderson finished for him. "And Steven's snatching some of your bucks. Now I begin to understand you."

Talan was puzzled. "I wish I could say the same."

Nothing more was said about it. The next day, back in his role as teacher, Talan took Anderson out into the desert and gave him a sample of Orian ecology made simple for Terran students.

Anderson was frankly astonished at the number of things that lived in the apparently barren desert, and in spite of his professed boredom with the subject, he found he was taking an interest in the delicate interplay among the creatures that made their living from the desert's thin charity.

Talan normally kept these field trips confined to the early-morning hours, mindful that the heat affected his student severely. Whether Anderson had been particularly slow that morning or they had gone farther than Talan calculated, the sun was getting high by the time they were making their way back to the cabin. Anderson flopped down in the shadow of a rock and demanded a rest. Talan squatted on his haunches beside him, waiting.

The Terran had just decided that even lukewarm from his canteen, water was one of life's great pleasures when Talan jumped suddenly and made a small cry of pain.

"What?" Anderson asked, concerned.

Talan showed him the beetle, about as big as Anderson's fist, black as the ace of spades, with his head buried in the fur about halfway up the Orian's leg. It seemed to be digging in for a long stay and causing Talan no little distress.

Anderson raised his hand to swat it. Talan caught his wrist. "Let's get rid of the damned thing," Anderson said.

"Not in that manner, Bill Anderson."

Anderson was about to ask for suggestions when inspiration caught him. Thinking that desert creatures should have a healthy aversion to drowning, he upended his canteen over the beetle. It squirmed and wriggled in the stream of water and finally let go and dropped to the ground to immediately bury itself in the sand.

They both sat in the shade of the rock while Talan recovered his composure.

"That was a procedure which would not have occurred to me," the Orian admitted.

"It would have been easier to kill it," Anderson said.

"No."

After a while Anderson said, "I've been thinking about what you said last night."

"Indeed?"

"Maybe I do owe Steven a thing or two. Tell me about this plan of yours. Maybe we can make a deal."

Talan gave Anderson his most penetrating stare and thought it over for a minute. "What kind of deal did you have in mind?" he asked finally.

"Well, I'll tell you . . ."

"Please do."

Anderson took a deep breath and started again. "Since I got to Orion, I've wanted one thing most of all, and that was to go home. But I'm stuck here because of my heart. Okay? So, if I'm not going to get killed at it, I'll do your dirty work in return for a round-trip ticket to Earth."

Talan's ears flattened slightly. "We can meet your terms," he said coolly. "However, you must know there is undoubtedly an element of risk. It can be minimized, with your cooperation." He grew brisk and businesslike. "We propose to weaken Steven Black to a point where he can no longer hold his organization together, to stop his ships, to thwart his deals, to bleed off his funds as much as possible. We need a person within the organization itself able to supply the necessary information."

"Who's 'we'?"

"This I will not tell you. Under the circumstances, I feel discretion is called for."

"Thanks for the confidence."

"You have your doubts about people with causes. I have my doubts about people who work for wages. It is my experience, Bill Anderson, that a man who works for wages is loyal to whoever pays the highest wage."

The Western Desert

The night Talan left Anderson alone with his temper, he had entered the desert with the sense of having handled the Terran badly. Quite possibly he had destroyed in one moment of carelessness the months of work he had put into building Anderson's confidence. That he could lay his clumsy mistake down to the fact that he was much disturbed by his growing fondness for the Terran did not excuse him in his own eyes.

He had never intended this to happen. He was having difficulty enough reconciling his use of Bill Anderson with his responsibility to the man, without the added burden of friendship.

He did not need a friend, he needed a tool, and these rising feelings of sympathy and compassion toward Bill Anderson's innocent and absolute trust, so much like some small animal one had treated kindly, were a hindrance. They were clouding his judgment and threatening to make a friend of an instrument.

He would have found it easier if Bill Anderson could have remained nothing more to him than an example of humanity, a race that had long held his interest, albeit without admiration. Humans fascinated Talan for their ability to maintain a civilization that, if it was not the best example of such things, at least worked and did not require its members to forgo half their natures. Oriani denied their savagery; Terrans absorbed and worked around theirs. Talan would not have had Orion emulate Earth, but he would have like to learn how to deal with the beast that raged within, held in check, in his own case at least, only with the greatest of effort.

He had set off into the darkness at an easy lope, heading for the dune fields to the west. It might have been more efficient to keep a flyer at Memenoh, as Nefis, a fellow conspirator, had suggested, but Talan had been uncertain about Bill Anderson's ability to operate the machine and more certain that the Terran would eventually try, regardless of his ability. There was a foolhardy recklessness about Bill Anderson that might have elicited a begrudging respect if it hadn't meant that Talan must be constantly on the watch.

In any case, the run was not so very strenuous, and the activity helped to ease the tension.

The black, moonless Orian night did not hamper him. He was well adapted to his world and to finding his way by starlight. Nor did he concern himself about getting lost among the rolling ocean of dunes, one so like another an Earthling would have been unable to distinguish among them. Bill Anderson would have been hopelessly confused in a very short time. Talan, whose ancestors for countless generations had made similar journeys, possessed an instinct for desert navigation that he never thought to question. He knew where he was and where he wanted to go as surely as he knew up from down, and the mechanism by which he knew it needed as little consideration.

His senses were alert, though, for other presences in the night. The smaller animals scampered away at his approach, but some of the big hunters might have found him tasty. Once he had to stop dead in the deeper shadow of an outcropping of rock and quiet his breathing while a massive hirral padded on wide, silent feet across the flank of the dune just ahead of him, fortunately heading upwind.

His associates had been waiting for him when he reached his destination, their flyer hidden within the arms of a long crescent of sand. He had told them that he had been unable to convince Anderson to help them, and recounted the last conversation he had had with the Terran.

And they had given him more bad news. The council would not support their scheme.

"We have failed on both fronts," Nefis said. "I see no reason to continue."

"I think it is not entirely lost with the Terran," Eoli answered. She had made a study of human psychology and had offered her advice to Talan on more than one occasion. "He only needs motivation. Preferably something more personal than the Kazi threat."

"I do not easily imagine a motivation stronger than the loss of life and freedom, not just for oneself but for one's entire race."

"But you are not human, Talan."

M'row shook her head. "Without council support, is there any need? It is bad enough to manipulate this one, but to do so to no purpose . . ."

"Perhaps, with the mechanism in place, the council could be convinced," Talan suggested.

Nefis disagreed. "They are old people, Talan, set in their ways. They will not be quick to see a need for change. I doubt they can be persuaded."

"Let us make the attempt," Talan had said. And he had called Eoli aside and let her advise him.

When the others had gone, Talan did not immediately return to Memenoh. Instead he had spent a day and a night in the empty silences, regaining his sense of himself and searching for the strength to continue with his unsavory task.

He had needed a period of solitude to come to terms with his feelings. As much as he thought Bill Anderson needed time alone, he himself needed it more. The long period of close proximity had worn on his nerves.

Now he was making the journey again, while Bill Anderson slept and dreamed of vengeance and promises of Earth. Talan honestly hoped the Terran would be quick and sure enough to survive to claim his reward, but he was full of doubt. And, strangely, of regret. Knowing the need, yet he regretted it.

The conspirators met again, between the arms of the same dune that had sheltered them the last time.

"He has agreed," Talan announced, "for the price of passage to his homeworld. We were both wrong, Eoli."

The psychologist nodded her acknowledgment.

"The council?"

"Nothing has changed."

"Then we may have to proceed without their approval."

Talan received their disapproving stares and shook them off as a dog might shake off water. "There are preparations to be made, and they must begin at once. Nefis, the back trail must be carefully laid and must be persuasive. It should be as convoluted and confusing as possible without losing credibility. If Steven Black manages to follow it back to Midway, Bill Anderson is dead.

"M'row, I think we will be in need of your professional services, if you could come to Memenoh tomorrow."

Anderson had just finished cleaning up after breakfast when a flyer landed near the cabin and an Orian with a doctor's bag came in. Talan introduced her as M'row, the healer Anderson had met on Midway. He didn't remember her.

M'row looked her patient over with the attitude of someone contemplating the purchase of a piece of beef and poked and prodded and consulted a variety of instruments, most of which had functions totally unknown to Anderson. Finally she pronounced him as physically fit as one could expect under the circumstances. But she seemed to have her doubts about something else.

"The psychological profile is not promising," she said. "There is a lack of maturity, a hedonistic approach."

"You are not a psychologist."

"Call for she who is, if you doubt me."

Talan dropped his eyes. "I do not," he said. "Forgive me. Let us make the attempt."

"He is stubborn in many ways, with deep-seated patterns of violence, uncontrolled —"

"He is the tool we have."

"The risk is too great."

"The risk is mine alone. Why do you object?"

"The project is at risk, Talan."

"Without him, there is no project."

Anderson was greatly impressed with this dialogue. He might have been a hacksaw for all the consideration he was getting.

The healer put one shoulder up and leaned her head into it, with her face turned away. This, Anderson had learned, was the nearest thing to an Orian shrug. "I think it is unnecessary, foolhardy, and doomed to failure. However, if you are determined, I will do what I can to help. But the others must know that the risk is greater than anticipated."

"I leave it to you to see they are informed," Talan said.

"Are you part of this thing, Doc?" Anderson asked as he struggled back into his shirt.

M'row turned toward Talan for guidance and got none. She turned back to Anderson and shrugged again. "Yes."

"This whole idea is crazy, you know. There's no way it's going to work. There's got to be a better way."

The healer was busy packing her instruments and didn't bother to stop work to answer him. "I'm open to any suggestion short of murder."

That was a bit of a jolt. It was the second Orian who had admitted to Anderson contemplating killing Steven. Anderson might have been forgiven if he had started to suspect that Oriani weren't quite so dedicated to peace and tranquility as they let on.

Orion Space Central

It seemed like a century since Anderson had last looked down from the window of his apartment in Space Central, a dizzying height of two stories, into the restless street below. Not that it was a scene to particularly delight the eye: the gray street below, the gray wall beneath, and the gray office tower across. Nor had it changed significantly. It could have been the same people coming and going, hugging the shady side of Sundance Street, always restless, never content with where they were.

The scene hadn't changed, except that now the worst of the summer's heat was past, people and vehicles had claimed the daytime hours.

Anderson had changed. After months of isolation in the desert, he was pleased to see all the activity. But he no longer felt a part of it. A shuttle went screaming up, and the great boom as it crossed the sound barrier left him with that same heart-pounding startlement it had on his first visit to the port. He'd become accustomed to silence.

He had arrived about midday and spent half an hour showering, trying to wash the stink of the good ship *Igarg Garowl* off of himself, figuring on the Oriani to pick up the water bill, wondering all along if Talan's choice of that rusty Rigan freighter to carry him back to Orion was a matter of using whatever vessel could be found in an out-of-the-way place like Capara, or if Talan intended a few days' close company with those churlish sailors to be another lesson in Anderson's ongoing edu-

cation. He didn't think Talan left much to chance. The
Orian did take his role as teacher far too seriously.

Not liking the blowers for the dehydrated feeling they
left him with—Orion's climate did that all too well without help—he was drying himself with a towel in front of
the window and had just turned to rustle through
drawers to find a clean shirt when the door behind him
opened. Startled, he turned to confront the intruder. Samantha came sauntering in unannounced.

"Nervous?" she asked, smiling.

"Most people knock before they walk into somebody's place," Anderson said as coolly as he could manage with nothing but the towel to protect his dignity.

Sam looked him up and down, her gray eyes half
amused, half sulking. "I used to live here, too. Shall I go
out and come in again?"

"Don't bother."

"Thanks a lot." Reinstating her good humor with a
wave of her hand in front of her face, she said, "Anyway,
welcome home. This time I brought the wine." She held
up a bottle for Anderson's approval.

"That's nice."

"I'm overwhelmed by your enthusiasm." She put the
bottle down on a handy table. "Aren't you glad to see
me?"

"Sure. Of course."

"Well, say so, damn it. Try something nice and original, like 'Hello, Samantha, I'm glad to see you.'"

"Hello, Samantha, I'm glad to see you."

"Christ." She had come right up to him and was
kneading his biceps gently with her long fingers. "You
look good." She ran one finger slowly down his chest
and across his belly. "Aren't you ticklish anymore?"

"No."

"Oh?" Her eyes followed her finger on down. "I'm
glad to see you still allow yourself a few human weak-
nesses."

There are certain aspects of humanity no amount of
tough Orian training will disturb. Thanks to Talan and
M'row's efforts over the last ten weeks or so, Anderson
was probably healthier than he had been in a very long

time. Between them, the two Oriani had taken a drug-wasted body and cultivated it and cared for it and filled it full of vitamins and heaven-knew-what-all and worked the living daylights out of it. A prize racehorse couldn't have had more careful attention. They ended up with a pretty good approximation of a human male in prime condition—one who had been a long time away from anything even approximating a human female.

All Anderson's steely resolve not to get once more entangled with Samantha and her friends melted under her softly demanding kiss. She clung to him as if she had really missed him. He knew, of course, that she was a grand master of the art of flattery. It didn't seem important at the time.

After not so brief an interlude, they opened the wine. He found he hadn't lost his taste for that, either.

Later Samantha sat cross-legged on his bed like some pagan fertility goddess, combing out her hair all over the sweat-damp, rumpled sheets and watching him get dressed.

"You've changed, Bill," she said.

All kinds of alarm bells went off inside Anderson's head. "How do you mean?" he asked.

"Being away has been good for you. You're, I don't know, tougher, stronger."

"I've worked my way halfway around the galaxy. I've had plenty of opportunity to develop my muscles."

"I don't mean like that." She nibbled the end of her comb and a rare frown line grew between her delicate brows. But it vanished in a moment and she put the comb aside. "I was supposed to tell you Steven wants to see you right away."

"It would have been nice if you had mentioned it a little sooner," Anderson complained.

"Oh?" Samantha could put any number of twists on that little word.

"Come on, Sam, don't be like that. You know what I mean."

"Do I?"

"Yes, you do. You know how Steven gets annoyed with being kept waiting. I mean—oh, the hell with it. Come on, get dressed. We'd better go right away."

"Now you sound like your old self," Samantha said with some satisfaction.

Steven was in his apartment, lying on his cushions, a fat cat in a haze of cigar smoke, dreaming of cream. "Ah, Bill, good to have you back," he said a little too heartily. "It took you a while to get here," he added petulantly. He peered at Anderson through narrowed eyes. "You look well."

"A deckhand gets a lot of good, healthy exercise, especially on an undermanned Rigan tramp. I didn't get a whole lot of help in my hour of need, Steven."

"Well, now, you have to understand, we didn't know what had become of you, you see."

"You didn't bust a gut trying to find out, either."

"Take it easy, friend." Steven waved an order to Samantha to prepare some scotch. "We'll make it up to you."

The smooth, aromatic heat of the whiskey was good, but Anderson scarcely did more than sip the drink before putting it aside. Steven rolled his glass between his hands, his rings clicking against the surface. "So what happened on Midway? We haven't heard any news since the assassination of the Orian delegate was announced."

If Steven didn't have somebody on Midway keeping close watch on the progress of the conference, Anderson would eat his cigar. "Strangely enough," he said, "I didn't wait around to find out. In case you're wondering, I've been running like hell these last eight months, and I've been just one step ahead of Orian Security the whole time."

Steven pasted a small smile on his face, displaying a couple of tobacco-stained teeth. "Don't think I don't appreciate what you've done. But you're safe now. Relax."

"Relax?" Anderson howled convincingly. "I'm trapped. The first time I stick my nose outside of Space Central, I'm dead."

Steven's smile deepened, becoming genuine. "Where

did you want to go?" He levered himself to his feet and paused on his way to replenish his glass to chuck Samantha under the chin. Sam continued to stare unwaveringly at the new DeLeon painting on the far wall: Steven's latest acquisition.

"We'll have to see what we can do about getting Security off your tail. In the meantime, there's plenty for you to do here."

"You haven't done much to get them off your own tail," Anderson said. Steven turned and glared at him. He plowed on. "In the meantime, I need some money. I've been earning a sailor's pay lately, and it sure doesn't go very far."

"I guess not. I'll put a couple of thousand in the Government Bank for you right now."

"A couple of thousand? You owe me six times that much in back wages, damn it."

"What're you, my echo? I'll give you two now. When you've settled down and cooled off, we'll talk about it again."

Anderson had been dismissed. He stalked toward the door with a fine show of barely contained anger.

"Bill."

Anderson stopped with his back still to Steven.

"Do you want some pills?" Solicitude from Steven was about as common as handshakes from a snake. He had got the word and was checking it out.

"No."

Behind him, Anderson heard the long, slow release of Steven's breath.

"Where are you going?" Steven asked.

"Out," Anderson answered from the doorway. "To get something to eat, to get some decent clothes, and maybe to get drunk."

"You can do all that from here."

"Thanks, I'd rather do it myself."

"You're getting to be a pretty independent cuss, Billy boy," Steven warned. "'Just don't forget which side of your bread has the butter."

Anderson left Steven's apartment and went down to his old office in the warehouse. It looked as if it hadn't been touched since he left it. There was an inch of dust on everything. The computer terminal was still active, but the machine didn't have anything interesting to tell him. He wasn't surprised. Steven would want to back-track, probably reconstruct Anderson's history for the entire eight months; he hadn't gotten where he was on trust.

All Anderson could do was wait and hope—hope that Talan had succeeded in laying a credible trail and hope that Steven didn't push his investigations to extremes. Whatever trail Steven followed, it would inevitably lead back to Midway, and enough people there knew that Talan was alive and well to guarantee that with any in-tensive effort, Steven would learn the truth.

Anderson was mulling over his probable fate over a cup of ersatz coffee in the noisy, crowded Portside Cafe-teria when a young Orian sat down beside him.

"Do you like that brew?" he asked.

"Not much."

"I have a tonne of the genuine available, Earth grown, fine quality."

"You must be a wealthy man. It's worth a hundred thirty-five credits a kilo."

This exchange amused the lad to no end. "I am fasci-nated by this what you call cloak and knife."

"Dagger."

"Whatever. Why does Steven Black do his banking by courier?"

"He doesn't trust the communications network. He thinks the Com/Com Net can be tapped."

"We intercepted the courier. He had an order for two thousand. Your boss is a cheapskater."

"When I pushed him for more, he got quite hostile. I have a hunch his liquid assets are tied up somewhere." Anderson made a face over the insipid fluid in his cup and wished the kid really did have some coffee stashed somewhere.

"This matter of the funds being tethered..."

"Tied up."

"Whatever. Is it possible for you to discover the rea-son?"

"I'm pretty sure Steven won't tell me. I'm cut off from information about the organization for the moment."

"Cut off? As in amputated?"

"No, as in not having access."

The Orian thought this over for a moment, then gave an Orian-style shrug. "Whatever. Why is this?"

"Steven's natural caution, I think. I hope. I'll snoop around and see what I can find out. I've got to be careful, though."

"Agreed. It would be a waste to have you discovered so soon."

"From my point of view it would be a waste to have me discovered at all."

"Of course." The kid looked over his shoulder in the style of the best cloak-and-knife characters. "I had best leave you now," he said. "The Lleveci and the Rigan sitting together two tables away are following you. What you would call 'tails'?"

Anderson nodded.

The Orian wagged his own appendage slightly, considered the two watchers, and failed to make the connection. "Whimsical language," he said and left.

Anderson went back to Tradex Interplanetary. The muscleman doing duty as guardian of the inner sanctum tried to stop him, but Anderson avoided him without too much difficulty. He was just beginning to appreciate what Talan's training had been all about.

Unannounced, he burst into Steven's apartment.

If Steven was disturbed to have Anderson suddenly confront him at his desk, he gave no sign of it. The guard rushed in about a half a second later and grabbed Anderson's arm in a grip that could crush stones, apologizing to his boss.

"Get this monkey off me before I break his neck," Anderson told Steven. Steven smiled a little, as if the thought of such a contest touched some deep humor, and waved his man away.

"I'm not sure I approve of your newfound belligerence, Bill," he said.

"One thing I discovered out in the cruel world was

that unless you fight back, folks will walk all over you. I got a little tired of being stepped on. Which brings me to the point. I told you, I need some money."

"I gave you some. You saw me arrange it."

"I don't know what you arranged, but if you check with the Government Bank, you'll see that my credit balance is sweet zero."

Steven frowned and punched a button on the top of his desk. A distant electronic voice responded. "Send me Petrowski," he ordered.

"Petrowski hasn't checked in," the voice said.

The frown deepened. "Find him." Steven chewed his upper lip a bit. "Petrowski's always been a reliable man," he said.

"Maybe he's been mugged."

Steven gave Anderson a look that was richly deserved. Nobody in his right mind would attack Steven's courier, not in Space Central, not when the motive was nothing more than someone's pocket money.

"You'll get your money," Steven growled. "Now get out of here. I've got work to do."

Anderson decided to tour the organization and see what in-house gossip he could pick up.

When Talan outlined his plan, Anderson said it was on a par with trying to skin an elephant with a nail file, and then had to spend some time explaining both elephants and nail files. But even granted that knowledge, the Orian had said only, "We will make the attempt."

Talan had started work some months ago, and there was no doubt Steven was on edge. The whole organization was trembling in sympathetic vibration. Sitting in on a few coffee breaks and hallway meetings, Anderson discovered that some lesser lights had already packed their bags and taken off for friendlier environments. Steven hadn't even bothered to chase them down. But he was beginning to feel a little shorthanded. It wasn't many days before Anderson's time was filled to overflowing with Steven's little chores.

"I don't fancy being turned into a messenger boy, Steven," Anderson complained.

"Go," Steven said. "And don't give me a lot of back talk. Who do you think you are, anyway?"

Deciding that was a line of inquiry he didn't want Steven to pursue very far, Anderson went. A little humility might be less dangerous in the long run, and it wasn't so hard a thing to carry a message to John Walters at the IP Trade Center—though it would be nice if Steven would catch up with modern times and use the Net.

Just outside, Anderson quite literally bumped into the young Orian. While they dusted each other off and watched the reflections in the glass front of the building for suspicious-looking characters, the Orian told Anderson he had left a package for him at the Sississin. That was fine. Anderson had been intending to get down there and say hello to Issith anyway.

The Sississin hadn't changed. The dusty plastic plants waved stiffly every time the door opened or closed, the two Llevecis still pursued their game at one of the tables, and what little Anderson could read of the salamander face behind the bar told him that Issith seemed pleased to see him.

"Hhallo, Bill. Time iss long ssince you come."

"Issith, my friend. I've missed your cheap booze."

"Iss not cheap, Bill."

"Don't I know it." The impossibly green leaves wavered around them. "Listen," Anderson said. "The Rigan and the Lleveci who just came in together have been following me around all day, and I'm beginning to get tired of them. Do you suppose they might be getting tired, too?"

Imperturbable, the Roothian studied the two who had settled at a table a short distance away. "Iss possible," he said. He intercepted a waiter and in a short time Anderson's shadows were nodding over their drinks.

Issith motioned Anderson behind the bar and into the storage room beyond. "Ssomeone leavess thiss for you." Issith showed him, among the shelves and bottles, three heavy plastic boxes labeled "Pride of Peru. Fine Coffee. 1 kilo."

"Who?"

"One I do not know. An Orian."

It was just as well Issith didn't know the messenger. This was Talan's last resort. In one of the boxes, was a quantity of explosives; in another, the detonator. Crude munitions indeed from the cultured representative of a sophisticated civilization.

The third box had Anderson puzzled for a bit, until he had hefted all three. The third one was quite a bit lighter than the other two, weighing probably about a kilo. Then it dawned on him: A gift from his friend of the fractured idioms was a kilo of real, live, fragrant, beautiful, Earth-grown coffee. He blessed the lad in silent benediction.

Issith, standing nearby, looked perplexed.

"Samples from a deal I'm working on," Anderson explained. "Do you mind if I leave a couple of them here for a while? I don't want Steven horning in on this, and if I take them with me, he's bound to find them."

"Ssteven Black iss not one a poor vendor of cheap boozze should annoy."

"If he finds it, tell him I threatened you, or anything you like."

"Iss sstill a rissk."

"Maybe I can make it worth your while. Okay?"

"Iss okay, Bill. Becausse you are my friend."

By the time his two unwelcomed companions were rousing from their slumbers, Anderson was back in front of the bar paying Issith rather more than he owed for one untasted drink. His tails tottered out behind him, and he was careful not to lose them in the crowds.

Nothing much happened for the next few days. Anderson spent some of the time he could claim from running Steven's odd jobs in renewing his acquaintance with his landlord and discovered that Samantha had been paying his rent to hold his room for him while he was away. She had threatened the Caparan with dire consequences from Steven if he didn't stick to the bargain. Some time during that period, also, a sizable crowd of brassy-looking Terrans arrived in Space Central, looked around for a couple of hours, and then were whisked off in a cloud of pomp and circumstance. A lot of Terran expatriates, Anderson included, would have loved to get close enough to talk to them for a while, but there was a whole battalion of Security types keeping nervous watch, and they wouldn't let anyone get within shouting distance of the visitors. Scuttlebutt had it that they were some high United Nations muckymucks come to negotiate Earth's entry into the Interplanetary Community.

Steven became at least partially satisfied that Anderson's story was true and put him back to some real work. Just housekeeping chores at first—Steven wasn't ready to risk a very high level of trust yet—but it was a start. And Anderson preferred even donkey work on a regular basis to sitting around waiting for Steven to yell at him. That was too hard on the nerves.

Furthermore, he was possibly a little more clever with restricted computer files than Steven realized. He found out where at least some of Steven's money had gone. So he made arrangements to meet his Orian contact.

To all appearances, he just happened to drop in to the Sississin in the evening to join the shift-change crowd from the docks. It was a nice bunch to be with, everybody relaxed and friendly, and the dockers were typically the first with the off-planet news. But it was a crazy place for the kid to choose for them to meet. When the Orian had maneuvered himself through the press of bodies to get next to Anderson at the bar, Anderson told him so.

"Anyone who's been on this planet more than fifteen minutes knows Oriani don't drink. You take some awful chances."

"Anyone might expect to find one rotten apple in the container, as the saying goes," the kid said.

"In the barrel. That's not exactly how the saying goes."

"Whatever. You have something for me?"

"Um-hum. At least part of Steven's capital has gone to buy the freighter *Susan B.*" Anderson was speaking in a very low tone of voice, not wanting to be overheard, although in the buzz of the crowded bar, it didn't seem too likely. He would have sworn he could see the kid's ears growing bigger as he listened. "Lock, stock, and cargo," Anderson continued. "The cargo is mainly heavy arms and ammunition. The ship left Centauri July twenty-ninth, local time, bound for the Ellgarth Cluster."

"What would be its value?" the Orian asked.

"On the open market, the cargo would be worth about five million at Centauri. The ship? It depends. Anything from next to nothing to about thirty million."

The lad looked as pleased as if he had personally swallowed the biggest canary since the dawn of time.

"Incidentally, what was the outcome of the Midway Conference?" Anderson asked.

"A cease-fire was announced, with formal peace negotiations to begin in about thirty days, Orion time."

"Without doing all the arithmetic, I would guess the *Susan B* should arrive in the Ellgarth Cluster just about then."

"Steven Black intends to put a fly in the unguent?"

"Ointment. Something like that." Issith caught Anderson's eye. He took a quick glance over his shoulder. "You'd better get out of here. My tails have found me."

Anderson expected the boy to leave as quickly and as quietly as possible. Instead, he turned and exchanged a few pleasantries with the Sgat sitting, as much as Sgats sit, on the other side of him. Then he slipped off his stool and made his way casually among the tables toward the door. He stopped beside the Lleveci and asked him something. The Lleveci pointed down the street. The Orian nodded and went out.

Anderson liked the kid. He was bright, cheerful, and full of *Phaseolus* seed, though a fellow had to wonder why he would remember that when "beans" was so much easier to say. If the kid would only stick to his native language. But no way. He liked English, liked English idioms. He fractured every one he came upon.

He had a lot of nerve. If pure nerve could have gotten him through it, he would have been fine.

Samantha was waiting in Anderson's room when he got home.

"Bill, what's happening?" she asked before the door even closed behind him.

"I don't know. Is something happening?"

She gave a short sniff, as if testing the atmosphere. "There is," she said. "I can smell it. I'm scared."

She looked scared, uneasy, her nerves tight. But that could have been whatever drug she was playing with at the moment. She wandered aimlessly around the apartment moving things, picking up and replacing cushions, looking out of the window.

"Steven's in an awful temper," she said.

"How come?"

"Somebody's organizing some of the small businessmen into a sort of resistance movement. A lot of them have stopped paying their dues."

"Who's the madman?"

"I don't know. Steven has knocked a few shopkeepers around, but they're very determined this time. They're not talking. Steven suspects the Oriani have something to do with it. Of course, they say they don't know anything about it." She settled for a moment in front of the window and watched the street.

"Are you looking for something?"

"No. Why?"

"Never mind. Do you want a drink?"

She was hugging herself as she turned to face him, and the form-fitting jumpsuit she was wearing made her silhouette slender and dark against the light from the window.

"Would you take me out, Bill?"

"Right now?"

"Please."

"Sure. Where do you want to go?"

"Just out. Anyplace. Maybe we can find a party."

"Okay. Give me five minutes to shower."

She waited until the shower was going before she spoke again. "Bill?"

"What?" he shouted over the noise of the water.

"Do you like me?"

"Ah, come on, Sam," he yelled. "You know."

"Tell me."

"Tell you what?"

"If you like me."

She was playing a child's game and Anderson wasn't

too patient with it. "Damn it, Sam, of course I like you," he shouted.

She said something he couldn't hear, but when he came out of the shower, she was gone.

Next morning, Kurt Morgen stuck his head into Anderson's office. "Hi," he said. Then he came all the way in, presented Anderson with a cup of the stuff the cafeteria down the street alleged to be coffee, sat down on the corner of Anderson's desk with a similar cup of his own, and asked Anderson how he was doing, if he was finding it hard to get back into the swim of things, and so forth, being so obviously casual that Anderson's suspicions were raised almost at once.

"What's on your mind, Kurt?" he asked.

"I was just wondering, like maybe we could go down to the Sississin later? Buy you a beer."

"How come?"

"No reason. Something to do, eh?"

It was on the tip of Anderson's tongue to decline the invitation. He and Kurt had never been great buddies. That in itself suggested that there was more to this than Kurt was letting on, which was a good reason to accept.

"Okay," he said.

"Good. See you. By the way, Steven wants you upstairs."

Steven's temper hadn't improved a bit. When Anderson arrived upstairs Engtheladrihar, another of Steven's employees, was cringing in front of Steven's anger, leaning back on four of her legs like a sailboat leaning away from a gale. "Now I'll tell you something," Steven was saying. "You find it and find it fast, or you're going to be missing, too."

"What's up?" Anderson asked when a shaken Engtheladrihar had left the room.

Steven sat down at this desk and puffed furiously at a cigar until it glowed hot enough to melt lead. "The *Susan B* is lost."

"What do you mean, lost?"

"I mean lost lost. What the hell do you think I mean? She was supposed to take on fuel at Ynacy Station.

She's two days overdue there, and no one of these idiots I've got hanging around here knows where she is."

"Maybe pirates?"

"They wouldn't dare. We got an agreement."

"Agreements can be broken. Anyway, it's a pretty old ship. Maybe she just broke up."

Steven glared at Anderson through the smoke. "Haven't you got anything to do?"

"Sure. Lots of things."

"Go do them then. And see if you can't give Engtheladrihar a hand tracing that bloody old bucket."

It was while trying to trace the *Susan B* that Anderson discovered that Captain John Walters of the *Star King*, a man who had successfully run Steven's errands for something like fifteen years and managed to keep his nose clean, was then in conflict with the Port Authority regarding a log entry that was at odds with the Port Authority's calculated number of hours on his engines since their last overhaul. While he argued it out with them, he was directed to keep the *Star King* in orbit. It was costing Steven well over a thousand credits a day to keep her there.

Anderson was beginning to believe that it might actually be possible to nickel and dime the king of Space Central to death. But it was going to cost a lot more than Talan thought it would.

A day or so previously, Steven had sent a couple of men out to pick up one of the local merchants who had recently stopped paying his dues. Anderson had just enough time to warn the fellow, who ran. The men were afraid to return to Steven without him—Steven had been in such bitchy humor lately—so they followed the guy all the way to Owr-Lakh, where they were picked up by Orian Security. Steven grabbed the merchant's partner. He was found in an alley later with the back of his head missing. The game was getting a bit rough.

Anderson said so to his contact when they met once again in the Portside Cafeteria. "The whole idea of Talan's scheme was supposed to be that innocent people wouldn't get hurt."

"You are concerned for the safety of these people?" the Orian asked.

"I'm concerned for the safety of me. We're not talking about soldiers here. These are little people, shopkeepers, with families and Saturday night poker games."

"What is this 'Saturday night poker games'?"

"Never mind. Pay attention to what I'm trying to say. They won't take much pressure. It's a mistake to try to use them. They're only going to get hurt and in the end they'll collapse and wreck the whole thing."

"You underevaluate them."

"Estimate."

"Whatever. You did know one of Steven Black's lackeys was physically removed from the Home Grocery yesterday?"

"I know the Home Grocery burned to the ground last night. You figure how that could happen in this day and age. Four businesses in the same building went, too."

The kid didn't answer that. Maybe he didn't have an answer.

For all that Steven hadn't found the *Susan B*, and it seemed he never would, Anderson didn't feel too confident that Talan knew what he was doing. Talan, after all, had never lived in the port.

In the Sississin later, Kurt Morgen drew Anderson away from the crowded bar to a table in the corner where he had more confidence they would not be overheard, and commenced upon a long-winded and ambiguously phrased question about what Anderson, from his unique perspective, thought of his master's competence.

"What'd'y think?" he asked. "I mean, you been away for a while, so maybe you'd notice any changes more."

"Anyone can have a run of bad luck," Anderson told him.

Kurt scuffed the floor with the toe of his shoe. "Maybe luck comes to them that make it," he said. He was treading on dangerous ground, and he knew it. It was a measure of his unease that he was willing to risk it. Either that, or this apparent moment of disloyalty was

another of Steven's tests of Anderson's own dedication.
There was no way Anderson could know.

"Maybe, sometimes. Sometimes you just have to
have the breaks," he said.

"The boss looks tired."

"He is tired. He's been working hard lately."

"Well, none of us are as young as we used to be,
right?"

"If you're suggesting Steven is getting too old, let me
tell you he's just as tough as he ever was. If you don't
think so, try getting a little out of line. And let me know
where you want the body sent."

"I didn't say that. Steven's okay. Shit, lots of guys
older'n him are running big corporations. Lots of 'em.
It's just, well . . ."

"Well what?"

"Well, it's like the men, eh? They're, um, kinda nervous. When the boss gets upset, they start getting restless. Start talking about old girlfriends, about going
home, about places they never been they want to see,
stuff like that."

"Steven must feel confident you can handle the men."

"Yeah, I guess."

"Things will settle down eventually."

"Suppose so," Kurt answered, but he sounded uncertain.

A few days later Kurt defected with half a dozen
friends to Riga Port, intent on going into business for
himself. The Rigans, more pragmatic than the Oriani and
needing none of that kind of trouble, promptly informed
Steven of Morgen's whereabouts. Kurt Morgen became
a gory example for his men. The grumbling died down
and the ranks tightened up for a while. But Steven had
lost a good man, and he didn't have a replacement who
was as effective.

At the same time, Steven was casting around for a
way to make the Oriani lay off. And he was keeping a
close eye on the Terran diplomats who had been confer-
ring with the Planetary Council in Owr-Neg. Anderson
couldn't bring himself to believe that was any kind of a

coincidence, or that Steven was watching the brass for entertainment.

He expressed his worries to his young contact as they walked together along a crowded street. The kid's long swinging strides carried him easily through the obstructing bodies, and Anderson had to hurry to keep up.

"You must tell Talan," the Orian said.

"You tell him," Anderson said. "I can't go to Owr-Lakh. Steven expects me to get arrested the moment I step out of the port."

"Not to worry," the lad said. "Something can be worked up."

"Out."

"Whatever." His stride lengthened and in a moment he had vanished into the crowd.

The kid was right about one thing: Anderson was worrying too much. His nerves were strung out, he hadn't been sleeping well, and he was dog tired. He decided he would complain to Talan when—if—he ever got to see him. He thought just maybe Talan would let him off the hook, though he didn't think it was too likely. Talan was inclined to treat Anderson's limits as nonexistent.

Walking back along Sundance Street to his apartment, Anderson thought about those days on the desert and Talan's course of physical training that had felt like a concentrated distillate of kung-fu and the marine combat course. Once he had flopped down on the sand and told Talan that he had had it, that he couldn't move anymore. Talan had stopped beside him, seemingly sympathetic, but suddenly he had grabbed a wad of the flesh of Anderson's buttock and pinched it hard. Really hard. Anderson had jumped a good half meter.

"You seem quite capable of movement," Talan had said. "Let us continue."

As he waited for his apartment door to respond to his handprint, Anderson caught himself rubbing the spot on his rump, which had been sore for a week, and was glad Talan wasn't around to notice.

He threw himself down on the bed without bothering to get undressed and dozed away the hot afternoon thinking about earlier, better times, half dream, half memory. Suddenly he came to with heart-pounding suddenness and with the thought that he had heard someone call his name. But it was only the bell of the Com/Com link.

Still breathless and confused, he answered its summons. Steven's face was on the viewer.

"I want you here," the image said.

"Okay. What's up? Anything wrong?"

"Five minutes." The screen blanked and Anderson was left to silently curse Steven's anachronistic ways. Deals big enough to shake governments were made via the Com/Com Net, but Steven wouldn't trust it to preserve the secret of his middle name.

He splashed cold water on his face and presented himself as ordered in just slightly more than the specified time. He was directed down into the basement of the warehouse, through a maze of naked concrete walls, and into a small, bare room. The tableau that awaited him there made his blood run cold.

Anderson had left the happy-go-lucky young Orian in fine spirits just a couple of hours before. Now he stood bound between two of Steven's Rigan goons. His tail hung limp; his eyes were dull and glazed. Part of one ear was missing and blood had drooled down the side of his face, matting the fur and giving him a lopsided look.

Steven poked his cigar in the kid's direction, and the kid flinched. "This fellow says he knows you, Billy boy."

Anderson tried to keep his expression emotionless.

"Well?" Steven asked. He was watching Anderson intently.

Anderson's heart was pounding so hard he thought surely Steven could hear it. He took a deep breath and tried to keep the tremor out of his voice. "Steven, if you beat a man hard enough, he'll tell you anything you want to hear, just to get you to stop."

"Hmph. And just happen to come up with your name out of the clear blue, or green as the case may be, sky."

Anderson was thinking furiously, trying to produce a plausible explanation. But he had no way of knowing what the kid had told Steven, or how much.

The kid stirred between the Rigans. "The jig is out, Bill Anderson," he said in a thin, cracking voice.

"Up," Anderson corrected automatically. He was shivering cold in the heat of the evening. He could not see any way out.

The Orian started a shrug, but the movement hurt him and he aborted it half done. "Whatever. Steven Black knows about the coffee."

Coffee? But that was just a cloak-and-knife game. "Oh," Anderson said because he didn't know what else to say. The boy coughed and brought up blood.

"Leave him alone, Steven. I'll tell you whatever you think you need to know about it."

"You will?"

"Yes."

"Good. Then we won't need this one any more." He nodded at the Rigans, and one of them pulled a long knife from a scabbard at his waist, caught a handful of the kid's fur, and pulled his head back.

Anderson knew what was coming next and so did the Orian. The yellow eyes were wide and terrified and fixed on Anderson. But Steven's piggy eyes were on him, too. He didn't dare move. The Rigan opened the boy's throat in one swift movement. Blood gushed. A high-pitched scream ended in a bloody gurgle. The body thrashed for a moment until the Rigan dropped it.

The room spun around Anderson. His gut had turned to water, and his legs threatened to give out under him. He leaned against the wall and cursed in a dull monotone because there was nothing else he could do.

Kaz

Steven could not tell where the Kazi's attention lay. Its inexpressive insectoid eyes looked in no particular direction, and its blank features displayed nothing whatsoever. Still, squatting on Steven's desk, it managed to convey its displeasure. Nervously Steven twisted the emerald ring around his middle finger, tried to ignore the musty odor of it, and waited for it to say something.

Eventually the sparse, metallic voice from the device around its neck said, "Slaying the Orian was a serious error. Oriani react strongly to the loss of one of their own. You invite retaliation. You jeopardize your position here and your value to the empire."

"You seem to think you know an awful lot about the Oriani."

The forelimbs waved irritably. "Much is known," it said. "The study has been long."

"Well, you don't know spit about keeping an organization like this together. If the Oriani can come in here and do deals behind my back, how long before they suborn half my people? Somebody had to pay, and it was either the Orian or Anderson. And it just so happens Anderson is one of my own. He'll behave himself now, I guarantee it."

"It is well that you do." The Kazi did not go into its knowledge of keeping organizations together. As part of a race that had for some millions of years managed an organization of staggering proportions including a vast number of peoples in various degrees of subjugation or enslavement to the empire, it felt itself to be well informed on such matters. Exactly that knowledge and experience made it see the death of the Orian as a mistake on Black's part. The Oriani would not forgive and forget; they would extract payment in a way that possibly neither the Kazi nor Black would anticipate. Oriani were schemers on a level that commanded respect even within the empire. The Broodmother knew, any creature that would foul its own brood should be damned by the gods. Yet the Oriani continued, and one would be foolish to deny that they were formidable enemies. The Kazi saw a danger here that its hireling seemed unable to appreciate. It wondered if all humans were so dense. If so, they made poor allies. Study of other members of the race was indicated. It would relay this suggestion to the broodmaster.

"Anderson, you have further need of him?"

"He's good with languages and with numbers, handy to have around, but the operation wouldn't come apart without him."

The Kazi contemplated this information in silence. After a few moments the tinny voice said, "We have difficulty accepting the miraculous escape from Midway. Oriani are neither slow nor stupid. Either Anderson is a better man than we were led to believe, or less truthful."

"I'm checking," Steven answered quickly. "So far, his story holds up."

"We cannot spend much time here. It is difficult, always to be in hiding. Be quick about your checking."

"I can't be quick and be thorough, both," Steven complained. "So you better decide which you want."

The Kazi clicked its forelegs together in obvious annoyance. "We do not immediately see why we cannot have both."

"Take my word for it."

A long moment passed while the Kazi appeared to be considering the wisdom of doing that. When the metallic voice resumed it held a dryness that Steven had not been previously aware of—or perhaps he just imagined it. "This association Anderson constructed with the Orian hatchling now dead, you know the nature of it?"

"A small deal in black-market coffee. A triviality. Nothing to worry about."

"The Oriani do not deal in trivialities, nor in coffee. Dispose of Anderson. He is occupying time and attention beyond his worth." The Kazi shifted uneasily. The position it assumed to converse with Black was not particularly comfortable. "Perhaps not. We—" the Kazi hesitated as if it didn't know the right word "—sense . . . complications beneath the superficial. We do not accept illicit deals in coffee. And if the miraculous escape from Midway is other than it appears to be, there must be a reason for it. Preserve him for now, until it is decided surely."

"Make up your mind, will you?" Steven said irritably. "But I don't think Anderson has the wit to be involved in deep dark plots to bring down the empire."

"Do not make jokes about the empire."

"Touchy, aren't you?"

"Yes."

Steven shrugged, a gesture less casual than he would have liked it to be. He had stepped on dangerous ground. He caught himself looking up to see that his Rigan bodyguard was still nearby. He felt a bit foolish about that, yet there was a definite air of menace about the Kazi.

"Sorry," he said, a word that did not come easily to him.

"Watch Anderson closely," the Kazi instructed. "Employ more subtle means than you have until now. If the means are not available to you, they will be provided."

"Thanks loads," Black said sarcastically. Sarcasm was lost on the Kazi. But it shifted its position once again, and Steven thought that perhaps he would be wise to mind his manners a little more carefully.

"And what do you hear of the Midway Conference?" it asked.

"I hear it's in disarray."

"You are misinformed. Ambassador Meela, eater of eggs, is pursuing her lifelong ambition despite the loss of her hatchling. This is not our agreement. We are not pleased."

"Well, that's too damned bad. I'm doing my best. I've

sunk a lot into this project, and I've got other troubles. If you want things to move any faster, you're going to have to finance at least part of it."

The Kazi was quiet a moment. It had taken note of the human's growing peevishness and was beginning to doubt the wisdom of its choice of instruments to further the cause of the empire. In Kazi history, it had been shown time and time again that the quickest, safest way to bring dissension and revolution to new worlds was to recruit or buy a local leader and then stand back out of the line of fire in a supervisory capacity. However, Broodmother knew, like any other tactic, it was not unfailingly successful. Occasionally a local leader would renege, have second thoughts, become too ambitious, be incapable, or otherwise prove unworthy of service to the empire. On these occasions it was sometimes necessary to abort the mission and begin afresh elsewhere. This option must now be given serious consideration.

But, as its broodmaster had pointed out on many occasions, Orion was unique. All efforts to recruit a native had failed. Black was the nearest thing to an Oriani leader the empire had been able to entice into its meshes. And, the broodmaster emphasized, the Oriani had been actively opposing the empire with some small success. This not only delayed implementation of the empire's plans, it also caused some perturbations in the smooth control of worlds with which the Oriani had been able to establish contact. Some border worlds had shown signs of dissent, and valuable time and resources were being diverted to deal with these. The emperor wanted Orion stopped.

However, the Kazi was not so foolish as to let Black know of these considerations. Its position on Orion was precarious enough. While its concern for its own personal survival was less than might be supposed, and it would freely give its life in service to the Broodmother or to the empire if that was what was demanded of it, it was by no means suicidal. And it felt much safer with Black as an ignorant employee than it would if he were to become a nervous and enlightened enemy. The decision whether or not to go on with the present plan would be made elsewhere by those more qualified to decide. It would relay its doubts to the broodmaster, and the broodmaster would determine whether or not the situation was worthy of consideration at higher levels. This Kazi would continue on the present course until the decision was made and it received instructions.

"This was not our agreement, to pay your expenses," it said. "Our agreement was payment for the job done. You set your price."

"Half the job is done. Talan has been eliminated and the staid old boys of the Planetary Council should be sinking back into their conservative policy of noninterference. So give me half the money, at least."

"This was not our agreement."

"Then give me a little time."

Talan

A bump on Anderson's hip took his attention from the settling dust to the frowzy blonde standing very close beside him.

He was out on the street, trying to lose himself in the restless crowds, hoping that busy people hurrying about their frantic business would distract him. A few blocks down from Tradex where Kaelir Road crossed Sundance Street, laser cannon were being positioned to demolish a building, and he had joined the crowd of sidewalk superintendents.

A line of portable flags marked the boundaries of what the technicians considered a safe distance, but the observers weren't paying them much mind, crowding up close to get a good look at what was going on. The technicians, a group of frail Megadae, ignored the onlookers.

They were good at their work. The cannon fired, and for a moment it seemed that nothing had happened. Then the building fell in on itself, collapsing with a crumpling roar, and became a pile of rubble heaped in its own basement. The towers on either side remained untouched.

In a few days construction would start on a bigger and better building, one more round in the endless cycle of construction and destruction as the port reached up, as if to touch the ships it served.

"Hi, Sport," the blonde said. Her voice was a hoarse klaxon. She had hard, dark eyes like dry mud and a look of class gone to seed. "Lookin' for a good time?" she asked.

Several heads with smiles turned his way. "Not today, sister," he said and started to move away.

She stayed with him. "C'mon, Sport. Give a girl a break." When they had moved a little way from the knot of onlookers, her manner changed and her speech became softer, with a trace of cultured modulation. "My name is Mary-Ann Brady. I'm sorry about your friend."

"Do I have a friend?"

"Two of them, Bill Anderson," she answered coolly. "One who sold coffee and is dead. Another who wants to see you. He's waiting. Come along."

One who sold coffee and was dead. Anderson was mourning the kid privately as best he could. He dared not let anyone know how shaken he was. Steven was only interested in the price the pelt would bring from some ghoulish collector of furs from Brodenl.

It seemed particularly bad that he had never learned the kid's name. He had liked the young Orian, him and his mangled idioms. The kid had had guts, out there saving the universe like a comic-book hero.

Comic-book heroes never die. They never even get hurt.

People had died on this little adventure, but it had always been somewhere offstage where he didn't have to watch. He'd never had to stand by while one of Steven's henchmen pulled the victim's head back and cut his throat. The kid had expected him to do something. Something. His last scream hung on the air like a material thing. Anderson couldn't get rid of it.

The boy had been able to do far better by Anderson than Anderson was able to do by him. Steven was annoyed in a mild sort of way, but only because his employee had made a silly mistake.

"Coffee," Steven had complained. "Coffee, for chris-sake. If you're going to work deals behind my back, at least make it something worthwhile. There's another thing you'd better remember. Don't deal with the Oriani. They don't know how to lie."

A lot Steven knew about Oriani.

Anderson was sick to the teeth, over the lad and over the situation he was in. He was lonely and scared and he had a permanent pain in his stomach, as if he were getting an ulcer.

A vacuum truck arrived at the demolition site to sweep the air clean of the dust that was giving the setting sun a purplish cast. Port dwellers were welcome to make as much mess as they liked in the port, but the Oriani took a dim view of dirtying either air or water or anything that might find its way out of the confines of Space Central. Folks did what they could to keep the landlords happy.

The roar of the truck made conversation difficult. Mary-Ann took a few hesitant steps along the sidewalk, plucking at her garish dress as she waited for Anderson to follow.

Puppylike, he followed. He wasn't too surprised to be led up the wide shallow steps to the Seven Planets.

In her scarlet-and-gilt domain, the dowager queen of the Seven Planets flounced about with her feathers like a fancy bird, but the hand she held out for him looked like the claw of a primeval bird of prey. She was full of chit-chat, as if he'd come to take her youngest daughter to the school prom. But he didn't think it was exactly the idle chatter it seemed to be. She was a shrewd judge of people, for she sensed his impatience.

"Well, I have things to attend to, Mr. . . . ah . . ."

"Smith."

She didn't crack a smile. "Of course. Mr. Smith."

Anderson's face flamed as he followed Mary-Ann's exaggerated swing through the reception room to a broad staircase at the back. The balustrades were draped with tarnished lovelies of at least seven races who observed his passage with disinterested eyes.

Four flights up, Mary-Ann selected a door from a dim hallway lined with doors and motioned him into the room. It was small, barely big enough to contain the enormous velvet-draped bed, a small table covered with pots and jars and tubes, and one hard chair.

Talan was sitting uneasily on the very edge of the bed. When Anderson came in he got up and greeted the Terran in the Orian fashion.

Anderson interrupted him rather rudely. "What are you doing here?"

"Waiting for you, Bill Anderson."

"Oh, for Christ's sake. Are you out of your mind?"

"I think not."

"What a stupid chance to take. You'll get us both killed."

"I assure you, I will do my best to prevent such an occurrence. It seemed necessary to reestablish contact."

There was one large window in the room, covered with heavy draperies that had been pulled aside slightly to let a little light into the dim enclosure. It looked out onto a tumble of rooftops. Anderson spoke to the roofs glowing falsely golden in the dying light.

"Talan, about the boy. There was nothing I could do."

"This is understood."

"If I had made any move at all, it would have been both of us."

"Hear me, Bill Anderson. He knew the risk and accepted it. He would not have blamed you, nor do I. I understand your distress. Doing nothing is the hardest burden of all to bear."

Though Talan's words were comforting, Anderson mistrusted the Orian's motives. He had a feeling that Talan's efforts at human psychology were carefully calculated, and he wasn't at all sure that Talan was ever wholly honest with him.

He turned back to the room. Talan's features were impassive. Mary-Ann sat by the table filing her nails as if she were alone.

"Steven is beginning to feel the pinch," Anderson said.

"I thought he would be," Talan answered.

"He's in a deal with the Rigans. He's not going to be able to make the next payment. Most of his liquid assets are tied up in an arms shipment to Beta Ellgarth."

"I was under the impression *Susan B* had been quite thoroughly lost."

"It was. But you didn't think you'd stop Steven that easily, did you? The *Star King* left Centauri Colony bound for the Ellgarth Cluster five days ago, John

Walters commanding. You didn't keep the *Star King* tied up quite long enough. And if you have any idea that it might also get lost, you'd better know it has an escort, a Rigan gunboat and two Brodenli light cruisers, owned and operated by our friendly neighborhood pirates."

Talan looked through Anderson and out into space, as if he hoped to catch a glimpse of the *Star King* as it plowed doggedly along on a journey far longer than any it was designed to make. "How does Steven Black propose to meet his commitments to the Rigans?"

"I don't know."

"But you have your suspicions." It was not a question, it was a statement of fact, and a demand.

"Yeah, sort of. That bunch of brass-bound Terrans running around here somewhere. I think Steven has a notion to snatch a couple of them."

"Snatch?"

"Kidnap."

The focus of Talan's gaze shortened abruptly and came to rest sharply on the bridge of Anderson's nose. "To what purpose?"

"Ransom, of course. Enough to pay off the Rigans. He'll probably demand Orion stop interfering with his operations, too."

"Steven Black must know my government will not negotiate under duress," Talan said abruptly.

"Then he'll kill the Terrans, and at least some of the blame will land on Orion, and there's your Interplanetary Community all shot to hell. That'll serve him just about as well."

Talan's eyes dropped, nearly closed, and a long minute of silence grew in the room. Anderson could almost hear Talan's mind working, synapses opening and closing like antique electronic relays, making a hum just below the audible level.

"Why?" he asked.

"Why what?"

"Why would damage to the Interplanetary Community serve Steven Black? Why does he continue to promote the Ellgarth War even though, as you say, it must soon end because the combatants can no longer continue? It can be only a matter of when and how many more must die. What value does Steven Black find in it?"

"I think it has something to do with the Kaz."

"The Kaz?"

"Yeah. There's been a couple of them hanging around."

"Here?" For the first time ever Anderson saw Talan lose his cool a little. He looked as if he thought there might be one in the room with them and it wouldn't please him if there was.

"Yeah, in the port. I never get in on the meetings, which is fine with me. I really can't take to those guys. So I don't have much more than a hunch that they're connected. But I'd take a bet on it."

"They have grown so bold they come to our very doorstep," Talan said, but his words were not meant for Anderson. "It cannot be allowed. Can it be prevented?" He was silent for a while. "You do not know how the kidnapping is to be effected?" he asked finally.

"No, I don't," Anderson answered.

"Please make every effort to find out." Talan turned away, preparing to leave.

"Just a minute, damn it."

Talan's look of surprised inquiry put Anderson a little off stride. "Look, I want out of this. I'm getting an ulcer. I'm not built for intrigue. It's making me sick."

"I will see you are attended by a healer."

"I don't want a healer. I want out."

Talan put one of his hands on each of Anderson's shoulders, pulling the Terran around to face him. The blunt-clipped claws extended slightly as he held on. It was like standing face to face with a lion.

"I believe you have more strength than you imagine, Bill Anderson," he said. "I have need of you yet awhile. Endure a little longer." He seemed to be looking inside of Anderson for that strength he thought the Terran had. "Can you, my friend?"

Well, what could a man say? What, in heaven's name, could anyone have said? "All right," Anderson said. "A very little while."

So he was stupid. So he was flattered witless to have an Orian call him friend. So he was being used and didn't have the sense to resent it. A few months later it wouldn't have happened like that.

"I have no courier free for you," Talan said. "Can you meet me here occasionally?"

"It depends how often. I mean, this place—it's not the kind of . . . there's a limit . . ."

"I understand you, Bill Anderson. Let us leave it then until you have something to tell me. Mary-Ann Brady can find me when you need me." A hint of amusement or maybe embarrassment touched his words. "I suggest you remain here for whatever length of time is suitable."

He moved aside a wall panel and disappeared into the hole he had made. Mary-Ann left off her filing long enough to replace the panel behind him.

She explained to Anderson's astonished face. "It's a service crawlway. It comes out in the temple. That's in the same building, you know. The priests sometimes use it. That's how I knew it was there."

Anderson had heard that Roothians, while exhibiting a natural preference for their own kind, were not particularly fussy in that regard and could work themselves up to expend their passion into the mouth of almost any creature who could be persuaded to accept it. But the priests of the Immaculate Saint? They always let on that they were above such worldly things.

Nothing was as it appeared to be.

Mary-Ann resumed the care of her nails. She pointed with her file at the wall. "He's a cool one."

"Talan? Yes, he is. Sometimes I wish he'd get upset about something, just so I knew it could happen."

"Not me."

"Why? He'd seem less like, what, a machine."

"I bet if he got mad he could take you apart and put you back together without raising a sweat."

"Oriani don't sweat."

"You know what I mean."

The persistent slow *scritch* of the file was beginning to get on Anderson's nerves. Those nails should have been filed down to the wrists by then. "Where did you meet him?" he asked to get his mind off the sound.

"Here, in the port. A long time ago."

"It couldn't have been very long ago. You would have been a child."

"I was. A dumb kid. He gave me some advice I was too dumb to follow."

"Like what?"

"Like 'go home.'" She finally traded the file for a small jar of crimson paint.

"Don't do that."

"What?"

"Paint your nails. It makes your hands look gory."

"Oh, for Pete's sake," she complained, but, accustomed to the idiosyncrasies of men, she put the jar down.

The next time Anderson saw her, her nails were blood-red again.

Because Orion is far from its primary, its seasons are long. Summer slowly pulled itself to a burning close. Everyone said it had been an unusually hot summer. Anderson had never been anywhere where people claimed that the weather was normal. People said the fall storms would cool the air a little. The storms were a long time coming.

Samantha took Anderson's occasional visits to the Seven Planets hard. He should have known he wouldn't be able to keep them from her. If she didn't find out on her own, Steven would tell her just to see her hurt. No doubt her pride was wounded. Maybe the specter of age had begun to haunt her. She stopped coming around Anderson's place at all, but he saw her at the Sississin often enough, dressed to kill, spaced out on God knew what, hanging on some guy's arm, laughing at his weak jokes. He wanted to tell her, but he didn't dare. He quit going to the Sississin. But he couldn't avoid her icy glares around Steven's apartment.

Time dragged. Steven was wholly preoccupied with his problems, which were gradually growing worse. In an unprecedented move by Orian Security, members of the force came sweeping into the port and poked into dark corners and damp places until they found Steven's Kazi contact and saw it well out of Orian space. Everybody was excited for a few days, but things quickly settled back to normal when the Security team left.

Steven's Rigan debt began to loom large on his horizon. He had counted on his deal with the Kaz to pay off the Rigans. If he had any plans for the Terran VIPs, he was keeping them to himself.

At the tag end of the summer, Anderson met Barbara. She was a lonely lady, following her salesman husband around from place to place, one of those jaded travelers who spend a lot of time complaining that things were not like they were at home but always hoping that a change of venue would give their lives excitement. There wasn't much hope. She was a congenital dowd. Most of the time they were together, Barbara talked about Harvey, and about how her Earthside home was decorated, and how she wished she had children. She needed a juicy story to write home about, and Anderson supposed she got one, but the affair was pathetic for both of them.

Eventually Harvey gave up trying to sell communications equipment to the people who invented the Com/Com Network and Barbara vanished out of Anderson's life—not a minute too soon.

The Kazi returned with a friend. Or maybe it was a different pair. Who could say? They sneaked nervously about, avoiding contact with the Port Authority.

And Samantha turned up again. Anderson had just seen Barbara to the shuttle—and learned she was going to "do" the Centauri Colony on the way home—and was feeling relieved and ready to shower and go to bed with a resolution to stay away from tourists. He was in no mood to start reassembling his home.

Sam was sitting in the big easy chair, but she got up when he came in. The room looked as if it had been ransacked. Sam herself looked as if she had been put together in a hurry, strange for one who was usually meticulous about her grooming. She fiddled with her earrings and with her hair, and her pale eyes followed

Anderson as he walked around setting chairs and tables to rights.

"Aren't you going to say anything?" she asked.

"Yes. When did you take up house wrecking as a career?"

"Bill, please. I'm in trouble."

"There's a lot of that going around. Why don't you take your problem to Steven? He can probably do more for you than I can. I'm only the hired hand."

"No." When he made no comment, she went on. "I want to go home."

Anderson indicated the door with a sweeping wave of his hand.

She sat down again with her hands in her lap, her fingers twining about one another restlessly, and it finally dawned on Anderson that she truly was upset. "I mean really home. To Earth."

"I can't help you, Sam."

"You have to help me," she blurted out. She took a moment to calm herself before going on. Anderson stopped her with a finger to his lips.

"Sam, before you say something that's going to get both of us more trouble than we know what to do with, I'd better tell you Steven's had this place wired."

"I know." She pointed up at the ceiling. The overhead light fixture, which minimally disguised a scanner, was swathed in layers of towels held in place by one of Anderson's belts tied in a rough knot. She gave him from her pocket two battered bits of metal that might once have been bugs.

He picked a brass ornament off the floor where it had been abandoned and put it back on the table where it belonged. "How long do you think it will be before someone comes to check on that thing?"

"Not long," she said. She smoothed her hair with one hand. "So listen. Steven is pretty sure someone on the inside is tipping the Oriani about his operations."

A cold hand gripped Anderson at the solar plexus. In the next half second perhaps a hundred schemes of flight hatched, breathed one breath, and died. He shut his eyes for a moment and tried to remember some of the things

Talan had taught him. When he could talk without a noticeable quaver in his voice, he said, "It would take some rare kind of suicidal idiot."

Sam looked at him quizzically. "I don't think so."

"Anyway, what of it?"

"Steven thinks it's me."

"You? Of all people. Why?"

"I've been doing a little business of my own. Nothing very much, just something to set aside against my . . . retirement."

"Samantha, everybody in the organization puts a little something in his own pocket. And Steven knows it."

She continued to fiddle with her hair, twisting it into unsightly strings. "Steven had a tankerful of alcohol bound for Brodenl."

"We're not supposed to supply Brodenl. Interplanetary agreement. They get strange on it."

"I know. The tanker was seized at the perimeter of the system by a Brodenli patrol acting on information from Orion. The cargo was impounded, the crew chucked into jail. I happened to have a thousand liters in storage at Riga Port. A couple of Brodenli offered to buy it at quite a bit above the market price. I didn't plan it. It just happened that way."

"Sam, that's a hell of a story. What do you take me for?"

"Steven doesn't believe me, either. He thinks I engineered the whole thing."

"And you didn't?"

"No."

"Okay, just suppose there's a grain of truth in this somewhere, what do you want me to do?"

"I need protection."

"I'm only one man."

"You have friends."

"Friends?"

Samantha had regained some of her composure. She looked at Anderson levelly. "Don't you give me that stare of wide-eyed innocence, Bill Anderson. I know who the informer is. I had a long talk with Mary-Ann Brady. Checking up on the competition. You've been meeting a certain Orian who's supposed to be dead but seems very much alive, and you're hatching something up between the two of you."

"You know a lot, don't you?"

"Yes. I can help or—"

The doorbell interrupted her.

"Who?"

"Com/Com Net Maintenance, Mr. Anderson. There's some trouble in the system. We'd like to check your terminal."

"Come back tomorrow."

"We'd like to clear up the problem as soon as possible, sir."

Quietly Anderson told Samantha, "You've got about ten seconds to get undressed and get into the bed." He stripped off his shirt and carried it in his hand to the door.

"There's absolutely no privacy left in the worlds," he complained to the strange Gnathan standing there.

After one quick glance at the ceiling and one at Sam in the bed, the man kept his eyes carefully on his work at the link. Anderson couldn't tell if he knew what he was doing or not.

When he'd left, Sam grew agitated. "Steven must know I'm here."

"No doubt."

"I'm trapped. He'll kill me."

"All right. Calm down. Get dressed. I'll see what I can do."

She paused at the side of the bed long enough to touch his face. "Poor Bill. Someone's always using you."

He got Sam out onto the street, and they joined the crowds enjoying the slightly cooler air of evening. He tried to keep their pace to a leisurely amble in spite of the fact that every instinct he had demanded that they run. They stopped to look into shop windows and have a drink at a bar like any idle couple, until he was reasonably sure they were not being closely followed.

He guided Sam down a short, narrow alley and through an unobvious door, and so into the Temple of the Immaculate Saint of Roo. He told her to stay there in the blue light amid the tall marble statuary carved into symbols only a Roothian could understand, and wait until he found Mary-Ann.

Mary-Ann was never hard to find, and Talan was only a few minutes away by the underground transit system. In half an hour or so they were all together crowded into Mary-Ann's tiny room.

Mary-Ann looked very unhappy about Sam's being there. Talan's concern was shown only by a slight backward tilt of the ears. Anderson poured out Sam's story as fast as he could speak the words, ending with "I don't know what Steven might do to her. We've got to get her safely off planet as soon a possible."

"So you brought her here?" Talan said.

"We weren't followed. I was careful."

"But not careful enough to notice your companion was carrying a tracer." Talan reached out and gently unhooked the baubles from Samantha's ears. He displayed the two of them side by side in his palm. They didn't quite match.

The facial muscles of an Orian are not nearly so mobile as those of a human being, yet Talan managed to develop an expression usually found only on medieval paintings of saints, one of weary sadness and resignation at the endless folly of humankind. "It did not occur to you to wonder why you were not followed? You are so hopelessly a fool, Bill Anderson," Talan said.

The loose wall panel burst inward with a clatter. A wide-eyed Roothian climbed out of the hole. His priestly blue robes caught on the edge and he tugged frantically at them.

"You musst go," he hissed. "Quick. In the temple are they. Many." He freed himself with a rending of cloth. He took two or three hurried steps toward the door. Talan held his arm.

"They are also here," he said calmly.

"The window," Anderson shouted. He grabbed the chair, but after one ineffectual swing surrendered it to Talan. It took several precious seconds for the Orian to succeed in breaking the tough duraglass pane. The roof-tops looked very far below.

"Can you make it?" Anderson asked.

"Possibly, at risk of a broken leg."

"It's the only chance."

"Yes. And you, Bill Anderson?"

"I'm right behind you. I'll probably bust my stupid neck, but it's better than waiting around for Steven to do it for me."

The Roothian shouldered his way between them and looked down. "Iss too far," he complained. There were roars in the hallway and thunder on Mary-Ann's door.

"The females," Talan fretted.

"They can chance it or not, as they choose. Go," Anderson urged. Talan stood for a moment framed in the empty window, carefully avoiding the jagged edge. Behind them a blaster reduced the door to ashes. Anderson heard the thud of Talan's impact with the roof.

The Roothian was diddling in front of him. "Get going or get out of the way," Anderson yelled. The priest hesitated, then bolted for the door. The blaster roared again, and Mary-Ann screamed. Anderson made a desperate effort to climb out of the window.

"You'll never make it," a rough voice behind him warned. "Don't try. Turn around and move into the room."

He did as he was bid.

Steven's Llevci-Rigan team were in the empty door-way, weapons leveled. Beside them the house mother, her feathers awry, clucked in futile distress like a pouter pigeon among rapacious eagles. The charred remains of the Roothian lay a few paces in front of them.

Mary-Ann huddled in a corner, whimpering with ter-ror. Samantha was sitting calmly on the edge of the bed.

"The Orian is gone," Sam said. "Through the win-dow."

Reasonably certain that Steven wanted him intact, Anderson stood between the intruders and the window. But he bought Talan only a second or two before he was knocked aside. The Rigan strode to the window and stuck his gun through it.

With a cry, Mary-Ann launched herself at the Rigan, spoiling his aim and sending his shot into the sky. He hit her with all the strength of his free hand and raked the roof with blaster fire. In the glare of the resulting flames there was no sign of motion.

Mary-Ann lay in a heap beneath the window, her neck at an awkward angle, a little froth of blood at her lips.

Tradex

Anderson came to lying face down on a cool concrete floor. He'd been there before. He remembered the place. He thought he remembered the place.

He got himself up in stages.

The cage he was in—it was too meager to be properly called a cell—was all featureless concrete, about two and a half meters square and three meters high. A piece of lighting panel had been fixed to the ceiling and it gave off a thin, cold light. A tiny square table against one wall held a metal jug of water. Beneath it was a filthy, stinking bucket.

Near the table an oblong seam in the wall suggested a door, although there were neither hinges nor latches in evidence to confirm the suspicion. He threw his weight against the possible door. It gave not at all.

What had become of Talan?

He hit the panel with all the force he could muster and was rewarded with a muffled metallic clink and an injured shoulder.

If Talan had hurt himself jumping from the window, chances were his situation was no better, probably worse, than Anderson's. If not, he was quick and agile enough to stay ahead of any of Steven's heavies on the rooftops. If they hadn't anticipated the escape route. If no one had got a clear shot at him. If they hadn't surrounded the building. If . . .

Talan was his only hope. He paced his tiny cell: three steps one way, turn, three steps the other, turn. Even if Talan had survived, he wouldn't risk the bloody confrontation he feared on Anderson's behalf. Three steps, turn. If Talan survived. Three steps, turn. If . . .

He leaned against the might-be door and was surprised to have it move away from him, so that he fell into two pairs of waiting arms. All Rigans look about the same. He wasn't sure if he had met this pair before or not. It didn't matter; they weren't interested in social amenities.

They tied his hands together behind his back and hustled him down a long hallway and up long flights of concrete steps into a cool room whose brilliant lighting made his eyes water. But the smear of blues and greens on his left he knew for the new DeLeon painting, and he could make out Steven lounging on his air cushions. Nice of him to take a personal interest in my case, Anderson thought wryly. Samantha was somewhere in the room. He was vaguely aware of her.

Once before, a few hours or maybe days ago, he had been parked like this in the center of the room, waiting for Steven to decide to take notice of him. He had been knocked around somewhat by Steven's uglies, and Steven had pulled his mouth down in distaste over the blood on his carpet.

Steven gave him the same look now, as Anderson stood in bleary-eyed apprehension. Slowly and carefully, he got to his feet, made an appraising tour all the way around, and stopped in front, half a meter away. Anderson could smell the tobacco on his breath.

"You have got tough, haven't you?" Steven said. "Billy boy, you mustn't take too seriously all that Orian garbage about mind over matter. It's a crock." He smiled his wax smile. "I bet you still feel the bruises, eh?"

Anderson nodded stiffly.

"How long do you want it to go on?"

When Anderson didn't answer, Steven continued. "This is a game you can't win. You'd better level with me and trust my charity."

"Like I'd trust a Rigan to mind the butcher shop."

Steven's features hardened. "Tell me about the Merchant Security Force."

"I don't know anything about it."

"You've been working for them."

"I told you, I didn't know that."

"I don't believe you." Steven walked around Anderson some more, studying him up and down. "What are they trying to do?"

"I don't know."

"What did they offer you?"

"A sixty-forty chance at survival. I could go along with them or spend the rest of my life rotting in an Orian prison."

"You lost."

"I know."

"What was the Roothian doing there?"

"I don't know. I never saw him before."

"Who was the Orian? Where did he go?"

"I don't know."

Steven raised his arm as if to backhand his prisoner. The light glittered on those blasted rings and Anderson couldn't take his eyes off them. Then, abruptly, Steven changed his mind.

On a small table near at hand there was a pneumatic hypo with half a cc of clear amber fluid in it. Steven picked it up and nodded to his men. They each got a firm grip on Anderson. The syringe hissed and stung a little as it emptied its contents into his arm.

"I promised you three happy times at my expense, Billy boy," Steven said. "That's two. You get one more for free. Then we'll negotiate the price of the fourth."

"Steven, I can't tell you what I don't know."

Steven put the hypo down carefully. "I've heard some of the hopheads around here say that rystl helps them overcome the trivial little problems of day-to-day living so that they can think more clearly. I don't know about that. You don't seem to be doing too great in that department. Come along, Samantha, let us leave our very dense friend to his dreams."

Obediently Sam rose and followed Steven out. She might have paused as she passed by Anderson. He thought he heard her whisper, "I'm sorry, Bill." He thought he could see her features, strangely disembodied in his deteriorating field of vision, distorted by some inner hurt. But by then the drug was taking hold and he couldn't be sure of anything he thought he heard or saw.

The Rigans manhandled him to the head of the stairs. Before they reached the bottom he was unconscious.

He came out of it embracing his old friend the concrete floor.

All this had happened before, or would happen again, or both. It was like one of those plays where the story line is repeated over and over with different endings. His mother always said you couldn't trust a playwright. She was angry because his sister wanted to be an actress. His sister didn't care. He didn't care, either. Nobody cares. C'mon, Kaz. Here's a whole world full of people who don't give a damn.

He was meandering. He had to stop it. He tried to remember what Talan had taught him about handling that kind of problem. But the memory of Talan was the memory of a ghost, dim and distant, from some other existence. He became sure that Talan was dead.

That was the drug talking. He knew it was the drug. Knowing didn't help.

It was beginning to bother him that he had no idea how long he had been in that cell. There was nothing to differentiate day from night or Wednesday from Friday. He wasn't particularly hungry, so it couldn't have been too long. Or would the rystl account for that? A nameless fear clawed at him.

Reach for something real, something surely known, that was the key. Build on it. Steven was real, perhaps his only reality. Steven wouldn't rest until Anderson answered his questions. And once the questions were answered, the organization would have no more need of Bill Anderson.

Steven didn't know who the Orian was or where. So Talan had escaped the initial pursuit.

Samantha knew who the Orian was. Why hadn't she told Steven? Or had he only dreamed her in his apartment asking him for help? He lay down against his cold friend the concrete floor and slept, seeking Samantha-dreams.

* * *

As soon as she felt reasonably certain that Steven would be occupied for a few hours, Samantha took the underground transit to Owr-Lakh.

It was a crazy chance to take. Everything was against success. If the Oriani had connected her to Steven, and they must have through Talan, she was liable to be arrested the moment she surfaced. If Steven missed her, she'd have to come up with some kind of explanation of what she wanted in the Orian city. And if neither of those things happened, still her chances of finding Talan were vanishingly small.

Talan himself would undoubtedly be off the Com/Com Net, in keeping with the fiction of his death. But Ambassador Meela should be listed, if she was on planet and not out and about being diplomatic somewhere.

There was a link in the transit terminal. It was the only blessed thing there was in the terminal, which was otherwise only a wide spot in the tunnel with a stairway to the surface. Unfortunately, the link spoke only Orian. Sam spoke only English. It was no help at all.

Frustrated, she made her way up the stairs to the surface. All she had wanted from the machine was an address or whatever. She wanted to carry out her mission face to face. Maybe some of Steven's paranoia had worn off, or maybe she just thought she could be more convincing in person.

She found herself blinking in the sunlight in what appeared to be an extended park with some few buildings in it. She wasn't familiar with Owr-Lakh. She had never been there before. Bill had told her something about the city, how it was laid out, but it didn't help much. The occasional pedestrian looked at her curiously. She felt very much out of her element and terribly conspicuous, which turned out to be not all bad, because then she felt she had nothing to lose by asking dumb questions of everyone she met. Eventually she came across an Orian whose curiosity outweighed his natural caution and who explained in halting English how she could find the ambassador's home.

Sam could see a degree of aloofness in the low stone

buildings of Owr-Lakh with their windows tucked up under their brooding eaves. The ambassador's house, almost lost in the growth of its garden, wasn't significantly different from its neighbors.

Once in front of the rough sort of lawn that sloped down toward the walkway, Samantha didn't know how to proceed. Should she march up there to the house and knock at the door, or what? Despite having lived a large fraction of her adult life on Orion, Samantha knew practically nothing about the Oriani.

She was saved from having to decide by the appearance of an Orian female at the door.

Ears pricked with curiosity, the Orian moved down the path through the garden toward Sam. She was a dignified lady, getting on in years, a bit gray at the ear tips and grizzled across the shoulder blades. "Ambassador Meela?" Sam asked.

"Yes."

"My name is Samantha. I have to see Talan."

Meela regarded her gravely. "Surely you know my son is dead."

"I know he's not dead, and I have to talk to him."

"How do you propose to do that?"

"Don't play games with me. I know Talan is alive; I saw him myself not two days ago, and I want to talk to him. It's about Bill Anderson. Please, it's important."

"Why do you suppose Bill Anderson is of importance to my son or to me?"

"You met him on Midway, ambassador, and he has been working with your son. I know what you've been doing in the port, how you're trying to beat Steven Black. I know Bill was helping you. Now he's in trouble, big trouble, and he needs you to help him."

Meela thought it over while Samantha worried. If the ambassador firmly refused to tell her where Talan was, she was stuck. She didn't know what she could do.

"I see," Meela said. "You are well informed, Samantha. Perhaps you should come inside."

Sam followed the ambassador into the house. She got only a fleeting impression of the appointments of an Orian home, one large room divided by draperies and screens, sparsely furnished to give a sense of both privacy and space. Then they were outside again, behind the building, in an open, patiolike space in the plantings, and the object of her pilgrimage was lying curled up, sleeping like a baby in the sun.

She was furious with him that he could look so relaxed under the circumstances. She wanted to go and kick him awake, to make him get up and face the seriousness of what was happening.

Any such action was unnecessary. Talan was up and alert almost immediately.

The Oriani, mother and son, spoke together briefly, and then Sam was alone with Talan, and he was contemplating her presence with slightly cocked head and cool reserve. He said nothing to her, in greeting or otherwise, but simply waited for her to explain what she was doing there, eroding her self-confidence with his silence.

"Steven has Bill Anderson," she said.

"Yes."

"He's killing him a little bit at a time, Talan," she said. She thought she saw the Orian wince. "You have to get him out of there."

"You are unhappy with your handiwork, Samantha?"

If a few well-chosen words could wound, Samantha would have been bleeding. "It's not my fault. I didn't know. I really didn't," she protested.

He didn't answer. "Look, it doesn't matter about blame, does it? Bill needs help." Talan said nothing. "Well, look at it from a practical point of view. If he doesn't get it, sooner or later Steven is going to know everything that Bill knows. What's that going to do to all your fancy plans, eh?"

"Very little. Bill Anderson knows very little."

"Steven thinks different. Damn you, Talan, don't you care? We have to get Bill away from Steven."

"If you know how to do that, I would be interested to hear about it. Otherwise, I do not believe we have a great deal to say to one another."

"I do know," Sam answered.

Ter-Lakh

Anderson woke with his heart pounding, thinking he had heard a noise. That was crazy, because no noises penetrated the thick walls of his cage. But there was a noise, the tiny grating sound of the door opening. They were coming for him again, and he was still muggy-headed from the last time.

Despair overwhelmed him. There was no way out. He couldn't even give in, because he didn't have what Steven wanted. He pushed himself to his feet, surprising himself that he retained enough sense of his own dignity to want not to be found lying on the floor.

But it was not the Rigans who came in—it was a brace of agitated Oriani. A third stayed by the open door, watching the hallway. Confused and frightened by this unexpected turn of events, Anderson backed into a corner.

Seeing his fear, one of them spoke to him gently. "Come, Bill Anderson, we will leave this place." The Orian held out his hand as if asking for the confidence of a child. Anderson couldn't move to accept it.

"The drug is still with him," the second Orian said. "We have no time to lose." He tried to take Anderson's arm. Anderson pulled away. The Orian stopped, baffled. Not knowing how to proceed, the two of them stood there, watching the wide-eyed Terran watching them.

The third man left his post by the door and strode up to Anderson. Grabbing his shoulder, he pulled him roughly out of the corner and motioned the other two to stand one to each side. Stunned by this breach of etiquette, they made no move to comply. "Quickly, now," the third man commanded. "We depend on speed."

Stumbling along between the two, Anderson was hustled into the hallway, down its length opposite to the way he had journeyed with the Rigans, through a door, up some steps, then through another door. They emerged in a dark alley. It was night and the sounds of the busy city roared in Anderson's ears. Nearby, a ground freight vehicle sat with its engine idling, muttering to itself. One of the Oriani jogged around the side and slid into the driver's seat. A hatch in the cargo bay was opened and Anderson was pushed into a black, cramped space between the crates. The other two Oriani followed, closing the hatch between them.

The darkness was absolute. There wasn't room to take a deep breath. Anderson could feel panic rising as he struggled for air.

The engine shifted into a steady, throaty purr.

In a few moments it was idling again and he was urged out among the windburned stones and thorn-plants of the desert's edge. One of the Oriani went to the cab of the vehicle and spoke briefly to the driver. Then the truck turned back toward the glow of the port city and left them standing in a choking cloud of dust.

"We must wait," someone told him, "until they pick up the trail."

To Anderson this seemed an unwise move, and he said so. Despite the Orian's reassurances, he was not all that reassured. They waited anyway, with much swiveling of large ears and murmured conversation. In a few minutes, which seemed a very long time, he was steered, stumbling blindly, down a slope to where a flyer was waiting. Interminable minutes more dragged by until the little machine was airborne. By then even he could hear the drone of another motor. He had an awful feeling that these Oriani were on a suicide mission. The other machine was closing fast.

They skipped along the dune tops at increasing speed, heading for Owr-Lakh. Then, suddenly, they picked up a lot of speed and altitude, and turned eastward.

The flyer was a vehicle peculiar to Orion. It was the

pogo stick of air transportation, and Anderson knew
something about its limitations. To the east lay the En-
Tiree Mountains, a brawny young range whose lowest
passes were maybe 200 meters above the flyer's ceiling.
And that was where they were headed, into a sky-high
fence that ran the whole length of the continent.

The Orian piloting leaned back to hear what his companion was saying.

"They are closing too fast. They will be in range in
about seven minutes."

The flyer's engine whined as it put forth all the power
it was able, and they fled on a beeline toward the black
cardboard mountains silhouetted against the oncoming
gray dawn, leaving an infrared trail a blind man could
follow.

A few bolts of lightning flashed around the mountain-
tops.

The flyer's engine stopped whining and started
screaming. It was hot enough to glow. Their speed
dropped to almost nothing.

Nobody but Anderson seemed to get very excited
about it. The pilot feathered the engine and they began a
long, slow, silent glide through the darkness.

They made a rough, unpowered landing into the scrub
brush on a hilltop on the western flank of some raw giant
of a mountain. Shaken but undamaged, Anderson stumbled out of the wreck and slid and rolled a short distance
down the hillside. His legs were trembling.

One of the Oriani came and asked him how he was
and told him that the pilot was unhurt. Until then he
hadn't given them a thought.

"Where are we?" he asked.

"I am from Owr-Marl. I don't know this region," the
Orian said. "Somewhere near the Ter-Lakh caves, I believe." Thunder interrupted him. When it rolled away, he
continued musingly. "I am a sociologist by profession. I
had thought to come to this oldest of the birthing places
one day to study. I had anticipated other circumstances,
however."

The pilot came sliding down the incline. "There is
shelter among the rocks farther up. I think it best we

move there if you are able, Bill Anderson. There will be rain."

"It never rains on Orion," Anderson said.

The Orian didn't bother to answer. The fat drops hitting Anderson's face were argument enough.

They had just taken refuge in the hollow beneath a sheltering ledge in a darkness deeper than the graying night when a motor became distinguishable over the now nearly constant rumble of thunder: a machine bigger than a flyer. The Oriani exchanged glances.

There was no warning of anyone's approach until a small group stood silhouetted at the entrance of the shelter. Anderson recognized the voice of one of them as they greeted his companions and crowded into the shelter out of the rain.

"Talan. You're alive."

"I believe so," Talan answered with some amusement. He turned to the others. "Our adversaries are nearby and—"

"How did you find us so fast?" Anderson asked.

Oriani did not interrupt each other. Talan's irritation was evident, but it evaporated quickly. Anderson was excused because he wouldn't know better. Humanity was not expected to exhibit the niceties of manners. "In your present condition, Bill Anderson, I think I could track you across the continent by scent alone. However, it was not necessary. The flyer is still detectable to infrared scanning."

Half a dozen people had crowded in behind Talan and there were tail waggings of mirth at Talan's remark.

"Then Steven's men will be able to find us, too," Anderson said.

"Let us hope so," Talan answered. Again tails wagged.

Unwilling to be the butt of any more jokes, Anderson retired to the depths of the shelter, making his way over and among the rocks as best he could in the gloom. His feelings were hurt. All this might be a big laugh to the Oriani, but it seemed damned unfunny to him.

"Bill?"

He was surprised to see Samantha. "How did you get

here? What are you doing here without your Rigan friends?"

"Are you all right?" Samantha sat on a nearby boulder.

"Get the hell out of here and leave me alone."

"Please don't. I'm trying to help."

"You've helped me all I can stand and then some. Go away."

She seemed genuinely distressed. "All right," she said. "But I want to tell you, I didn't know I was being traced to Mary-Ann's."

"Uh-huh. I bet you were so upset you chewed off one whole fingernail."

"What should I have done, joined you in the basement?"

"Christ, no, you bitch. Lick the foot that kicks your ass. What the hell? Keep Samantha healthy. That's all that counts."

In her furious retreat, Samantha jostled Talan against the stone wall as she passed him.

"You are being unfair to one who has been of considerable help to us in this matter, Bill Anderson," Talan said.

"Yeah?"

"She knew the building and was able to get us into it. Without her help, we might never. . ." Talan stopped. He could see that Anderson's whole body was shaking.

"M'row, attend," he called to the healer.

After poking and prodding gently for some time, the healer produced a hypo. Anderson cringed at the feel of it.

"Bodramine to ease the symptoms," the doctor said. "You remember it." She turned to Talan. "He is back on the drug. He does not appear to be seriously injured otherwise, but I would like a Mediscan report."

"How urgent?"

"Moderately."

"We have lost contact with the others. I hesitate to leave this place until we are in touch. On the other hand, it may be necessary to leave very quickly. I cannot give you the skysled."

"Understood."

As the sedative action of the Bodramine took effect, Anderson's insides began to unknot. The rain poured down, and the sound merged with a sort of dream.

It had rained on the desert, a fierce, driven rain that a fish could live in. Water poured down slopes in rivers and filled the wadis that had for long seasons gone begging for a hint of moisture. The rain stopped as suddenly as it began, and the desert steamed like a devil's cauldron. By evening, everything was dry except the deepest troughs between the dunes, where the sun didn't reach.

A day or so later, Talan had taken Anderson out into the desert to show him how the desert bloomed when rain came, part of his unending effort to educate the Terran into an understanding and appreciation of his new world.

Among the sudden growth a small plant had flung itself into life in one of the troughs, as desert plants will do when given a little water. It consisted only of a short stem, two or three spiky little leaves, and one large carmine bud nodding on top. As the light faded into evening, the bud slowly unfurled. A sweet, haunting perfume filled the air.

Anderson had bent to pick the lovely thing and take it home with him. Talan stopped him. "Wait," he said. "Watch."

Short moments before the swift Orian twilight would turn into night, a creature appeared planing on the wind. At first Anderson thought it was a bird, so great was its wing span, but as it came nearer he could see that it was an insect, beating against the breeze now, hovering for a moment on powder-blue, almost translucent wings. Slowly it settled on the waiting flower.

Then it was dark. The insect was gone and the flower already wilting. As Talan guided Anderson's stumbling footsteps through the black, moonless night, he had murmured, mostly to himself, "It is a generous world that has such moments in it."

But that had been a long time ago, lifetimes ago, and maybe it was just a dream, like the sound of the rain beating on the roof of the rocky shelter.

The healer was bending over Anderson, offering some slightly sweet liquid from a canteen. She allowed him only a mouthful, though he wanted liters. Partially screened from view by a fallen rock, Sam slept, her head pillowed on her hands. From a point near the entrance of the shelter, a babble of many Orian voices mingled with the sound of the rain.

"There is no sign of pursuit."

"Have patience."

"It is light. Perhaps Steven Black has decided these are not worth the trouble."

"He cannot afford to think so. His organization is held by fear. If one can defy him and escape retribution, others will be inspired to attempt it. He will come."

"If so, we are ready."

"The weather is against us."

"It is also against Steven Black."

"We have had no communication from the others."

"The storm. It is too early to be concerned."

"I lack your confidence, Talan."

"So you do, Nefis."

After a few more mouthfuls of the doctor's insipid fluid, Anderson drifted back into sleep, luxuriating in the absence of pain—and woke to Samantha's sudden scream and the closer, grating thunder of falling stone.

He realized almost too late that the granite slab that had been their roof was tipping down on him and he scrambled to his knees to hug the mountainside as it fell, cracked, and fell again, confining him to a cramped triangle. The dust stung his nose. Through the dust he could see an occasional dim shape hurrying and he could hear Oriani voices shouting in confusion.

A blaster, a big one, fired, and more rock crashed down. Then there was the sound of many weapons, some distant, some very near.

Abruptly, it was quiet.

His ears throbbed to the ominous silence. Gradually, after some minutes of intense listening, he became aware of the continuing patter of the rain.

He moved enough pieces of broken stone to be able to push his way out of his corner. The place where Sa-

mantha had been sleeping was two meters high in rub-
bled mountain. The front of their erstwhile shelter had
vanished except for some gravel underfoot. A dead
Orian lay there with most of his front burned away and
his fur still smoldering.

Outside, he could see nothing except the wreck of the
flyer down the hill and the restless gray veils of rain rip-
pling over the valleys like the robes of damp spirit folk
marching solemnly to the order of some arcane ritual.

He moved stones from Samantha's rocky bed, seeking her, not finding her, and used them to make a cairn
for the dead Orian. Though he had no idea how the Oriani treated their dead, it seemed a proper thing to do.

A proper thing, and the only thing, and once it was
done, he was at a loss.

He wandered around the slope of the hillside looking
for the others. The rain beat down on him. The sodden
brush and rain-flattened groundcover gave no indication
that anyone had passed that way. He could see no sign of
the skysled that was supposed to be nearby. Eventually
he risked calling, but there was no answer except for a
distant roll of thunder from the storm moving off. He sat
down on a wet boulder to try to evaluate his situation.

The first fact to face: He was alone on the mountain, a
long way from anywhere. He would need food and
water. For the moment, water was no problem. It was
pouring out of the sky and lying here and there on the
rocks in pools. Food might be harder. Such plants as he
had knowledge of were predominantly desert species not
found on the mountain slopes. His chances of catching
one of the bright-eyed little creatures that inhabited the
brushy thickets were virtually nil. He even considered
insects, but they would be every bit as chancy as unknown plants.

With the prospects of a long famine ahead and already
feeling weak, he could think of only one possibility for
survival. He knew that somewhere in this range there
was a catch basin and water treatment plant that supplied the city of Owr-Lakh. Whether or not it was
manned, he didn't know. But even a fully automatic system would need at least periodic checks, and some pro-

visions must have been made for the technicians. Communications, for example.

There was only one hitch in this flash of inspiration. He didn't know exactly where the plant was or even in what direction he should begin to search.

The rain was faltering as he began to climb upward, looking for a vantage point. By the time he reached a high rocky bench free of brush, the sun had burst forth in all its glory, and he felt he was in a planet-wide Turkish bath.

The valleys were filled with mist, and the mountains floated in them. To the south an escarpment rose, sheer, shining, inviolate. To the north the hills fell away, some of them with only treetops like coarse whiskers showing now and again in the rolling fog.

Once he thought he saw in the shifting mists the glint of sunlight on metal. It could have been anything, of course, including his imagination, but at least it gave him a direction.

The going was rough. The terrain varied from outcroppings of bare rock, still wet and slippery, to hillsides covered with small trees and thorny bushes, to stands of mature forest, the first he had seen on Orion, dark and eerie with the mists hanging in shreds among the branches.

He walked a long time, until the sun climbed high into the sky and burned its way to the valley floors. Heat and humidity combined to bring sweat pouring off him, sticking his clothes to his skin and stinging his eyes.

The lower he went, the less open forest there was and the more tough, thorny thickets of man-high brush barred his way. He didn't catch sight of his objective again from these lower hills and had begun to doubt he had ever seen it. He began to doubt his direction also, for he found after some time that he had been unconsciously following the easier going in the wake of some large animal that had broken a trail through the undergrowth.

He was about to abandon the track and seek a tall tree or high hill from which to reorient himself when he realized that there was a streak of blood on the leg of his

pants. Not his blood; he had no open wounds. Therefore, it must be the animal's. There was more blood glis-
tening on a tuft of leaves just ahead. The beast was
bleeding hard.

Thinking that the animal couldn't be far ahead, he listened for it with held breath, but he couldn't hear anything. He began to follow the trail once more, thinking
only of a piece of meat roasting over a fire and not how
he would handle a wounded animal nearly as big as himself with nothing more than a dry stem, hastily broken
from a nearby bush, for a weapon.

He found a place of bruised leaves and bent stems
where the beast had rested and, beyond, branches that
were still swaying when he reached them. He expected
to catch sight of the creature at any time, but it wasn't
until he was at the margin of a small natural meadow that
he spotted the pile of damp fur half-hidden in the foliage.

It lay unmoving, perhaps already dead. Anderson ap-
proached cautiously, acutely aware of the noise he made
doing so. The beast stirred. He raised his club, hoping to
get in one good solid blow before it mustered the
strength to either attack or bolt.

"You are going to kill me, Bill Anderson?" Talan
asked.

A rock fragment had made a deep ugly gash in Talan's
thigh, and he had another cut behind one ear. With water
from a nearby pool and strips of his clothing, Anderson
washed and bound Talan's wounds as best he could.

"I was certain you were dead, Bill Anderson. I could
see nothing other than a pile of stones where you had
been sleeping," Talan said.

"I had time to get out of the way a little."

"There is a water reservoir about three kilometers
away, over the next hill. I was trying to reach it. There
will be food and shelter there, and a Com/Com link."

"I don't think you can make it. You've lost a lot of
blood. You're as weak as a kitten."

"Kitten?"

"The young of a small domestic animal. They look a

lot like—never mind. Can you walk at all? Put your arm over my shoulder and lean on me."

Talan tried hard, but by the time they had limped across the little meadow, he was exhausted and had started to bleed again. He slumped to the ground and sat panting with wilted ears and lolling tongue. Anderson dragged him bodily into the brushy shade of the meadow's edge and leaned him against the bole of a solitary gnarled and battered tree. Then he sat in the shadow himself and wiped the sweat out of his eyes.

Talan's ears came erect briefly, and his nostrils dilated. "There is a hunter nearby, following our trail," he said.

"A hunter? Someone hunts on Orion?"

Talan thought about it for a while. "A predatory animal," he explained.

"Dangerous?"

"Yes. I think it is confused by your scent, but it is coming."

"How big is it?"

"Thirty to thirty-five kilos."

"Good Lord. How can we handle an animal that size?"

"The urah is an efficient killer, but a cautious one. It will most probably circle around until dusk before attacking. If it attacks at all. It may be sufficiently worried by your presence to seek its meal elsewhere."

There was nothing to do but wait and hope. Anderson used part of the time to worry a large knot of root from an upturned tree, which made a substantial club. But it seemed very inadequate.

"Can you get up the tree?" he suggested to Talan at one point.

"Not with only one useful leg," Talan answered. He displayed the nails of his hands, clipped short and blunt, level with the ends of his fingers. "There may just be something to be said for the primitive condition."

"This is a hell of a time to think of it."

"You could climb the tree, Bill Anderson."

"I'm not much of a climber."

Talan turned his yellow eyes on the Terran, reading,

Anderson suspected, more into the statement than he had meant by it. He went on looking for a couple of handy-sized rocks.

Either it was desperately hungry or the urah knew nothing of what sort of behavior was expected from it, for the sun was still high when it suddenly burst out of the underbrush, a hurtling ball of tawny fur heading straight for Talan.

Anderson's rock deflected it only slightly, so that instead of its charge bringing its fangs slashing against Talan's neck as it passed, it collided with the Orian, knocking him on his back.

Talan hugged the shaggy head tightly to him, sinking his teeth into an ear to keep the doglike fangs turned away and, with his good leg, brought the powerful and unclipped hind claws up to rake at the beast's belly. By the time Anderson could get a clear blow at its head, Talan had it disemboweled.

When Anderson pushed the still-threshing carcass off the Orian, he got a good look at the long tear in its abdomen through which its bloody entrails protruded. "Remind me never to wrestle with you," he said.

"I will," Talan answered in a soft, breathless voice, and then he passed out.

Using the urah's tough gut for cord, Anderson began constructing a crude version of a travois from some straight clean deadfall and the limber branches of some of the shrubbery. He wasn't too efficient at it. His hands had started to shake again.

He chewed at bits of the animal's liver while he worked. It was warm and bloody and gristly under the teeth, but it was the only part of the stringy carcass he could bite.

Night was near before Talan roused. He looked dubiously at Anderson's handiwork. "You cannot pull it very far, Bill Anderson. You are weak yourself."

"We can't stay here. Who knows how many other hungry forest folk are hanging around?"

"You do not see well at night."

"Well enough."

"I cannot permit it. You must go to the reservoir and send help back."

"In your condition," Anderson pointed out, "I could lay you out with a rock. But it would be much easier if you could hang on."

Talan finally bowed to the need, but he would not accept the piece of urah liver he was offered.

"My people do not eat meat," he said with finality.

"Is that so? You've got a carnivore's teeth if I ever saw any."

Talan looked hurt and embarrassed. There was a long pause before he answered. "Be that as it may, I cannot."

"You've got to get some kind of food into you. Look, it's not as if the animal wasn't dead already. We had to kill it. Why let it go to waste?"

"No." He would argue the matter no further.

Progress was slow. The legs of the travois caught in every exposed root and every obstructing little bush. They stuck between trees. Anderson had to stop often to rest and to allow bouts of shaking to pass. In the darkness he blundered into holes and into thorn bushes, stumbled on rocks, and bogged down in a mud puddle left by a drying rain pool. Every cough and grunt in the darkness, every rustle of leaves, struck panic into his heart. Talan slipped in and out of consciousness and, when unconscious, tended to fall off his rough vehicle.

Dawn found them only at the rocky crest of the hill. Below, the waters of the artificial lake gleamed dully in the gathering light, looking very near until one saw the buildings and realized the scale.

"We're not going to make it," Anderson said, not knowing whether Talan was awake or not.

"We will. It is, as the English idiom says, downhill all the way..."

What Talan might have said after that, Anderson never knew. He had sunk down onto the stone as if it were the softest of feather beds and slept.

He roused to the sun burning his back, and Talan's insistent nudging. "Let us continue, Bill Anderson," Talan said. "I will walk awhile."

The Orian managed perhaps a hundred meters down

the slope before collapsing with a muffled groan. Anderson rolled him back onto the travois and began again to tug his burden along, a few centimeters at a time, too numb to consider the futility of it, too numb to do anything but tug and rest, tug and rest, until at some distant time, he found himself up against the wall of a building and was unable to think how to continue.

He had no real recollection of getting Talan inside, dressing his leg, and getting some food and fluid into him, along with an antibiotic, dosage by guess and prayer. He found a small cache of minor tranquilizers among the supplies in the first-aid kit and swallowed a number of them along with a generous liter of cool, marvelously pure, refreshing water in an attempt to relieve his own discomfort. His next clear memory was of another dawn, of an aching body and a sense of something wrong.

The tranquilizers hadn't been terribly effective. He might have been nailed into his bed of hay, so painful was the thought of leaving it. His muscles were cramping and his gut hurt. But some small worry in the back of his mind wouldn't let him stay put. Several frowning minutes passed before he could pin the feeling down.

It was quiet.

The station should have been full of motors and pumps, agitators, aerators, and what have you, but there was no sound of machinery. He dragged himself out of the bed and touched a lighting panel. Nothing happened.

Part of the living quarters had been set aside to serve as an office. In it, the Com/Com link sat, all its telltales dark. The dials and gauges of the process monitor that occupied most of one wall stared blankly back at him.

In the bedroom Anderson found Talan struggling into a sitting position on the edge of his box. The Orian gave Anderson a bleakly questioning look.

"Steven has been here ahead of us," Anderson said. "There's no power. We've got to find a way to get out of here before he decides to come back."

"It's reasonable to suppose Steven Black has closed all possible exits. However, if this place were being watched, we would be already dead. I think we are safe enough for the moment. I am more concerned for the time being with the fate of the others."

"I didn't see anyone else, except one dead Orian, back on the mountain."

"Nefis. He lacked confidence, and rightly so. I have consistently underestimated the speed and ferocity with which Steven Black moves when he is prodded."

Anderson sat down beside Talan. "Okay," he said. "Now will you tell me what's going on? I've been dragged halfway around the planet without so much as if you please, dumped on a mountainside, shot at, attacked by wild animals, and generally treated less than nicely, and I think I've earned an explanation."

Talan's ears flattened, giving him a wounded look. "If I knew what was going on, Bill Anderson, I would be delighted to tell you. At the moment, all I can convey is what was planned."

"Okay, what?"

"It was intended that you should be followed in your flight from Space Central."

"That I figured out for myself."

"The pursuing skysled, though faster, would be less maneuverable than a flyer. With the original course set for Owr-Lakh, the pursuers would report to their base and then attempt to overtake and bring down the flyer.

"With the sudden course change, it would overshoot the turn. By the time it recovered, determined the new direction, and reported that, its reinforcements should have been en route to Owr-Lakh. It was planned that they would be intercepted in the desert.

"The original pursuer we expected to be able to force down near the mountains, which we did. It was thought that in this way we would have in hand a significant fraction of Steven Black's port-based forces."

"So, what happened?"

"I cannot say. I believe the reinforcements crossed the mountains south of our position, flew north in the shadow of the primary range, and attacked us from the rear. Certainly we had no indication of their presence until a few seconds before the attack. I would not have believed they would attempt such a maneuver in the storm. How they knew to do so, I do not know."

"Let me take a guess. How much of your plan did Samantha know?"

"That is not the answer, Bill Anderson."

"Oh, yes, it is. I'd bet money on it."

Talan looked at Anderson as if he couldn't fathom the meaning of what had been said. "Does it matter?" he asked.

In some way it did. Sure knowledge of Samantha's betrayal seemed to Anderson to be important. It was like picking at a scab, this wanting to know how stupid he had really been, to plumb the depths of his foolishness.

But he didn't try to explain all that to Talan. "Besides which," he said, "you don't realize how well Steven knows you. He's made a thorough study. He knows you wouldn't risk a fight in the city. I would say you got off lucky."

"Lucky?" Talan actually winced. "I suppose so. A poor thing to depend on, luck."

"Well, you're sure as hell no kind of field marshal."

"This is true," Talan agreed. "I am a diplomat by training. I find this work as difficult as it is unpleasant." He struggled to his feet. "Have you looked at the link? What's wrong with it?"

"No power."

"Yes, you said that, didn't you?" Talan swayed slightly.

"Get back into bed. You're not going anywhere for a while. I'll see what I can do."

For once the Orian didn't argue, but settled back on the hay. "There is little time," he said.

Later, Talan's uneven gait brought him to the office where Anderson was working over the Com/Com link. He sat down gingerly and watched. "I had no idea you were acquainted with things electrical."

"My mother always wanted me to be an engineer. Anyway, this is pretty crude. I've swiped batteries from every piece of equipment in the place that had any to offer. I think we've got enough voltage here. But at best, thirty seconds of operation time."

Talan took over the board. "Code is more efficient than voice," Anderson reminded him.

"Yes," he said. After a tiny hesitation, he flipped the link on. A telltale glowed orange, warning of low power levels. Code rattled out from under Talan's fingers. The telltale turned to red and faded, and the hum of the machine faded with it. Talan glared at the useless board as if in furious frustration. But when he spoke, his words were calm and collected.

"Now we must move. No doubt Steven Black has locators monitoring communications. He will be here shortly. It would be better if we were elsewhere when he arrives."

Anderson shook his head. "Neither of us is in any shape to travel. We'd be sitting ducks. I think we'll have to wait and hope rescue arrives before Steven does."

"There is no chance of it. We cannot even know how much of the message got through."

"You got a better idea?"

"Yes."

"Well?"

"A few meters of rock will shield us nicely from scanners. These hills are predominantly limestone formations, riddled with caves. One entrance to a chain of them is about a half kilometer farther up the mountainside. We can take refuge there and be comparatively safe."

"If we get that far."

"Yes, if we do."

"And if Steven doesn't know all about these caves. There isn't a lot he doesn't know about."

"I doubt he knows them as well as the people who have for a thousand generations been born in them. Furthermore, I doubt Steven Black himself is in the field. He would not risk it. And his minions are not noted for either their intelligence or their comprehensive knowledge."

Some time later Anderson thought that perhaps he should have been offended, but he didn't think of it at the time. "I don't fancy being trapped in a hole in the ground," he said.

"Perhaps you fancy being dead," Talan answered coldly. "The longer we argue here, the greater the danger."

There was no arguing with that. Assured by Talan that there was water where they were going, Anderson gathered up a small supply of food, some antibiotics, and what tablets remained of the tranquilizer that had been doing an inadequate job of keeping him from shaking himself to pieces, and they left the building and started to make their painful way up the hill. They had succeeded in skirting an intervening corner of the reservoir and started the more difficult climb along a faint trail up the mountainside before the flyer first appeared, hovering distantly against the sky.

Still extremely weak, Talan was leaning against the trunk of a stunted tree that had somehow managed to anchor itself in the rock. "We are discovered," he said breathlessly.

"I noticed."

"The entrance is directly ahead. If you hurry, you can reach it before the flyer comes."

"And spend the rest of a short life lost in a mess of caves? No, thanks. Come on. Give me your hand."

They struggled up another few feet.

"Jump!" Talan shouted suddenly.

Anderson dived behind a boulder, and Talan vanished to the other side of the path seconds before the very ground they had been standing on was blasted into rubble. The flyer's engine whined in protest as it pulled up tightly against the face of the mountain.

Anderson yanked Talan to his feet. "Come on. Before he gets turned around to make another pass."

During the flyer's second pass, they both were sprayed with dirt and rock.

"You all right?" Anderson asked.

"Some bruises only. Bear a little to your left."

They reached an opening among a tumble of fallen boulders with the sound of the flyer close behind. Then

Talan was urging Anderson deeper into the cool darkness of the cave.

Behind them, a few thousand tons of rock crashed down, sealing off the entrance.

"Now what?" Anderson asked of the darkness.

"Now I rest," Talan said, and that was all he said for some time.

The darkness was complete. Afraid to move, Anderson settled for counting the echoing drops of water falling somewhere inside. Somewhat past a thousand, he fell asleep.

When he woke, the water was still falling and he was aware of Talan beside him.

"What are you thinking, Bill Anderson?"

"I'll be damned."

The silence was a continuing question.

"That's some question for a time like this." The darkness waited, patiently. "I'm thinking it must be my fate to be buried under some bloody mountain."

"I did not take you for a believer in fate."

"Remind me someday to ask you what in hell you do take me for."

"I will. Come now. Let us make our way to the lower region. When the others come for us, they will look first there."

"I can't see a thing."

"I can. I will guide you."

Anderson felt his way along, one hand on the cool damp wall of stone, the other clutching the end of Talan's tail as he limped ahead. The Orian obviously knew where he was going. They squeezed through passages scarcely wide enough to admit them and walked unseen paths through echoing empty spaces, going mainly downhill, and finally came to a place where the darkness was relieved slightly by an eerie glow.

"A lichen produces the phosphorescence," Talan explained. "My people call it star spawn."

They stopped to rest by an underground pool. "Talan," Anderson began. "What do your people do here? Why would they come here at all? There's nothing here."

"We do what needs doing. It is nothing that can concern you." His tone did not invite a continuation of this line of inquiry. It puzzled Anderson. A born teacher, Talan had never refused to answer or even evaded a question before.

They left the glowing lichens and entered a narrow defile that showed a point of light at its end. It opened out on a large cavern. From an opening in the roof some twenty meters above, a shaft of sunlight fell, an almost tangible thing. Irregular colonnades of rough, strange beauty had been constructed over the ages by lime-laden water. Some of the columns, after the slow crafting of millennia, were still unfinished. Talan leaned against one of them, resting his injured leg.

"This is as far as we can go," he said.

"So what do we do now?"

"Await assistance. It will come, sooner or later."

"Great. What's that supposed to mean?"

"Sooner, if our message was received; later, if not."

"They'll never find us here."

"They will."

"I'd like to know how. Unless there's another opening that goes someplace, we're trapped here."

"The other openings lead deeper under the mountain. The passages have many branches and turnings, but no exit. Please do not attempt an exploration. If lost, you might not be found for some time." Talan's voice lacked its usual timbre, and he seemed to be wilting.

"I think you better lie down for a while. You don't look too good."

Anderson pillowed Talan's head on the remains of his shirt against the foot of one of the columns. For a while then he was content to lean back against the stone wall and let his fingers idly trace the smooth grooves in it while he watched the Orian sleep. The tranquilizers might have had something to do with that.

The grooves seemed too regular to be natural. Anderson turned around and backed away from the wall to get a look at them, stumbling over a stone in the process and sending it clattering across the floor.

The grooves marched across the wall in a long line like ancient runes.

Anderson became aware of Talan's yellow eyes on him, following his train of thought. "This looks like some sort of writing," Anderson said.

"Yes, it is." The Orian closed his eyes as if to return to sleep.

"I don't know the language."

"It is very old and long dead," he murmured sleepily.

"Can you read it?"

"Yes." Impatience gave the word a tiny edge.

"What does it say?"

Talan's eyes opened again, partially. The nictitating membrane pulled across them made the Orian's expression distant, as if the man inhabited another space entirely. "It pertains to certain laws of an archaic society. I will sleep now."

Anderson was also tired, but too strung out to sleep. A nervous edginess, anticipated but delayed by the demands of recent events, now manifested itself. With nothing more than Talan's slow even breaths to keep him company, he paced among the fantastic columns, coming back repeatedly to the long line of hand-high characters carved by an ancient, forgotten artisan. In places, a corrosion of lime had blurred some of the letters, but most of the lines were clean and fresh-looking. One could almost hear the ring of the chisel, as if the craftsman still labored in these echoing, empty spaces. What inspired a society to record its canons in such a place?

He heard a sound, or thought he did: a tiny cry like an animal in pain. It came from the direction of a low-roofed passage where the pillars crowded into an almost impassable fence. He went to the mouth of the passage and listened.

He heard the distant wailing, forlorn and hurting.

He wiggled his way among the limestone pillars, pausing between movements to listen. Remembering Talan's warning, he would not have entered the passage, except that the cry came again, definitely the voice of some small thing suffering.

Bent almost double and feeling his way along, he followed the sound. The passage changed direction and the stygian blackness was relieved slightly by the glow of a growth of star spawn that grew more abundant as he proceeded until he entered a chamber whose roof and walls were almost covered with the phosphorescence.

A rough bench had been carved out of one wall by some rude tool. About a meter from the floor and something less than that wide, it was occupied by a listless female Orian who panted with tongue hanging.

Staggering around on the floor on bowed and shaking legs were six newborn kittens, still wet, blind, aided on their head-bobbing search for their mother by nothing other than instinct and determination. One little fellow had run into the wall near where Anderson stood. Unable to go forward and having no concept of reverse, the baby set up a fearful howling that seemed impossible to issue from such small, weak lungs.

Anderson called to the mother. "Are you all right? Can I do anything to help?"

She snarled at him like a lioness at bay, ears flat back, fangs exposed. He was so startled that he backed up a few paces and nearly fell over the stalled baby. He picked it up to keep from stepping on it.

Uncomprehending, he tried again. "What's wrong? Do you need help?"

Eyes aflame, she gnashed her teeth. Still growling, she slid down off her perch and started toward him. It didn't seem to Anderson that he could back up nearly fast enough to keep the distance between them. It didn't seem as if he would be able to turn around and flee forward either. His startlement had him pinned facing her.

The female stopped and squatted down near a baby that had given up the struggle to find her and had collapsed into a tiny whimpering fur ball. She considered it a moment, ran a hand over its damp fur, picked it up and held it close to her until its crying was stilled, then, to Anderson's great horror, bent down and bit into the wet thing's neck and gave it a shake. The baby's death scream was cut off half done. Anderson's own scream of protest died in his throat. The roaring of blood in his ears almost drowned out the crunching snap of small bones breaking and the sound of cartilage being crushed under sharp teeth as the mother began methodically to eat her own child. She had forgotten all about Anderson, if, in fact, she'd ever really been aware of him.

Anderson backed out of the chamber on rubbery legs and hurried down the passage as fast as he was able. He still had the baby in his arms.

He took a wrong turn somewhere and came within a step of falling into a barely visible underground pool. He squatted down beside the water to catch his breath and try to get his bearings, stroking the baby's soft, damp fur and talking to him as much to calm himself as to reassure the new Orian. The baby nuzzled his bare arm, took an experimental bite, and, finding it not to his liking, began to whimper. Anderson offered him a finger dampened in the pool. The baby sucked madly at it, but it was unsatisfying.

Anderson could only think that Talan would know better than he what ailed the mother and what to do for the helpless, untended kittens before she killed them all. He could feel his gorge rise at the thought of it, but he really didn't have time to be sick. A sense of urgency on behalf of the small ones drove him. Forcing calm on himself as Talan had taught him to do, he began a deliberate search for the passage that would take him back to the cavern where Talan slept. Motion frightened the baby, and nothing would dissuade him from clinging tooth and nail to Anderson's bare chest.

Whatever had possessed the woman to come to this place to bear her young, she was as much trapped as Talan and Anderson were. She had to have help, whether she wanted it or not.

As much by dumb luck as good management, Anderson found his way back to the pillared cavern.

Talan was awake, on his feet, about to start looking for Anderson.

"There's a woman back there," Anderson said breathlessly, "with new babies. There's something wrong. I don't know what. She wouldn't tell me. I think she's gone crazy or something. She's killing them, Talan. She's killing the babies. We've got to do something, for God's sake. They need help."

He was as unprepared for Talan's reaction as he had been for the mother's. He had never seen Talan angry, or known him to be capable of anger. The Orian's ears flattened tight to his head. The fur on his neck stood upright and his tail lashed his flanks. His eyes grew narrow and hard, and Anderson could see a startling number of teeth.

"Give me the infant." Talan's words were quick-frozen icicles.

Stunned, Anderson just stood there with his jaw hanging and the squirming baby in his arms.

"Give me the infant," Talan said again, advancing on him.

"Now, wait a minute. What's the matter with you? Are you listening? They need help. What's the matter, for Christ's sake? I'm trying to tell you, the mother is sick, maybe mad. The babies, and the mother, too—they need help."

Talan took the baby out of Anderson's arms none too gently by the scruff of the neck. The little thing hung limply and squalled. Anderson grabbed Talan's arm. "What are you going to do with him?"

It still hadn't sunk into Anderson's thick head that his friend was a savage animal. Talan's free hand lashed out in a blow that sent Anderson sprawling and left long welts across his neck and shoulder. If those claws had been long and sharp...Anderson didn't want to think about it.

There comes a point at which the mind will accept no more shocks.

Talan disappeared with the baby into the blackness of the passageway. The baby's cries grew fainter and fainter until Anderson could no longer hear them.

It had to be one of those nightmares when all the natural laws break down and the solid earth shifts beneath your feet and the people you have known and loved turn out to be demons in disguise.

Shifting shadows in the beam of sunlight caused Anderson to look up at the opening in the roof of the cavern. It was ringed with Orian faces looking down. For the first time he was aware that a streak of cruelty marked those impassive features.

Talan returned without the baby.

Owr-Marl

Dawn was about to break over Owr-Marl. Somewhere a bird whistled a few preparatory notes, high-pitched and melodic.

In a house on a low ridge near the edge of the city, Anderson rose from his hay bed and made his way between the other sleepers, who were curled into furry crescents, their tails draped over their flanks. He moved carefully, so he would not disturb them.

Those youngsters were a tolerable presence, less dreadful than their elders. If Talan was going to keep him imprisoned on Orion, these jailors were acceptable company, filling the house with the busy good humor of youth. The four were students at the academy, and they had adopted Anderson as a sort of household pet, called him "Old Frog"—or the Orian equivalent, which identified a somewhat larger amphibian and had no ethnic connotations—in view of his furless condition, and took their role as wardens not too seriously.

He went out into the garden. The sky was flushed orange all the way to the zenith. The bird started up in earnest. Near his feet, a tiny rustle announced one of the half-tame small creatures who inhabited the garden. It made a cautious inspection to see if he had anything for it, then vanished back among the shadows and the grasses. When Anderson had first arrived on the scene, the bright-eyed little beasts had been terrified of him and wouldn't come anywhere near. Now they accepted him as a part of the household and an excellent source of tidbits, a situation that disturbed the neighbor across the

hedge who thought that feeding the animals made them
dependent and so was not in their best interests. Anderson didn't care much what the neighbor thought. He was
badly in need of a friend.

As silently as one of the little animals, Ayyah came
into the garden.

Ayyah was his favorite among the students. She had
studied Terran culture in the course of her work, and
used him to test out her theories. She was a small, big-
eyed, serious girl with silvery fur and tufted ears.

Anderson thought she might be annoyed with him because he had neglected his household chores, but she
had something else on her mind. Together, they watched
the first sunlight spill down the brooding mountain that
cradled Owr-Marl in its lap and blaze off the windows of
the Academy of the Arts, which crowned the hill across
the valley. The valley was green then, in the winter of
that hemisphere. After the long, blustery, storm-ridden
fall, winter had a peacefulness of more moderate temperatures and occasional gentle rains.

A pedestrian was making his way up the path from the
valley.

"You did not sleep well, Bill Anderson?" Ayyah
asked.

"I was dreaming."

"Yes. Not pleasant dreams, I think. Several times I
heard you cry out." She moved uneasily beside him.
"You are unhappy in this house?"

"No, quite the contrary. If I'm to be kept prisoner on
this planet, I'm glad this is the place. I enjoy you kids'
company."

"We are not children. None of us is more than three
seasons away from maturity." Ayyah studied the grass at
her feet as if she had never seen it before. Imminent
adulthood seemed not to please her.

"Talan comes," she said.

"I don't want to see him."

"Speak to him, Bill Anderson. It will cost you nothing." She looked away. The pedestrian was near enough
to recognize. He had a carryall slung over one shoulder

and walked easily, with no sign of the injury to his leg. He looked up and saw Anderson looking down at him.

"I don't want to have anything to do with him."

Ayyah left him, making it plain that nothing would be forced—except his presence on the planet which was deemed necessary by his erstwhile friend.

Anderson could have left before Talan had climbed the rest of the way up the hill, but he didn't. He didn't bother to try to figure out why not.

Talan came into the garden and greeted him. Anderson turned away, which was about as insulting as anyone could get on Orion without actually hitting somebody. If he was offended, Talan didn't let on, but simply waited for Anderson to acknowledge his presence. Oriani were patient people. Talan would wait all day if need be.

"Go away," Anderson said.

"You are well, Bill Anderson?"

"I'd be a damned sight better if you'd leave me alone."

"Your work at the academy pleases you?"

Actually, it did, although Anderson wasn't about to admit it to Talan. Working with languages was what he did well. Most of the time the garbled output of the computers made him sure that machine translation would never be accomplished, but every once in a while a few phrases came out straight and it looked as if he might just possibly be making progress. Besides which, he could mind his own business, do his own thing, and have very little contact with any Orian, and that suited him just fine.

"Look," he said. "You obviously have something on your mind. Why don't you just spit it out and get it over with?"

"I have a letter for you. It arrived on a freighter from Gnatha yesterday morning. I fear it has been a long time en route." Talan dug in his sack and presented a battered envelope that looked as if it had been all around the galaxy as it was transferred from ship to ship until it made its way to Orion. Anderson took it and turned it over in his hands. He didn't recognize the handwriting.

"Why would one use such a primitive means of communication?" Talan asked. He seemed genuinely curious.

"It's cheap and it's private," Anderson said.

"I see." The Orian turned away, looking out over the valley. "I thought you might be interested to know that the Terran delegation got off planet without incident. It would appear Steven Black could not muster the resources he needed to effect a kidnapping. But I do not doubt you were right, that he had it in mind."

"Oh, hooray. So you've got your Interplanetary Community?"

"Not so easily, I think. There will be much negotiation yet to come. Politics does not move swiftly on Earth. There are too many rival factions each concerned about its own power. We have planted a few seeds for later germination, which is as much as we could have hoped." If Anderson didn't know better, he would have said that Talan sighed before he continued. "The Merchant Security Force has fared better. I think Earth will soon join the other members, and perhaps we will be able to clear the pirates from the traffic lanes in that region. It is progress of a sort. Any extraplanetary dealings Earth has are bound to make it more receptive to the concept of the Community."

"I want to go home, Talan."

"I'm sorry, you cannot."

"That was the deal we made. I had your promise."

"You are still angry?"

"I'm angry. I'm appalled. I'm horrified. I'm disgusted. I want to go home, and I'm damned disappointed that you don't keep your promises."

"I had at no time envisioned this eventuality, Bill Anderson. I am certain others of your race would be no less appalled and horrified than you are. I fear your people would recoil from us and all that I stand for, regardless of its value. I must do everything I can to prevent this from happening while delicate negotiations are proceeding. Surely you can understand that."

"I'm not so sure it would be such a damned bad thing."

"I believe you. This is exactly the problem."

"So what do you want from me?"

"I had hoped... Time heals many wounds."

"It ain't going to heal this one. So get the hell out of my life, will you?"

"As you wish."

Talan left the garden and went into the house, spent some time with the youngsters, and then went the way he had come, walking down the mountainside. He had made the grand gesture and been rejected. Anderson didn't expect to see him again.

He waited to open the letter until Talan was gone. It was from Barbara, of all people, dated only ten months before.

Dear Bill:

I wanted to tell you once more what a wonderful time I had on Orion because you were there. And I want to tell you something else, though I don't know how you will take it. I'm pregnant. Don't panic. I don't expect you to come rushing to my side. I don't want that. I only wanted you to know, I've just returned from the doctor's, and our daughter will be born early in April, TSD, probably before you get this letter. She will be born on Earth, or Harvey will live to regret it. Harvey is bemused but cooperative. We will give her a good life, I promise you. I'm very, very happy. Thank you, Bill.

Love,
Barbara

Anderson sat down on the brow of the hill where the garden ended, gazed out over the valley, and tried to imagine himself as a father. He kept remembering his own father, a strong, intelligent, battered man who would do anything to see that his precious children got out of the slums, and who had hanged himself in his cell rather than go to jail when he was arrested for bribing the registrar of a blue-ribbon school to accept his youngest son, whose only notable value was a talent for languages.

Anderson was not the man his father had been. It was just as well, he tried to persuade himself, that his daughter would have Harvey to look after her. Anderson had understood from Barbara that they had money and property, and that Harvey worked only to entertain himself. The baby would be well cared for.

He wished he could see her just once.

The following day, Ayyah got him out of bed early and took him once again into the garden. She said there was something she had to do.

"I have delayed too long already and my father grows impatient with me. But it is not an easy task he has given me. How shall I begin?"

"What's your father got to do with anything?"

"Listen to me." That was a bit startling. How did Ayyah come to see herself in the role of teacher? Anderson wasn't at all sure he wanted to be lectured by a mere slip of a girl. Ayyah gave him no chance to argue.

"It is not by accident," she said, "that you found lodging in this house. It was not by mere chance that you were invited to work at the academy. This was arranged by my father in the hope that it might make your presence in our midst more tolerable to you."

"What's your father to me, or I to him, that he'd go to all that trouble?"

"A friend. My father is Talan. He considers you his friend. In spite of the time you have spent among us, I think you do not yet appreciate what that means to an Orian. It is a lifelong commitment, Bill Anderson, not lightly made."

"Are you my friend, Ayyah?"

"No," she said bluntly. "I am my father's daughter."

A long minute of strained silence stretched between them before he could bring himself to speak. "Talan and I parted company on less than friendly terms," he said carefully.

Ayyah regarded him quizzically, as if his statement

had no bearing on the point at issue. Behind him Anderson could hear the sounds of the waking household.

"If you intended to apologize for your father," he said, "I don't want to hear it. There's nothing you can say that will make me feel any different."

Dismayed, Ayyah's gaze turned down to the grass.

"Look," he said. "I don't hold your father against you. Nobody chooses his parents."

Once more silence strained to bridge the growing distance between them. Ayyah leaned against a small tree and looked off into an empty distance. In words muffled by some suppressed emotion Anderson did not understand, she said, "I understand even on Earth friendship implies a certain obligation."

"I guess it does."

"Oblige my parent, Bill Anderson. Take a short journey with me this day. It need not cost you more than two hours of your time."

"Well, if you put it that way."

"I have put it that way."

"All right, damn it. Tell me where we're going and when you want to leave."

"Where we are going," Ayyah said coolly, "you will learn soon enough. We will leave at once. I have asked Lawr to accompany us. He has agreed, provided you have no objection."

"Why should I object?"

"Why indeed?" Ayyah asked.

"No objection intended, but why do you want him along?" Anderson asked, thinking the answer might give him some clue to what was going on.

"We are mated," Ayyah said, and would explain no further.

They left the flyer on a ledge near the base of the mountain. Though the distance to be traveled on foot was not long, the path was steep and rocky. Anderson was panting by the time they stopped to rest on a reasonably level place. There a few wind-battered trees maintained a precarious roothold in a skiff of soil lodged among the rocks and offered meager shelter from the sun. Even in the dead of winter, Omnicron Orionis was more than warm enough for him.

There had been little conversation en route, and most of that had been short, cryptic phrases between the young people. Then Ayyah addressed herself to Anderson. "We have arrived," she said.

"Arrived where?" He had grown more than a little annoyed by the whole effort. He supported himself by holding a rough, crooked, head-high branch, and tried to catch his breath.

"Come," Ayyah said, taking Anderson's hand in her own and leading him along a barely discernible path among the gnarled and stunted trees. They stopped before a pair of columns rough hewn from stone and capped with a tremendous flat rock, standing before an excavation into the mountainside.

"This is Ter-Marl," Lawr said. "You will find some such place, either natural or constructed, near every center of population on Orion."

Although the excavation had been left utterly unadorned by any sign or symbol of its makers, it gave the impression of great age. The stones looked worn, as if perhaps the passage of time itself had abraded the surface, giving a foothold to mosses and vines that hung down in long loops and bloomed tiny purple flowers among the sparse leaves.

Still holding his hand, Ayyah conducted Anderson through the opening that in a short distance opened out into a chamber of some extent with a roof so low that, though he was in no danger of bumping his head, he felt as if he needed to bend down to avoid striking it. All the light there was came in through the entrance and it took a few moments before he was able to make out several square openings in the far wall of the chamber, gaping like the mouths of so many mine shafts. Along the wall to his left ran a long line of characters that looked familiar.

"I've seen those before," he told the girl.

"In Ter-Lakh," she said. "The language is dead; it has been forgotten, all but this. It says: 'This is the law, and you shall have no other; only the strong shall survive, one to every birthing. Who shall fail this convenant shall die, with her family, an agent of war, famine, and disease, an enemy of the people.'"

"My God," Anderson said.

"Come," Lawr demanded and, giving him no time to ponder the meaning of it all, urged him into one of the tunnels. It was black but short, and a growth of star spawn glowed at the other end. They entered a room such as he had seen at Ter-Lakh, with a rough stone bench carved out of one side. This one was, thankfully, uninhabited.

"This is where our children are born," Ayyah said. She was becoming agitated and could hardly keep still.

Lawr's words came to him as from a distance. "Our ancestors were cave dwellers. We have never quite been able to free ourselves from the caves. As some animals may spend their whole lives on land yet must return to the sea to breed, so we must return to these places to bear our young. In spite of our pretensions to high civilization, we can do nothing but obey the dictates of our nature." The boy's words were bitter and without hope.

It was incredible, yet Anderson could not doubt those two earnest young Oriani watching carefully for his reaction.

"What about the writing out there, the law?" he asked.

Ayyah shuddered. "You must understand," Lawr said. "Our children are born five or six at a time. Our world is not a generous one. It is hot, dry, and mineral poor. We have the potential to breed ourselves out of existence in one generation. To destroy some arbitrarily gives no regard to future generations. Reducing the number of birthings diminishes the gene pool, with unknown consequences. We are a race that weakens easily; this geneticists surely know. We do what we must do."

"Which includes killing unwanted children. Is that what you're trying to tell me?"

Ayyah had been padding restlessly about the small room. She continued to pace as she spoke. "After a birthing, the mother waits up on this ledge until she can be sure which of the infants is the strongest and most fit to survive. She destroys the others."

"Good God."

"She is near madness at this point, blindly following her instincts, more beast than person." Ayyah took Anderson's hand and held it between her own. Her eyes begged for his understanding. "It is our way. We have no other."

Anderson jerked away from her and got a little distance between them. He felt dirtied by being there with them, contaminated with the horror of it. The runes in the outer chamber were carved so deeply into the stone that they might outlast the ages.

Until the day in Ter-Lakh, he had believed the Oriani to have one of the most stable, prosperous, and gentle societies in the known universe, so gentle that it often seemed foolish. That it could be based on such a brutal foundation seemed impossible, yet these children were telling him that it was and asking for his acceptance.

How could he accept it? Because Orion exported technology and diplomacy, two valuable commodities? The interstellar community would be poorer without them. A world crowded to the limits of its endurance would offer neither. Because he owed his life to Orian technology and would do so again and again? He owed his life to the dead children and an ancient, brutal law.

"There has to be some other way," he said.

Lawr answered. "You can be certain we have explored everything possible through the years, from breeding restrictions to genetic engineering."

Ayyah looked at Anderson, the pain of her heritage stiff in her face. "At least twice in my lifetime, I must face the agony and the madness. If there were some other way, would I not be the first to embrace it?"

She seemed so distressed, so haunted by these visions of her future, that he actually wanted to comfort her, but he had no comfort to give.

"This is not an easy thing," Lawr said. "It has never been, and will never be, easy. But we owe our parents, who suffered this on our behalf, and we owe our children, who must accept the world we give them without recourse."

"Somehow you manage to make it sound very dutiful and sane," Anderson said, "but you're trying to rationalize infanticide. You're trying to tell me it's right and proper and sane to murder babies. Your own helpless little babies."

"Give us an alternative, any alternative," Ayyah cried, "and become the everylasting hero of my race."

Both Orian faces had set into hard masks of tragedy, teeth clenched, eyed downcast. "Let us go from here," Ayyah whimpered. "This is an evil place."

They left Ter-Marl and all of them were glad to be gone.

Being alien, Anderson came to believe, was largely a state of mind. Whereas he had previously felt reasonably at home and comfortable with the young people, he now was uneasy among them. He would see a couple of them with their heads together over some record or paper and find his skin prickling. Seeing them enjoying some tail-wagging good banter, he would slink angrily away, furiously resentful of their ability to enjoy themselves.

His work suffered, too. Fortunately, he was under no pressure on that score. The academy, having once established his potential, seemed willing to wait indefinitely for its realization. Though it bothered him to have the project grow away from him, he could summon neither the energy nor the enthusiasm to stay on top of it.

He didn't go to the house very often except to sleep. He spent most of his waking hours in the academy, alone in the office that had been assigned to him, staring at the computer terminal, snapping at anyone who came his way, accomplishing nothing. During the day, he brooded. Many nights he walked the pathways of Owr-Marl, feeling a lot like he had felt when he'd first come to Orion. He lost a lot of sleep and a little weight. He could not resolve the dilemma nor shake off the depression.

The Academy

The grizzled, arthritic old Orian who was nominally Anderson's supervisor waited patiently on the other side of his desk for Anderson to take notice of her. Like Talan, she would wait forever. The only way to get rid of her was to give her what she wanted. Silently he handed over the record containing a copy of the results of the latest fiddling with the translation program. It was complete garbage, but she could figure that out for herself.

"It is improved?" she asked after a moment.

"No."

"It would appear we are proceeding in the wrong direction, Bill Anderson."

Anderson didn't answer.

A silence stretched out between them.

"You are displeased?" she asked then.

"Yes."

"How may I be of help?"

"I want to go home."

"It is not possible."

"Get out. Get out and leave me alone."

She hesitated a fraction of a second. "As you wish," she said, and left Anderson to wonder if she had children, if she had at some time lain in the caves in Ter-Marl, had at some time bitten into the necks of frightened, helpless babies. The disgust and the loneliness descended upon him afresh. The words on the computer terminal in front of him blurred and became meaningless. He stared at them without seeing them.

Over the top of the monitor, through the windows in

the front of his office, he could see her going down the hall, her stiff, halting gait making progress slow.

It might go on like this forever, he thought, or until the depression drove him into madness or to some desperate measure. A man couldn't live like this, surrounded by beings that turned his stomach by their very presence.

He turned away, swiveling his chair around so he could see the mountain that dominated the view in the outside window. Only a small part of the 8700-some-odd-meter slope of dark, jagged rock fit in the scene. Ent-Kowal Itahi, its name was. The Mountain that Touches the Sky. The Orian characters on his terminal screen formed that name, and the English characters below were the computer's translation, an interelemental obscenity that even the computer should have found ludicrous.

He swiveled the chair a little farther to face a cabinet and opened a file drawer, looking for the printout of the latest changes in the program. Then, abruptly, he changed his mind, shoving the drawer closed. Tired and sticky and grainy-eyed, making no noticeable progress, he decided to quit for the day.

Turning back to the desk, he gathered up the notes and papers on its surface and tucked them into a drawer. No matter how sophisticated computers got, there were still things he liked to write down himself, on paper. But he had to keep these notes out of sight. The superefficient custodial staff would swoop up every scrap of paper of an evening and have it all recycled by morning.

He heard a small sound and looked up, thinking his supervisor had returned. Eventually she was bound to get fed up with him and send him packing. Not that he could work up much concern about it.

But it was a Lleveci coming down the hall toward him.

He wasn't particularly surprised to see a Lleveci. All kinds of folk used the academy or worked there. It was well known and well thought of. Even people with as few intellectual pretensions as Lleveci might find an occasion to be there.

What did surprise him was that the Lleveci stopped at the open door of his office and called him by name.

What also surprised him was that he recognized this one, although at first he doubted his senses. The last time he'd seen him was some months ago and half a planet away, standing in the doorway of poor Mary-Ann's room with the dead Roothian priest at his feet.

The Lleveci came in and grinned at Anderson from across the desk.

"You haven't been forgotten, Earthling," he said, and he hauled out of his clothing a long, narrow, slightly curved knife.

The overhead lights gleamed on the blade of quartz crystal, polished until it shone like diamond and honed, Anderson knew, by the Lleveci's own hand according to rituals and customs centuries old. The haft would be of carved black magnesite quarried in the volcanic hills of the assassin's homeland and decorated with scenes from his family history.

"Steven sends his greetings," the Lleveci said.

Between Anderson and the Lleveci there was only the desk with the computer terminal on it. Anderson had the presence of mind to hit a couple of keys and set the computer to going in circles. That would bring somebody sooner or later, to see what he was up to. Later wasn't going to be much good to him. If the Lleveci had brought a gun, he probably wouldn't have had time even for that. But the assassin had a notion for the artistry and ceremony of the blade. And perhaps for his own survival as well. Blaster fire might well bring everyone in the academy down on him before he could find his way out of the building.

Obviously, the guy wasn't stupid, and Anderson had no place to run, and it wasn't likely any of his colleagues were going to show up in time, if at all, since he hadn't been making them welcome lately. He got to his feet and pushed the chair to one side, out of the way.

The Lleveci took a swipe at him over the desk. Anderson jumped away, collided with the wall, and lost a chunk of skin off his belly.

At times like that a man can tell his stupid brain to

think of something, but all mental activity comes to a dead stop and the brain just sits there like a lump of meat—which was exactly what Anderson's brain was going to be very shortly if he didn't take some action. He could only think of two things: that he needed room to maneuver, and that his best chance would come if he could do something totally unexpected that would put his assailant off stride.

He did what he thought the Lleveci would least expect. He came across the desk toward his attacker.

That bought him about ten seconds while the Lleveci blinked and backed off a meter or so. Then the assassin lunged, point first.

Anderson managed to sidestep and let the lunge go by him. He tried to grab the arm, but not only was the fellow not stupid, he was quick, quick enough to ram the hilt of his weapon into Anderson's gut and send the Terran crashing into the wall.

Fighting for breath, Anderson scrambled and got turned around. The Lleveci waited for him, in no particular rush, holding the knife low and loose, watching him the way the matador watches the bull. Anderson took a kick at the knife hand. The assassin moved slightly to let the kick go by and, while Anderson was still off balance, moved in for the kill.

Anderson tried to slip under the thrust, wasn't quite fast enough, felt the cold crystal slide along a rib but didn't stop to think about it hurting, and brought his two fists clenched together down with all the strength he had onto the middle of the Lleveci's skinny neck. The Lleveci collapsed into a heap and stopped breathing.

Then Anderson became aware of the pain and the blood pouring down his back and the Com/Com link bleating, and someone coming at the trot down the hallway.

Much official fuss and bother ensued. Owr-Marl was not the port, and people attacking one another just didn't happen in Orian towns. The local authorities were at a bit of a loss, and the academicians were thoroughly scandalized. Anderson was muzzy from shock so he

never did learn how they worked it out. He answered
their questions as briefly as he could, and in the end it
was agreed that he could hardly have been expected to
stand peaceably by while some unprincipled character
stuck holes in him, so they tidied him up and sent him
home with a healer, who explained things to the kids,
applied bandages, and put him to sleep.

He woke up about midday, stiff and sore and thirsty,
with a definite sense of unease. He got up expecting to
meet impending disaster.

The house was quiet, the young Oriani gone about
their several chores. No goblins appeared out of the
woodwork, no ominous rustlings set his heart to pounding, no mysterious strangers lurked in the garden or hid
in the shadows from the noon sun. But it was only a
matter of time. Steven knew where he was, and Steven
wasn't the forgiving type. He'd try again.

Anderson had a feeling he should be on the move.
The next assassin might not be so clumsy or so direct.

He had to get away from there. He couldn't depend
on the Oriani; their police force was virtually nonexistent, and they would have a terrible time trying to understand the situation.

He had to get away from there, yes, but where could
he go and how long could it be before Steven found him
again? In terms of hiding from Steven, Orion was a small
planet, and Anderson was rather a unique part of it.
Wherever he went, he would stand out like a sore
thumb. There was only one place on Orion where he
wouldn't be as obvious as a drunk at a temperence meeting.

It was several days before he could work up the courage to actually get started.

When he finally set out, the plan was only half formed
in his mind. He was working on the basic Orian tenet of
strength in the unexpected, without much idea of what
he was going to do except that carrying the fight to Steven would be what Steven would least expect.

He let the young people think he was going to work
that afternoon, walked down into the main part of Owr-
Marl, and committed himself to the transit system.

The transit car surfaced outside of Owr-Marl and slowed for the series of tunnels that carried it through the mountains. Then it turned into the desert and ran dead south for 3000 kilometers until it dropped below ground once more outside of Owr-Lakh. Anderson didn't see the light of day again until the end of the line in Space Central, next to the IP Trade Center. The journey took minutely less than one Orian day, some twenty-one hours and an odd number of minutes.

Orion Space Central

Anderson knew that strange things were happening in the port as soon as he got aboveground. The first hint was the two Oriani at the exit, both wearing the electric-blue baldric of the Security Service. They didn't stop him, or even ask his name, they were just there, and that in itself was curious.

The street in front of the IP Trade Center was surprisingly free of pedestrians, and those there strode purposefully along, as if anxious to get on with what they were doing. Anderson wandered among them, head swiveling, getting in folk's way, trying to figure out what had happened to dampen the hustling, bustling burble of activity of the port down to a quiet drone.

Freight vehicles were on the street in their usual numbers, grumbling their heavy-laden complaints, generally moving more freely with fewer people getting in the way. But no drivers stuck their heads out of their cabs and cursed pedestrians. No pedestrians thumbed their noses and cursed back. Presumably business was still being done. But from the sour looks on people's faces, nobody was having much fun.

Nobody was huddled around a deck of cards in a doorway, and no one was shooting craps in the end of a blind alley.

Though he made himself look idle and interested, no one offered to sell him so much as a cheap timepiece, special for you, mister.

It was kind of eerie.

The various and boisterous folk who gave Peddler's

Lane its name had vanished and their dust had been swept out after them, leaving no sign they ever existed. But there were more Security types around. Anderson turned off on Sundance and went to the pawnshop.

The Caparan was as depressed as Anderson had ever seen him. He seemed close to tears, or whatever happened to be the Caparan equivalent. He raised all six arms toward the ceiling while he told Anderson his tale of woe.

It was as if, he said, they were trying to make Space Central into an Orian city. They were trying to make it neat and orderly and clean. He told Anderson that he was ready to pack it in and go home. Business was terrible. Anderson's old room was there if he wanted it, with his stuff still in it. There were no renters. Nobody stayed in the port these days. The Seven Planets and all the gambling establishments had been shut down. And most of the bars. A lot of other shopkeepers had simply given up when their markets evaporated. People came and went as quickly as possible. Word had got around. The Oriani were giving everybody a hard time.

Anderson told the Caparan he wanted a bed for the night, a change of clothes, and a shower, and he had credit in the Government Bank. The Caparan waved Anderson's offer of payment aside. The man was really depressed.

Steven Black was still around, the Caparan said, but not doing much. The word was that Steven had barricaded himself in his fortress at Tradex and was just waiting out the storm and trying to keep his Rigan creditors off his back.

The Sississin was still in business though it didn't seem to have a lot of customers. Issith looked more morose than ever, but he just shrugged when Anderson asked him how things were going.

"Iss bad now, Bill. Ssometime it getss better. I ssee thiss before. Ssoon the Oriani go away. Then everything iss ass it wass." There was a lot to admire in a guy like Issith. He knew how to roll with the punches. If the Oriani insisted on a bunch of new rules about the sales of intoxicants, Issith would go along with them, at least as much as was necessary to keep from being put out of business. But the sum result of it all was that even the Sississin wore a somber air, and Anderson didn't stay long.

Instead he spent some time across the street from Tradex Interplanetary in a doorway which, he discovered, he was sharing with a drunken Terran sailor. Shortly after dark, a Security patrol came by and one of the Oriani told him gravely that it wasn't safe to be alone on the street at night. When he was gone the drunk confided, articulating carefully, that if the patrol came by again and Anderson was still there, they would haul him off to a holding area to spend the night. It was all very pleasant and civilized, the sailor said—he himself had spent several nights there—but boring, and they wouldn't let one out until morning.

Anderson told the sailor that he wasn't planning to stay, which was true. Things were very quiet at Tradex. Most of the warehouse was dark. If his presence in the port was known, it didn't show. He went back to the pawnshop and went to sleep.

The next day he went to the Government Bank and arranged for the transfer of the majority of his credit to Barclay's, London, England, Earth. Then he hung around the IP Trade Center looking for a ship heading at least roughly Earthward and a captain who was recruiting. Deckhands were always in short supply on starships, so he anticipated no great difficulty on that score. And he found none. Before the end of the day he had a berth on the *Senator Davies* taking a load of crystal silicon to Gnatha, leaving in three days' time. It wasn't the way he would have preferred to travel. He had no doubt that staggering back and forth across the rim on freighters he would be a year or several reaching Earth. But the truth of the matter was, he couldn't afford to be fussy. He couldn't stay on Orion as long as Steven was there.

Could he get back to Orion before he needed another treatment for his heart? Only the gods could say. The first order of business was to stay alive long enough to need it. Afraid as he was to leave Orion, he was now more afraid to stay.

Anderson had left Owr-Marl with only the vaguest idea of what he was going to do and trusting that his appearance in the port would throw Steven off stride. His ruse must have worked, since he had a whole day undisturbed. But it didn't last as long as he might have hoped. By evening, Steven had apparently decided that nothing was to be lost by turning Anderson into the kind of example he liked best.

Because he had been more or less expecting Steven's goons to show, Anderson was sticking as close as was practical to the Orian Security types. He was just leaving the IP Trade Center after signing on with the *Senator Daves* when the two Rigans hove into view. The way they bore down on him, he didn't have much doubt as to what was on their minds.

Anderson ran headlong for the nearest Security patrol and set up as much fuss as he was able. In a very short time they were thoroughly surrounded by Oriani, and Steven's boys and Anderson spent the night in the holding area. Sure enough, it was all very comfortable and civilized, with food and coffee of a sort and books available, and it looked a lot like the common room at the YMCA except that males and females of a variety of races were dumped together indiscriminately, and the doors were locked.

Of course, the Rigans were perfectly capable of disposing of Anderson anyway, but nobody knew how the Oriani would react to murder committed on the premises, and the Rigans were unwilling to risk it. But they swore a lot and made Anderson very much aware that his life expectancy was short.

In the morning everybody was turned loose, but Steven's goons lost their weapons to the greater good. And Anderson had to figure out how to keep his skin intact for another two days.

He also had to figure out how he was going to keep ahead of Talan. He was sure that by this time the kids back at the house had figured out he wasn't just wandering the streets of Owr-Marl, that he had actually left.

And however much he might doubt the efficiency of the loose Orian social structure, they did have the best communications system that had ever been devised. What one of them knew, they all could know in the length of time a radio wave took to travel to and from any of the geosynchronous communications satellites, of which there were a great many.

Two Orian days—forty-three point some odd hours—isn't so very long a time. But for Anderson, they stretched on like eternity. Any moment might bring the Rigans back, alerted now to his tactics. With any breath, Talan might show up and drag him back to Owr-Marl where he could sit and chew his fingernails and wait for Steven to follow.

In any place on Orion other than the port, Anderson would be as obvious as a pumpkin in a gravel pit. On the other hand, camping on Steven's doorstep was not the most comfortable place to spend the next forty-three point some odd hours. What he really needed was a distraction, something to keep everybody busy for a little while.

A notion formed in the back of his mind and began to take shape. He needed something exciting and noisy and he remembered the stuff Talan had given him—when? It seemed like a century ago.

He took a chance going back to the Sississin. Steven and Talan both knew his habits well, knew what he liked to do and where he liked to go. But there was one minor advantage to having nothing to lose. He could take chances no one in his right mind would take, accept risks his opponents would naturally assume any rational being would discard out of hand.

He asked Issith if he still had the coffee samples.

"Ssure, Bill. Comess who here for coffee?"

"I need them, Issith."

Issith shrugged. "Iss here." He took Anderson into the back room. Anderson picked up the two plastic boxes and persuaded Issith to let him out of the rear of the building. He felt minutely more secure in the alley among packing crates and disposal units than he did on the bare, empty streets. As far as possible, he stuck to the shadowy alleys.

As much as he had sought them out the previous day, Anderson now became positively paranoid about avoiding the Security patrols, convinced in his own mind that by then every Orian on the planet was looking for him.

But at least he knew an Orian when he saw one. Steven's men weren't so easy to identify. He wound up trying to avoid every creature that moved, hoping to make the passage from the Sississin to the narrow lane that separated the now-dark and empty Blue Moon from the Tradex building unobserved, wondering all the time how successful he was being. He saw eyes everywhere, and had no way of knowing if eyes also saw him.

He reached Schats Street with a sense of relief that turned out to be premature. He was halfway down the alley when a soft, inquisitive Orian voice called his name.

"Bill Anderson?"

The Orian was coming down the alley toward him at a lope. Anderson fled toward the Tradex building, stopped at the first door he came to, and demanded entry.

It came as a mild surprise to him that the door opened to his command. That should have made him suspicious, because from the outset it had been a worrisome thought in the back of his mind that there was the distinct possibility he would not be able to get into the warehouse at all. When getting in turned out to be easy, Anderson just assumed that with all he had on his mind these days, Steven had simply forgotten to change the instructions about whom the doors should admit. Of course, he should have known better. Steven never forgot anything.

Anyway, he was in and the Orian was outside. If the Orian was going to wait, like a cat waiting at a mousehole, there was nothing he could do about it except hope his diversion would be sufficiently startling to attract the Orian's attention while Anderson made good his escape. Preferably by another door.

The warehouse was dark, with only a single panel lit near a flight of stairs. Anderson moved in that direction, needing a little light for his work.

He dumped the coffee out of the boxes, got the charge and detonator, and looked around for a likely place. The smell of coffee was marvelous in the air. It seemed an awful pity to blow up the precious beans. He probably wouldn't have been able to do it for anything less than survival.

He found a stack of perhaps a hundred polycarb barrels nearby, labeled "enthanol, 95%, 100 L." He thought he remembered that alcohol would burn, though he had never tried to burn any. That, too, seemed like a waste.

He put charge and detonator together, snugged them down between the barrels, set the fuse, and took off like a scared rabbit—and all but ran into an enormous Rigan who was just a shadow in the gloom, making his way carefully down the aisles between stacks toward Anderson, weapon drawn.

Rigans are slow moving, but not as slow as Anderson might have wished. He dived behind a couple of aluminum boxes only to have the top one disintegrate around him. The Rigan was between him and the nearest door. Anderson was so conscious of the fuse timer that he was sure he could hear it ticking away. Of course, the damned thing didn't tick, but he could hear it anyway.

Anderson squirmed his way deeper into the stack of boxes, trying to find a way around the lethal obstruction. Rigans might be slow, but they're not stupid. This one puzzled over the situation for a minute or two, then started blasting away at boxes at the bottom of the stack. It didn't take many before the whole stack collapsed on top of Anderson and he was buried under a ton of Steven's very expensive cigars.

The boxes fell against one another. Anderson wasn't badly damaged, but he wasn't going to get out from under them in any reasonable amount of time. The Rigan was digging after him, pitching boxes aside as if they were made out of Styrofoam.

And then the charge went off.

It wasn't a very big explosion; Talan had envisioned quite a different scenario when he had given the stuff to Anderson. But it was enough to all but deafen a man and send a lot of junk flying. The roar of the fire that followed was almost as loud. Alcohol burned just fine.

Anderson was surprised that he wasn't dead, and that he was still able to scrabble, to get himself free, and that his instincts still operated sufficiently well that he was trying to escape without even thinking about it. But the smoke was getting thick, and the air thin and hot, and one leg wasn't working, and the wound in his back had opened up again, and it was so hard to breathe that it just didn't seem worth the struggle after a while.

And then someone was madly pushing stuff aside and grabbing him by the collar of his shirt and pulling him out from under, completely heedless of the pain in his back and the protests of the damaged leg. And he thought the Rigan was damned dedicated, but that it would be no worse an end than cooking to death.

And then he was somewhere outside and for the first time ever the Orian atmosphere was cool and sweet.

There was a while in which he did nothing much but breathe, and was grateful to be able to do that. Later he started to take notice of what was around him.

He was lying on the pavement in front of the Blue Moon amid a gathering crowd. Across Schats Street, Tradex Interplanetary was going up in flames. Firefighting equipment was on the scene, but finding the street too narrow for easy maneuvering.

Talan was bending over him, looking strange with patches of soot on him and the fur around his snout singed brown and curly. Anderson tried to say something but his throat was glued together. Talan gave him a mouthful of something wet.

"How did you get here?"

Talan cocked his ears and gave the question a moment's consideration. "I borrowed a flyer from the academy," he said as if he didn't at all understand why Anderson was interested.

"You're crazy," Anderson croaked. "I don't understand you at all."

"You do not, Bill Anderson?"

"I do not." Anderson got another swallow. It was

good stuff, whatever it was, but it was making him feel a
bit light-headed.

"What about me puzzles you?" A healer was hovering
around wanting to take over, and Talan was about to
move aside. But Anderson held him.

"You save bugs and kill babies. You risk your stupid
neck to save my life just so you can keep me prisoner. It
doesn't make sense."

Talan removed Anderson's hand from his arm. "I believe the saying is: that makes us even. All that is required of you is that you do nothing, yet you consistently
refuse to do so at some considerable peril not only to
yourself but those who care for you and all others
around you. Three are dead, and to what purpose? This
makes no sense at all to me."

He started away.

"Talan?"

The Orian stopped and looked back.

"Who's dead?"

"A Rigan and a Terran whom I do not know. And
Steven Black."

"Steven's dead?"

"Yes. He was asphyxiated by the fire. Perhaps you
have performed a service in spite of yourself, Bill Anderson."

They took him to the Medical Center in Owr-Lakh to
recuperate, back to where his Orion adventure had
started. Ee had left the hospital, but Hairy the physio-
therapist was still there, taking up where he left off the
last time and making the same disapproving sounds. The
only difference was that now Anderson could talk to
him. He discovered that Hairy had nothing much to say.
Hairy seemed to be a person for whom muscles were the
only reality.

They told him that the Midway Conference was making progress after a couple of false starts, although it
would probably be years before anything was really decided. They told him as if they thought he should be
pleased to hear it. He thought probably he should be. It
would be good to have people not killing each other. But

it was so remote from him that it made no dent in his despair.

The last time he'd been at the Medical Center, he'd been lost and lonely, a man with no future. That's how it was again. His escape plan wouldn't have worked anyway. By the time he had arrived at Space Central from Owr-Marl, the Port Authority had already been informed, and he wouldn't have been allowed off planet. The *Senator Davies* would have left without him even if he hadn't blown himself up.

When the healers at the Medical Center declared him fit and healthy, he was sent back to Owr-Marl to take up his work at the academy. The youngsters had abandoned the house across the valley, and he had it all to himself. Once settled in Owr-Marl, he was free to do anything he wanted to, except that the transit system was forbidden to him. Three thousand kilometers of desert separated him from the spaceport.

He never saw Talan again.

He never got to see his daughter.

Kazi-to-Kazi communications were accomplished without need for artificial sound makers. A combination of a semaphoric waving of the forelimbs, body attitude, and the controlled release of pheromones got a message across quite handily. The two that kept to the shadows of the IP Trade Center discussed the loss of Steven Black and the unfortunate cease-fire in the Ellgarth Cluster while they waited for a chance to board their shuttle unobserved. They kept a nervous watch while they waited. The presence of Orian Security in the port had complicated their lives considerably.

They were leaving Orion on a Gnathan vessel, the first stop in their very long journey to the Kazi homeworld. The journey had been arranged by their broodmaster because they had much to tell the emperor and council. While it was true that they had failed their mission in Ellgarth, they had stumbled upon a mote of information that might prove more valuable in the long run, and perhaps alleviate the irritating Orian interference that had plagued the empire this last century or so.

The Ellgarth worlds were still weak, after all, and could be taken by force of arms if necessary.

But a weapon against Orion, that was worth having.

Neither of the Kaz boarding the shuttle could explain it, but they had come to believe that an enmity existed between Terrans and Oriani. They had seen it with Steven Black, who roundly hated every native of the planet. And they had seen Anderson, at first apparently favorably inclined, grow cold and distant toward the one he had called friend.

Terrans appeared to be a fast-breeding, quick-tempered, violent people. Find a way to exploit this animosity they seemed to hold toward the Oriani, set the Terrans against the Oriani, and the eaters of eggs would have their hands full for the foreseeable future.

It might take some study; not a great deal was known about humans. A year or a century, but it was little enough to invest in an idea the two felt had considerable potential. They were sure the emperor would agree.

Epilogue: The Ambassador

The aide, Rawlir, was upset.

Talan closed Bill Anderson's book and put it aside. He dragged himself back to the present and with some difficulty addressed himself to Rawlir's concerns. And it was difficult. He found he didn't want to know how bad things were. A typically human way of thinking. He was privately ashamed of himself.

"There is no good news," Rawlir said when he was sure of his superior's attention. "The United Nations General Assembly will vote on the resolution later today or early tomorrow morning, depending on how long the representative of the Union of Soviet Socialist Republics continues to speak against it."

Talan stood, stretched, and walked around the office a little to get the blood moving again.

"I did not expect an ally from that quarter," he said.

"Nor do we have one," Rawlir answered. "The resolution was drafted by the Eurocom-North American faction and the Union of Soviet Socialist Republics therefore opposes it as a matter of principle."

"We will be given no opportunity to defend ourselves?"

"None."

"And the vote?"

"We will lose it. We are already declared guilty. The vote is only a matter of form."

Talan bowed his head, defeated. For a moment he and Rawlir stood silently, side by side, mourning all the lost effort and anticipating the ultimate indignity coming

251

when the United Nations would ask the Orian Embassy to vacate Terran soil. A diplomat could fail no more than this. Talan felt all the weariness of all the long days of all the years descend upon him. He felt old.

"We should start making preparations," the aide suggested.

"Tomorrow is time enough. I will be in my quarters if you need me."

"Sleep well," Rawlir said.

Those last two words bothered Talan as he walked down the freshly polished marble floors of the hallway. A silly expression, a Terran expression, he thought, doubly silly under the circumstances. Are they making Terrans of us then? Perhaps it was time to go home. But not like this. Not like this.

Farther down the hallway, a short round woman switched off the floor polisher she was guiding and waved to him. He returned the greeting, Orian fashion, recognizing the supervisor of the janitorial staff. She had a title—everything on Earth had a label—but he couldn't remember it. He did remember a name.

"Bessy Breckenridge."

"Good evenin', Mr. Ambassador."

"Things are well with you?"

"As well as you could hope, sir."

"You look tired."

"One of the kids was off school with the flu today. I didn't get all the sleep I'd like."

"Yes, you have several children. Four, I believe."

Bessy Breckenridge beamed up at him.

"Perhaps you could answer a question for me?"

Bessy nodded and smiled some more.

Talan had long since learned that a vigorous bobbing of the head signified assent. "I have reasons for not seeking an official explanation. Could you explain to me by what criteria the Eugenics Council might refuse permission for breeding?" The ambassador found it a difficult question to ask, and Bessy was astonished to see him looking down at the floor like an embarrassed schoolboy.

He mistook her moment of silence for reluctance to

answer. "I'm sorry," he said. "I have no right to ask you such a thing."

"Oh, no, no, sir, that's not it at all. It's just, you see, I don't know. My youngest is twelve, born before the council was ever dreamed up. Lucky for us. No way that bunch of fat old men'd see the likes of us bringing children into the world, me with my rheumatism and my Gordie deaf in one ear."

"I had no idea your children were that old."

Flattered, Bessy smiled more broadly than ever. "I'm an old woman, sir. I've been workin' here thirty years, come spring."

"You have found your work pleasant?"

"Oh, yes, sir. I've been happy here."

"It doesn't bother you to work for aliens?" Talan found the word strange when applied to himself.

"Not me. I'm not like some folks. You're my third ambassador, and every one has been decent to me. I'm not one to hold a man's race against him, if you know what I mean."

"Are your duties pressing? Can you spare me a few minutes? I would like to talk to you if you have the time."

Bessy Breckenridge continued to beam while she assured him she had all the time he needed. It's not because of your peerless charm, Talan reminded himself, it's because of this curious concept of social levels. She's flattered because someone of your level is reaching down to someone of hers.

Strange that I can talk easily to this individual, even though all I have to tell her is that her long labor is ended, Talan thought as he guided Bessy Breckenridge into the library, yet I have had so little success in communicating with groups. In humans, the group mind seems wholly foreign to the individual. And I have learned this too late.

Then he turned his whole attention to the woman, intent on planting such small seeds for the future as he could manage in these difficult circumstances.

He did not keep Bessy Breckenridge long; the need for rest weighed down on him. But in spite of that, and in spite of Rawlir's good wishes, the ambassador did not sleep well. And the morning was hectic, filled with minutiae, all seeming to need his personal attention. He was glad to be able to escape for a while in the afternoon to keep an appointment he had made the previous day.

He stood before the rundown apartment building. In the street, aimlessly restless humanity surged around him, jostled him, and scarcely paused to notice the alien in their midst. On the steps in front of him a heavy, unkempt woman sat staring at him incuriously over the battered pram that held her fretful infant. Sounds of a quarrel issued from within. Somewhere nearby, a radio blared the raucous sounds Terrans professed to find pleasing. To the ambassador's sensitive ears, it was a noise scarcely endurable.

The whole neighborhood was pervaded with noise. And with smells—unwashed bodies and illness and garbage and food poorly prepared and kept too long. It was an ugly, dilapidated place, centuries out of its time, an incredible anachronism in the heart of a modern city.

For this, the ambassador marveled, the Eugenics Council strives to breed a race without flaw; for this hopelessness, for this desperation, humanity needs perfection.

In the street motors roared and horns blatted as impatient truck drivers complained of slow progress in congested surface traffic. Talan turned to the two security men who had insisted on coming with him when he left the embassy. His bodyguards had been frightened and concerned about the entire venture. They had tried first to dissuade him, and then had come very close to threatening. The mood of the people was bad, they said, since the news of the *L'rar* affair had been made public.

L'rar had been fired upon and had fired back, destroying its attacker. The records of *L'rar* showed the attacker to have been a light cruiser with Terran markings. The crew maintained the accuracy of the records. But a Kazi transport claimed to have picked up debris of an unarmed factory ship en route to Io. None of the debris ever became available for inspection, still Earthlings accepted the Kazi account for reasons known only to themselves. Nothing any Orian could say about possible Kazi motives seemed to have any effect. The Oriani were perceived as the murderers of innocent Terran workmen, and no one wanted to hear from them. *L'rar* was at LunaPort now, undergoing repairs and being gutted down to the hull to provide accommodation for all Oriani personnel within the Terran system. *Personae non grata,* all.

The official mood had percolated into the streets. There had been what the news media were pleased to call 'incidents.' Radio broadcasts had been particularly active in spreading news of 'incidents.' Radio. In spite of all the improvements made in communications, humanity's love affair with its radios continued, undiminished.

Now that the ambassador had left the relative safety of the armored embassy car, his guardians were doubly unhappy. They scanned the street with wary eyes and even when Talan spoke to them, they didn't interrupt their careful effort to see danger from wherever it might come.

"I would like the two of you to wait for me here," Talan said.

"No way, Mr. Ambassador. We're sticking with you." Brian McInnes didn't take his eyes off his job. But he meant what he said. He was a good man, loyal, capable, serious about his work—and rock stubborn.

"This is a private matter," Talan insisted.

"You know us," McInnes answered. "We're discreet."

"I must demand you accompany me no further. I have no wish to frighten these people. The two of you and your ever-ready weapons make a rather threatening presence."

"Who, us?" McInnes asked, smiling to the street. "We're a couple of pussy cats."

"Really."

"Hey, no offense, eh? You know what I mean."

Talan could see that he was going to have to take a different approach. "Brian McInnes, I know you for a man skilled at his profession. You must realize that I could leave the embassy at any time without your knowledge and make this journey on my own. If I cannot get your cooperation now, that is exactly what I will do. Do you understand me?"

McInnes finally looked at the ambassador. He had had some difficult charges in his career, and this was one of them.

"God damn, Mr. Ambassador, you're not giving me a whole lot of choice."

"That was my intent."

Two small crowds had gathered. One was pressing around the embassy car in the street. With fuel a rare and expensive commodity, any private vehicle on this mean street in this decaying district was an oddity worthy of attention, and the embassy car was more elaborate than most. The chauffeur, who had been left with it, had his hands full preventing small boys, and bigger ones, from stripping bits off of it and packing them away.

The other crowd had assembled around Talan and his bodyguards, the argument finally rousing numbed brains to take notice. The crowd started to rumble as it grew, and from somewhere out of it a rock came flying. The rock bounced harmlessly on the pavement, but its meaning was clear. "Orian," someone shouted from the safety of the group. "Orian," as if it were a curse.

Talan was hustled into the comparative safety of the building. The three of them crowded the cramped entry that was largely occupied by a flight of wooden stairs leading up. "Okay, okay," McInnes growled. "You win. Let's get this over with before there's a bloody riot or something. Here's what we're going to do. Bob will stay here and watch the door. I'm going upstairs and check out the hallway. Then you come up. And when you go into the apartment, leave the goddamned door open. I want to be able to get in there if I have to. And make it fast. Two of us can't stand off a mob."

Talan indicated his acceptance. He had won as many concessions from Brian McInnes as was possible, and if he was to be completely truthful with himself, he would have to admit that in spite of his declaration of independence of a few moments before, he would have been more than a little apprehensive about entering this district alone.

Melissa Larkin had been told to expect the ambassador, but still she was nonplussed by his appearance at her door and stumbled over her tongue as she introduced John. John's mouth hung slack as if he had doubted until that moment that Melissa had meant what she said when she told him the ambassador was coming.

The young people had done what they could to make the tiny, dim room presentable, but the overall impression was still one of faded wallpaper and sagging drapes and incredible squalor. Melissa apologized. "Until we're assigned a living space," she explained, "it's either an unregistered room like this, or living separately with our families. But you didn't need to—I could have come to the embassy—a courier—I didn't mean to—"

Talan stopped the outpouring with a gesture. "It does me good to get into the real world once in a while. This is an excellent excuse to take advantage of a last chance to see Earth outside of the artificiality of the diplomatic community."

"You're leaving Earth?" Melissa asked.

"Yes." The young people looked puzzled. "I take it you have not been paying undue attention to the news media of late. Understandable." The youngsters flushed, and Talan regretted having embarrassed them even in a small way. "We have been required to do so by the Terran governments, severally and in concert." His thoughts wandered momentarily to other problems. "Unfortunate that their only moment of agreement should be this."

Melli brought him back to matters at hand. "I'm sorry," she said and sounded as if she meant it.

Once again the individual is at odds with the group, Talan thought. It is a matter that should be given some study. And he filed the thought away in the back of his mind for future consideration.

"I have brought the documents you require," he said. "These are the originals, the medical records and the psychological profile, prepared by the healer in Owr-

Lakh. These are translations, certified at the embassy, which you will need for your bureaucracy."

Melissa accepted the sealed records in the palm of her hand and marveled at how small they were to contain her whole fate. She glanced at John. John shrugged, but he looked more concerned than he wanted to let on. How trustingly they place their future into my hands, Talan thought, and how simply I betray their trust.

"As far as I am able to determine," he said, "there is nothing about your grandfather's physical condition that should cause you difficulty. Your grandfather's heart condition was due, apparently, to a rare allergic response to an outdated procedure for controlling tooth decay by inducing in individuals antibodies to *Streptococcus mutans*, one of the organisms responsible for tooth decay in your race. A few persons were found to produce antibodies which also attacked their own heart muscle. The technique is no longer used, I understand, having been replaced by safer, more effective methods.

"However, regarding the psychological profile, I am unfortunately the bearer of unhappy news. It seems that toward the end of his life, your grandfather was quite mad."

"No," Melissa cried.

John caught Melissa's hand between his own and the two youngsters stared at each other in agony. Talan ignored the display as best he could.

"That can't be right," John said.

"I'm sorry. I cannot reasonably doubt the healer. I have read Bill Anderson's manuscript." Since all the hands in the room were occupied, Talan set the heavy book down on the least crowded edge of a small, rickety table. "It recounts, quite seriously, I believe, circumstances which never arose, events which did not and could not happen."

"Fiction?" John and Melissa said almost together.

"Perhaps. But I think not."

"But—" John started to protest.

Brian McInnes appeared in the open doorway. "Hey, man, we got to get out of here. There's a riot developing, for Christ's sake."

"I am responsible for that?"

"Hell, no. In these damned ghettos, people are so bored they'll riot over what somebody said somebody said on the bloody Tri-D just to relieve the monotony. Any old excuse will do. But we don't want to get caught in it. So move it, Mr. Ambassador."

"Yes, I am ready."

"Now, wait a minute," John said. He made a motion as if to take Talan by the arm, but thought better of it at the last minute and let his hand fall limply to his side. "I can't believe what Bill Anderson wrote is one great big fantastic hallucination or something. It seems so—I don't know—authentic. And there are real people in it, you—"

"My grandmother," Melli put in.

"And I remember reading about the Midway Conference in my history classes," John continued.

"As I read of the Centauri Accords in mine," Talan said. "Which does not mean I believe that a Terran named Robin Hood buckled on his swash and saved the entire solar system from tyranny and injustice single-handedly."

"Yeah, I see what you mean," John admitted reluctantly. "Just the same, I'm not so sure that you're not just saying that because Anderson's manuscript puts you guys, you Oriani, in a pretty bad light."

"John Richards," Talan said wearily. "I am at this moment, on this world, in just about as bad a light as it is possible for me to be in. Nothing you care to believe about Bill Anderson's delusions will affect that greatly. If you choose to believe in the madness of an entire race rather than the madness of one man, it is your privilege to do so."

"Ambassador," McInnes urged.

"They say that Orians don't know how to lie," Melissa said almost to herself.

"What purpose would be served, Melissa Larkin? I must go. I wish you well."

Out on the street, a squad of police had arrived and were holding the crowd at bay. Talan, as he entered it, felt his hackles rise. He had a strong, instinctive urge to take to the rooftops to get above and away from the howling hostility. Instead he allowed himself to be pushed by rough, urgent hands into the embassy vehicle. Before the door closed behind him he caught a snatch of grumbling from a policeman unused to the sensitivity of Orian ears. "...wish the smartass VIPs would stay behind their fences where they belong," and his companion replying, "Damned Orian. We should let them..."

Talan turned to look back at the building he had just left. It had been built of wood, perhaps a century before. The fire protection was poor; he had seen that even in the few moments he had been inside. When the incendiary device he had planted in Melissa Larkin's apartment ignited sometime during the next morning, the flames would spread rapidly. He was taking a terrible risk with lives not his own.

He was disturbed with himself for this moment of doubt. All the moral agonizing should have been completed last night, when he had calculated the cost a dozen different ways and come to the same conclusion over and over again. The manuscript had to be destroyed, and destroyed in a manner that would not call attention to it. He must take some risk now for the opportunity of repairing shattered Earth-Orion relations at a future time. He had done what he could to minimize the damage, choosing a time for the event when there would be fewest people in the building. He should be able to accept the need and live with it without regret. But regret was there.

He forced the tension to drain out of him as the vehicle lifted and took them away. Even Brian McInnes, seated in front beside the driver, relaxed enough to joke with his comrades. The story he was telling revolved around the sexual practices of the Kaz and relied more on ribaldry than factual information. It was a subject that seemed endlessly to fascinate Earthlings. Talan didn't get the point of it. Neither, it turned out, did Bob Lee, the other guard, sitting beside him.

"I thought the Kaz laid eggs," he said.

"Aw, for Pete's sake," McInnes answered, annoyed. Then he twisted around and leaned over the back of his seat, and asked Talan, "Hey, yeah, Boss, I been meaning to ask you, why do the Kaz call Oriani eaters of eggs?"

The expression was new to Talan, and it took a few seconds before the meaning of it sank in. When it hit, it was like a physical blow that shocked the ambassador numb. He couldn't breathe. He could only stare at Brian McInnes like a stunned thing while the blood thundered in his brain. And then it was as if all of his vitality gathered itself together to huddle somewhere deep inside and leave him weak and shivering.

McInnes draped one arm over the back of the front seat and levered himself around to better see his charge. "You okay, Ambassador?"

The Kaz. The thrice-damned, long-studying, patient Kaz. Somehow they had discovered what the Oriani wanted most to keep hidden, and they were telling the Earthlings. Quietly, as rumors, making folklore of it, so dreadfully much more efficient a way of provoking belief than an official statement would be.

And so all of his work, and his mother's work before him, and the sacrifice of Bill Anderson and the young people he had just left, all of it was meaningless, pointless, futile. Everything he had ever done was undone. The game was lost, not just for now, but for all time.

"Talan?" McInnes asked.

Talan fought to pull himself together. "Yes," he said after a long moment. "Quite well."

"You sure?" McInnes asked, his suspicions aroused by the uncharacteristic roughness in the words.

"I am well, Brian McInnes. Do not alarm yourself on my behalf. To answer your question, the expression is a term of contempt among the Kaz. It has as little meaning as would your calling me a son of a bitch, a thing which is obviously not the case."

McInnes grinned. "Okay, I was just wondering." He turned back to his conversation with the driver.

Talan leaned back in the seat and closed his eyes, alone with his pain.

"They say that Orians don't know how to lie," Melissa Larkin had said. I've learned to do it so well, Talan thought. And what has been gained for that?

He could rest now, and he felt wounded to the quick and much in need of rest. Away from Earth, with its teeming billions.

It would be good to get home. His long struggle was ended. He had done all that he could do, and lost. There was no need to fight any more. He found a sort of morbid comfort in that, as one might find in contemplating suicide.

It would be nice to live again where noise was not so all-pervasive, in a city that did not stink, in a place where solitude was respected, in a society where lies were not necessary, at least not so much.

About the Author

LESLIE GADALLAH was born in a small town in northern Alberta on October 8, 1939. The next day her father joined the air force and went to war. She graduated from the University of Alberta in 1960 with a B.Sc. in chemistry and spent the next fifteen years or so plying her trade and raising a family before abandoning the practice of science for the opportunity to write about it.

Ms. Gadallah has written popular science extensively for newspapers and radio, and served as a technical editor for the Alberta Research Council for a number of years. This work represents her first foray into the field of science fiction.

Ms. Gadallah lives with her family on a small farm just outside of Edmonton, Alberta, which they share with four cats, five chickens, a horse, and an uncertain number of rabbits. There they pursue the firm but distant goal of becoming independent of the supermarket.

Sci-Fi fans will love
the latest
by
Steve Miller
and
Sharon Lee